THE LAW GIVETH

JE GURLEY

THE LAW GIVETH

ISBN: 978-1-925493-12-2

JAKE'S LAWS

1. Aim high; shoot straight.
2. Long noses often get lopped off.
3. A fool and his life are soon parted.
4. Don't bring home more problems than you left with.
5. In a lawless land, the biggest gun makes the law.
6. Bad people deserve bad ends.
7. Trust yourself first; others seldom.
8. Use the tools you've got.
9. Always have an exit strategy.
10. Serve revenge in big doses.
11. Be willing to lose it all.
12. Stay focused.
13. First things first.
14. The heavier the burden, the less likely someone will want to share it.
15. Shit not only happens; it happens often.
16. If it you break it, you buy it.
17. Love isn't just cruel, it's string your guts out on a clothesline to bake in the sun cruel.
18. Shit sticks to everything. Fling it at your own peril.
19. If you're going to bitch slap someone, have a pistol in your hand.
20. If the day sucks, call it Monday and start your week there.
21. Trust your instincts.

1

June 10, 2017, 8:00 a.m.   Hatch, New Mexico —

Six heavily armed men moved on foot with military precision toward the center of town. Three provided cover fire for the three advancing in *defilade*, moving silently, hugging the sides of abandoned buildings to avoid detection by zombies or anyone else that might feel like shooting strangers in uniforms. Each man wore black clothing. The dark color was an effective camouflage at night, but it was now early morning and all it did was soak up the summer sun's rays. At a hand signal from the group's leader, two of the men broke away from the formation and raced ahead down an alleyway to reconnoiter the area.

One of the two men was Jake Blakely, former Arizona Pima County Deputy Sheriff. To say he was unhappy with their present circumstances would have been a gross understatement of his ire. Ideally, the group should have reached their target well before dawn and been in position at first light. Zombies did not sleep, but they could see no better in the dark than could humans, making infiltrating the town less dangerous at night. Unfortunately, a washed-out bridge had delayed them, and the team leader, Captain Luis Lambrini, would not postpone their mission. His orders were to survey the town of Hatch, New Mexico, to determine the feasibility of reclaiming it as a site for a new community for survivors, and he intended to do just that.

Jake and his companion took turns covering each other as they leapfrogged across empty streets toward their target, the municipal building three blocks away. Jake crouched low on the left side of a narrow alley reeking of decayed garbage across from their target, searching for any signs of movement. Other than three Staggers-infected Shamblers mindlessly ambling up and down the street a block away, the area was deserted. It was too easy. He believed wholeheartedly in *Jake's Law #21 — Trust your instincts*. His innate sense of self-preservation had saved his ass on numerous occasions. Right now, his ass felt exposed. He had a bad feeling, an itch between his shoulder blades that would not go away no matter how much he scratched.

It was not just the eerie silence lying over the town like invisible, sound-dampening fog. He was used to silence. He eyed the rusting, dust-covered cars and pickups lining the streets, but it was more than the lack of early morning delivery vans or commuter traffic clogging the streets. Nor was it the absence of bleary-eyed housewives preparing breakfast for husbands soon off to work, or the children laughing and frolicking on their way to school. It was summer, and schools would normally be out, but school had been out for a long time now. It had been almost two years since the Staggers Plague. The zombie apocalypse had swept through the land, leaving only the bones of thousands of dead towns and silent cities. He remembered a line from Alice Cooper's song, *School's Out: School's out forever. Damn right!*

It was not the disconcerting silence or the late mission launch that had him on edge. It was the absence of zombies. Zombies infested every city he had investigated so far, the new cockroach of the post-apocalyptic world. Zombies were not immortal creatures. They could starve to death, but it took a long time. Only three Shamblers seemed too much out of the ordinary. Where were the fast Lopers? There should have been either more zombies or more live people. Something wasn't right and it bothered him.

"I don't like it," he whispered to his companion, Howard Estes, a 42-year-old former bank manager from Wilcox, Arizona.

Estes looked over at him frowning. "What's wrong, Jake?" he asked, annoyed by Jake's hesitation. He was eager to get the job done and return to Marana. They had been in the field for five days, and he was tired of canned beans and bacon.

"Where are all the zombies? Hell, there aren't even any dogs roaming the streets."

Since the zombie apocalypse, dogs and coyotes had taken over territory once inhabited by man, feeding on corpses. Packs of either branch of the canine family sometimes took down zombies. Wild dogs were as ubiquitous after the apocalypse as Starbucks had once been.

"You should be happy there aren't any zombs. Let's do this."

Jake shook his head. Estes was competent with a weapon, but he carried too much excess baggage, harbored too much anger and resentment at the deaths of his wife and children by the Staggers Plague. That made him both restless and reckless, two dangerous traits in a world where patience and caution kept you alive. He was not Jake's first choice as a recon partner, but few people chose to become Arizona Rangers. The pay sucked, the hours were long, and the chances of dying were high. Having a natural immunity from the Stagger's spores wouldn't stop a bullet or a zombie.

"Something's not right," Jake insisted.

He could see Estes' edginess in his nervous hands caressing the trigger of his weapon. If Estes was eager to get himself killed, that was his business, but Jake did not care to join him. Estes usually deferred to Jake's judgment, but the two-year anniversary of his family's death was only two days away, and the bitter memories lay heavily on his mind crowding out caution.

He growled his annoyance. "Come on, Jake! For God's sake. Three slow zombs, and they're a block away. We check out the building, report back to the captain, and eat breakfast. Then we go home. It's a sweet deal, a simple in-and-out."

It sounded easy enough, but one thing Jake had learned since E-Day, his personal End of the World Day when the president of the U.S. had finally declared Martial Law for a country descended into chaos: Nothing was ever simple. Simple had died with three hundred channels of crap on the television, drive-thru fast food, the World Wide Web, and romantic walks in the park with your best girl. He lived life by a set of self-imposed hard and fast rules, Jake's Laws. Two applied to this particular situation. *Jake's Law #3 — A fool and his life are soon parted.* Estes was being a fool and was trying to drag Jake along with him. The other was *Jake's Law #7 — Trust yourself first; and others seldom.* He had long ago learned to trust his gut instincts, and they screamed for him to crawl his ass back out of town.

He tried reasoning with Estes, to make him question the obvious. "Why aren't there more zombies in town? Why no corpses, no skeletons, or no fucking dogs?"

Estes sighed. "It's a small village, less than 1,600 people according to the last census. Maybe they all died in church, or maybe they left town when things got rough. Hell, maybe they're having a fucking picnic in the park, and we weren't invited."

Jake dismissed Estes' caustic reply, though he did like the part about the picnic. His instincts had kept him alive in through two tours of Afghanistan, twelve years as a Pima County deputy, and two years of zombie apocalypse. "That's a lot of maybes."

Estes snorted. "Look, I'm not sitting here roasting in the sun while you think about it." He cocked the lever of his Winchester .30-30 to chamber a round and stood. "I'm going in. You can sit there all day for—"

He never finished his thought. The side of his head exploded like a kicked Jack-o-Lantern. Blood and brains sprayed the paint-peeling wooden wall beside him. His eyes rolled up as if he were trying to stare at the small hole that had suddenly appeared in his right temple dripping blood down the side of his face. The report of the heavy caliber rifle echoed through the empty town a second later, as Estes slowly crumpled to the ground at Jake's feet. He twitched once, twice, and then went still. His eyes stared up at the clear blue sky, but they didn't see anything. *He finally made it to be with his family.*

Estes' death did not strike Jake personally. The impatient bank manager turned Arizona Ranger had been a comrade but not a friend. He no longer had friends. Friends died, and he had seen too many deaths in his lifetime to allow anyone else get under his skin. Almost instantly, the com receiver in his ear burst into life.

"What the hell was that?" Captain Lambrini shouted at him.

Jake winced at the feedback screeching in his ear. "Estes is down. Sniper. Sounded like a .243 Browning," he reported succinctly, keeping his voice calm and controlled, a trait that had drawn comments of 'cold fish' and 'ice water for blood' from his fellow Rangers. He didn't mind. It made it easier for him to remain aloof. He preferred keeping as much distance between himself and others as possible, a personal buffer zone.

He hugged the ground and peeked around the corner of the building, ready to jerk his head back if he saw anything. "From the angle, the shot had to come from the municipal building, left corner front window."

Jake waited impatiently while Lambrini considered his options. The captain was deliberate and cautious. Normally, both traits were desirable in a leader, but when quick decisions counted, it was irritating. "Hold your position. We'll be there in two mikes."

A bullet ripped a divot from the cracked asphalt beside Jake. The sound was different this time, a heavier caliber weapon. The shooter from the left window had no line of sight at his position. The shooter was not alone.

"The hell with that. There are at least two shooters. I'm engaging."

"Blakely! Hold—"

He ripped the ear bud from his ear and let it dangle from the receiver clipped to his belt. He didn't need Lambrini's useless chatter in his ear. If there were more than two shooters, one of them could move between him and his team and cut him off, leaving his ass hanging in the early morning breeze. To make matters worse, the shots had attracted the zombies' attention, rousing them from their aimless rambling. Now, like vultures, the smell of Estes' blood drew them to his position, staggering like drunks from the parasitic infection slowly eating away their brains. By their emaciated condition, the slow moving Shamblers had not eaten in a while. They would eventually die without sustenance, but they weren't dead yet and still posed a deadly threat. He was immune to the airborne spores, but without immediate medical attention, a zombie bite was certain death.

He waited until the three zombies were in the street between him and the shooters, and then leaped up and ran straight at them. One zombie went down almost immediately, its chest blown away from behind by a shot meant for him. He sidestepped a second zombie's reaching arms, spun the third one around, and shoved it ahead of him with his foot to use as a shield. Its head exploded, scattering wads of the tiny, wire-like parasitical Staggers worms all over the asphalt. He carefully avoided the wriggling bloody gore and leaped for a 1995 Chevy pickup lying on its side up against the curb. He landed heavily and rolled behind it just as bullets tore up the street behind him. Another bullet ripped through the thin bed of the truck bed beside his head, sending shards of rusty metal flying. One lodged in his cheek. *Great! All I need is tetanus.*

He plucked the metal shaving from his cheek, hugged the ground, and crawled to the front of the truck where the heavy engine block and metal chassis offered better protection. Peeking through the grill, he detected slight movement at the edge of a window on the right side of the one-story building, a shadow within the shadows. Like Estes, he carried a lever-action Winchester 1873, a sentimental affectation the territorial governor insisted on for the Rangers, but his was an Italian-made Uberti .44-40. He preferred the heavier 240-grain .44 caliber over the normal .30 caliber round for the extra punch it offered. It was in line with *Jake's Law #5 — In a lawless land, the biggest gun makes the law.* He always wanted the biggest gun on the block. There was no such thing as too much firepower. Right now, he wished he had a LAWS rocket.

The shadowy figure was very cagy, moving back away from the window between shots, but he possessed the fatal flaw of most amateurs; the shooter moved to a steady rhythm beating in his head. He methodically sighted and fired, slowly targeting along the truck's hood with each shot searching for a gap through the mass of metal before retreating to the shadows. Jake had learned one important lesson with the First Recon Battalion in Afghanistan — never let the enemy know where your next shot was coming from. It made you a tempting target for a sniper round or an RPG.

Jake watched the shooter for a couple of minutes, matching his internal rhythm to the shooter's pattern. In his mind, he could see the shooter slide back the bolt of the rifle, load a bullet, slide the bolt closed, and move to the window. After the next shot, he began counting down; then, he stood, hoping like hell that the first shooter wasn't aiming at him, and sighted through his 20X scope at the spot he knew the first shooter would be. He did not rush. He took a deep breath and exhaled slowly, as he gently squeezed the trigger. At one, he fired. The window exploded just as the shooter stepped in front of it. Jake had a quick glimpse of a bearded man's startled expression as shards of glass peppered his face, followed by the heavy .44 caliber slug tearing through his skull.

Jake dropped down behind the truck just as the second shooter's shot gouged a crease in the truck's faded blue, left front fender. He smiled when he heard answering fire. His reinforcements had finally arrived. Lambrini had not been too far off on his two minute ETA. Fighting down memories of Afghanistan, Jake cocked his rifle, took a deep breath, and sprinted across twenty yards of open ground for the building's front door, expecting a bullet in the gut with every step. At the last moment, he veered sharply and fired through the plate glass window beside the door. He leaped head first through the shattered glass, rolled across the floor, and came up on his knees, pointing his weapon toward the shooter's position. Through the office's open door, he saw the shooter, alerted by the breaking glass, turn away from the window to face him.

Jake eased the pressure on the trigger slightly as he saw the shooter's face. The kid couldn't have been more than fifteen with a bad case of acne and no face fuzz marring his thin cheeks. He was shirtless and barefoot in dirty jeans, and his ribs pressed tightly against his sallow skin. He looked as if he had missed more than a few meals. His dirty, long blond hair hung in filthy curls to his shoulder. In his trembling hands, he held an old bolt-action Browning .243 caliber deer rifle with a scope. Jake's anger rose when he realized the kid was the one who had shot Estes. Still, he did not want to kill a frightened teenager who should have been hunting his first deer with his father or hanging out at the mall checking out girls if the world had not ended about the time he hit puberty.

"Arizona Ranger, kid," he called out. "Drop the rifle."

The kid hesitated when he saw the sun glinting off the badge on Jake's chest. For a split second, Jake thought it was over and began to breathe a sigh of relief, but he stopped short when the kid raised the rifle to his hip and pointed it in his direction. He no longer looked like a frightened boy. He looked like a predator with cold, lifeless eyes. He reminded Jake of a younger version of Levi Coombs, the man who had almost killed him. He swore softly to himself. He had almost forgotten *Jake's Law #12 — Stay focused.*

He fired two quick rounds into the kid's chest. At close range, the .44-40 slugs ripped out his back, painting the faded grey wallpaper with splashes of crimson blood. The kid stumbled backwards into the wall and slid down it to the floor, leaving a glistening blood smear across a two years out of date calendar depicting a roadrunner perched on a branch of a palo verde tree, head cocked to one side as if listening for the kid's last gasping breath. His dark brown eyes were open, staring at Jake, no longer cold. They were frightened and pleading. A tear rolled down one cheek. His lips moved, but no words came out.

"Damn you, kid!" Jake shouted, but the boy did not hear him. He was dead.

At the sound of glass crunching, he turned, weapon at ready, and saw Captain Lambrini step through the broken window. His face was grim as he stared at the dead boy.

"I told you to hold," he shot at Jake.

Jake cradled his rifle in his arms and glared at Lambrini. "I was too exposed."

"You could have retreated and waited for us."

Jake's irritation at the senseless death of the boy bled through his words. "There were two of them," he snarled. "There might have been more. I couldn't take the chance you guys might leave my ass hanging out."

"Dammit, Jake, you've got to learn to trust your team."

Jake's Law #7 raced through his head — *Trust yourself first, others seldom.* "Yeah."

Lambrini stared at the dead boy and frowned. "He's just a kid."

The captain's misplaced sympathy for the dead boy irritated him. "He's old enough to blow half of Estes' head off. I gave him an out, but he wouldn't take it."

"Did you have to kill him? Couldn't you just wound him? You're a good shot."

Jake frowned and shook his head slowly. Lambrini was a rarity, a man of honor dedicated to rebuilding a crumbling society using the law. He was a good organizer and a likable person, but he was pitifully out of his depth when it came to dealing with the lawless. He hated to kill. A good heart just made a bigger target. It irritated

Jake that Lambrini thought he had killed the kid for no good reason.

"If I have to shoot, I shoot to kill," he replied. "Life's too short for regrets. If someone's got to die, it won't be me."

"What happened with Estes?"

Jake shrugged. "He got careless."

Lambrini shook his head. "Dammit, Jake! He was your partner. You should have looked after him. We didn't need to lose another man."

Harry Deacon and Gerald Cray strode down the hallway from the other end of the building. Deacon carried the other shooter's rifle. He dropped it on the floor, barely glancing at the dead boy; then, laid a box of cartridges on the table. "One more body back there," he said, jerking his thumb toward the other end of the hallway. He smiled at Jake. "Clean head shot. That's a Kimber 8400 he was using."

Jake looked at the box of .325 Winchester Short Magnum shells and shook his head. "A damn elk rifle. No wonder it was punching a hole through the truck like a cardboard box. I'm glad he wasn't a better shot."

"Is the building secure?" Lambrini asked.

Cray shook his head. "The front is. There are still several rooms in the back we haven't checked yet."

"Don't stand around admiring Jake's work," he snapped. "Go check them out. Where is Andrews?"

Mitch Andrews, a twenty-six-year-old former Army National Guard helicopter pilot was the sixth man of their recon team, Team Charlie. He had almost as much military experience as Jake, and should have been the team leader instead of Lambrini, but like Jake, Andrews shunned responsibility and preferred to follow orders.

"Checking the outside perimeter."

Lambrini nodded. "At least someone's following proper procedure."

Jake pulled his Colt revolver from its holster and placed one round in the kid's head. Lambrini jumped at the unexpected shot so close behind him. He whirled on Jake.

"What the hell, Jake?"

"In case he had the Staggers. I didn't want him coming back to life and biting you in the ass." Then, he brushed past Lambrini to join Deacon and Cray.

"When we get back, we have to talk, you and me," Lambrini shouted after him.

"Sure thing, Captain."

He had fired the pistol just to irritate Lambrini, wipe away some of his smugness. There was no way the dead kid was coming back to life. The Staggers parasite hijacked the body's autonomic functions, but it wasn't like in some zombie movies, no headless corpses walking around or skeletal creatures. It looked supernatural, but as the medical professionals had explained so often during the plague, it was simply a process of a natural parasite-host infection. Not that he cared. Zombies were dangerous; therefore, he killed them whenever possible.

The three pushed through the swinging double doors into a long, dark corridor. A dirty window in an exit door at the far end of the corridor barely admitted enough light fend off complete darkness. A water fountain stood against the wall between two doors marked with the AIGA symbols for men and women's bathrooms: a white stylized figure of a man, and a female in a wide dress, or possibly a Scotsman in a kilt. Jake could not remember the last time he had seen a woman in a dress.

Deacon pressed the lever on the water fountain. No water came out. "Figures," he said.

Jake opened the men's restroom door, and the stench of overflowing toilets and reek of stale urine immediately assaulted him. Deacon caught a whiff, rolled his eyes, and took two steps backwards. "Damn! Somebody's got some intestinal problems." Light filtered in through a small outside window with frosted glass, allowing Jake to determine quickly that the two stalls were empty. The foul odor wafting from the commodes discouraged further investigation. He closed the door tightly behind him as he left.

"We should weld that shut," Cray said.

The women's restroom was a little better, but the smell was still overpowering. Roaches scurried away out of sight beneath the sink cabinet when he opened the door. He grimaced. He hated roaches more than he hated zombies. If zombies ate roaches rather than people, he might like them a little more. Paper towels overflowed a garbage can in the corner. Scented hand soap had leaked from a dispenser above the sink, forming a hardened amber puddle on the counter. A frozen stalactite of soap hung from the nozzle. The soap's once floral fragrance had deteriorated over time to a scent reminiscent of decaying floral displays in a funeral home.

They moved on. The first room held only a few pieces of dust-covered office furniture and a row of metal filing cabinets along one wall. A faded calendar from 2015 bore handwritten notes scribbled in the daily boxes for each day up until the first week of June. Understandably, after that, the boxes were blank. Things had gotten too hectic and dangerous by then for business as usual. Most cities were already under siege by thousands of Staggerers. When the president had declared Martial Law, most government offices closed their doors for the last time.

The second room was substantially similar to the first with a minor variation in furniture placement and choice of wallpaper. In the third room, the furniture had been shoved against the wall. Boxes of canned goods and cases of bottled water were stacked haphazardly in the cleared space in the middle of the room. It appeared as if the two men simply ate through the contents of one box and then moved on to the next box. *Not much on variety*, Jake thought. Empty bottles of booze littered the floor. Dirty pots and pans sat on a desk beside a Coleman propane camp stove. A garbage can overflowed with paper plates and white plastic eating utensils. Maggots crawled through the garbage, looking like fat, disgusting, white Staggers worms. The odor was not as bad as the restrooms, but it still turned his stomach.

"Guess they don't like doing dishes," Deacon commented, smiling. Then he whistled a long, low note. "Look at this stash." He pointed to a cardboard box sitting atop a filing cabinet filled with dozens of bottles of pills looted from a drug store. Jake recognized several bottles of Class II narcotics.

"Guess they don't like facing reality either," he said, a jab at Captain Lambrini.

The fourth door was locked, but Jake heard furtive movement inside. It could be a third shooter, a roomful of zombies, or a frightened squirrel, but he was not taking chances. He nodded to Deacon and Cray, who immediately slipped into professional mode and took up flanking positions on each side of the door to cover him, while he crept closer. He counted down silently from three using his fingers. On one, he kicked in the door and dropped low, while Deacon took the high position, covering one side of the room, and Cray covered the other.

High-pitched screams startled him so badly he almost fired. Inside, three women, two of them barely in their twenties, lay handcuffed to metal beds. One, naked except for a ripped bra pulled down to expose her large brown breasts, barely glanced up at him through half-closed eyes. Her body and face were a mess of bruises. Some were new and dark, others old and fading. Rows of cigarette burns, some fresh, ran in a line up the inner thigh of both legs ending just below her pubes. The other two women pushed as far away from the door as their handcuffs would allow.

"Jesus Christ!" Deacon groaned when he saw the silent, tortured girl, his voice filled with outrage. His hand gripped his rifle so tightly his knuckles whitened.

The sight infuriated Jake as well. His gut clenched in anger. If the kid had anything to do with this torture chamber, he was glad he shot the bastard. "Check those two dead bastards for the keys," Jake told Deacon. To the women, he said, "It's okay, ladies. We're Arizona Rangers. We're here to help you."

He lowered his rifle and held out his hand. He was not sure they understood him, but at least they stopped screaming. He gently covered the naked girl with a blanket. She flinched when his shadow fell across her face, but otherwise she did not move.

"They drugged her," the older woman in the bed beside her said.

Jake looked over at the woman who had spoken. She was in her mid-forties, not magazine cover beautiful but not far from it. Her curly, bright red hair came out of a bottle, and her darker roots were beginning to show. She reminded Jake a little of Maureen O'Hara in *The Quiet Man* opposite John Wayne. She was slightly plump but far from fat. She had taken care of herself at one time, but no longer. He saw that a lot. The apocalypse killed the incentive for anything except basic survival. Some even tired of that effort after a while. Of course, handcuffed to a bed made proper grooming difficult.

"There were three of them," she said. "They stole a lot of drugs from the pharmacy and downed them with booze." She nodded her head toward the girl in the bed beside her. "I don't think they even know what they were giving her. Before the drugs, she fought back, cursing them in Spanish. The older one didn't like that. He liked hurting her though, the bastard."

Hearing that there was a third man somewhere around, Jake keyed his mic. "Captain, we found three women prisoners. One of them informs us there's a third man unaccounted for." He heard Lambrini swear in his ear bud, and then say, "You stay with the women. Tell Deacon and Cray to search the area, but for God's sake, be careful. Andrews, do you copy?"

A quick click of the mic indicated Andrews had heard, but wanted to remain silent and not give away his position. Jake turned his attention back to the older woman. "Did they drug you too?"

She chuckled. "Hell, I've gotten worse from my husband, God rest his zombie-ass soul. He had a short temper and quick fists, and I have a sharp tongue. I just laid back and took it like a man. Did you kill the kid?" she asked. Jake nodded. Her face became a mask of rage. "Good! He enjoyed calling me a filthy whore while he squeezed my tits. He loved to pinch my nipples until I yelled in pain. People like that didn't deserve to live through the plague when so many good people died. I hope he rots in hell."

Jake agreed with her. He had encountered more than his share of bastards that should have died early on. One in particular, Levi Combs, and his band of merry killers had almost killed him. They took from him everything he had worked so hard build, including his girlfriend, Jessica, forcing a nighttime showdown in the zombie-filled Tucson Mall to rescue her. He lived, and Combs was dead. He supposed that was what it always came down to: one person lives; one dies. He had been the lucky one that night.

"He'll rot," he replied. "What about you?" he asked the other girl, a young blonde, who had stared at him the entire time since he had entered the room. "What's your story?"

Beneath the bruises and the dirt, she was pretty. She might have been a cheerleader at the local high school or the girl next door. He supposed it didn't matter to the two corpses in the other room. To them, the women were just things to use, receptacles for their wanton lust. The bastards who had done this were worse than the zombies. At least zombies ate flesh because their disease drove them mad with an insatiable hunger.

She ignored his question. "Got a cigarette?" she asked, leaning forward so that her young pert breasts showed through her blouse. "I'm dying for a cigarette."

He ignored her cleavage. "I don't smoke, and you're too young to start."

She stared him boldly in the eyes. "I'm older than you think."

"I think you're about sixteen and frightened as hell. Now, how did you get here?"

Some of her forced composure left her. She slumped back on the bed. "They killed my father." She wrapped her arms around her chest and hugged herself. "I try not to think about the rest."

"She's been here three weeks," the older woman said. She nodded toward the semi-comatose girl. "She's been here two months as far as I could make out. My Spanish is about good enough to order *Dos Equis* and tacos."

"What about you?"

She chuckled, but Jake detected no humor in her voice, just sad acceptance. "I'm the latest addition to their harem. They found me a week ago in a hardware store looking for a pair of boots."

"Are there other survivors in town?"

She shook her head. "I don't know. I was passing through on my way to Albuquerque and stopped for supplies. That was my first mistake."

"There's a few groups scattered around the farms outside of town," the young girl replied. "They went into hiding when these three showed up."

"Why aren't there more zombies?" he asked. It still nagged at him. For a town of Hatch's size, there should have been hundreds of them. So far, he had seen only three.

Her face went grim, as if the memory hurt. "There were about thirty of us survivors. We lured the zombies out of town with loud music and slaughtered cattle in the bed of a pickup and down into the Placitas Arroyo. Then, everyone started shooting. It was …

awful." She covered her face and rocked on the bed. "They didn't scream or cry out as we shot them down. They just made a sort of low mewling noise, like baby goat or something. Then we burned the bodies. Some of them were still moving as they burned." She looked at Jake defiantly. "I knew some of them, but I didn't care. They weren't people anymore were they. They were just ..." She wrinkled her face, "things. Are you sure you don't have a cigarette?"

Lambrini walked in. He seemed nervous, unsure what to say to women who had suffered repeated rapes for weeks. "Uh, I contacted HQ. The recovery team will be here in a few hours. They'll have medics, if you ... Uh, we're going to clear Hatch of zombies and make it a farming community again. We'll get the farm equipment factories operating as soon as possible. You'll have plenty of food, and we'll post guards to keep out the, uh, riff raff. We're establishing farming communities and factory towns all over Arizona and New Mexico. We're rebuilding America one safe haven at a time."

"That's all well and good, but who's 'we'?" the older woman asked.

"The government, Miss ..."

"Call me Hilda. Is there one, a government I mean? I thought it pretty much folded at the end."

Lambrini shuffled his feet. "Well, we have a collection of regional civilian governments with territorial governors appointed by the military." He pointed to the five-pointed star on his shirt. "The Arizona Rangers are assigned to enforce the law and reconnoiter suitable sites to commandeer, uh, fortify with a military contingent and a civilian population."

Deacon came back with a key for the handcuffs. He unlocked the cuffs from the women's wrists. Hilda sat on the edge of the bed, rubbing her chaffed wrist. "If it's all the same to you, I'll be on my way to Albuquerque if you can spare a little food and water."

She stood, a little wobbly from her confinement, and walked over to the sedated girl. She began stroking the girl's cheek gently. The girl blinked a few times but said nothing.

"I'm afraid that would be impossible at this time, Miss, uh, Hilda. Albuquerque is still too dangerous."

"More dangerous than this," she snorted, waving her hand over the girl's body. "Give me a gun, and I'll take care of myself. Fucking bastards! I wish I could have shot the motherfuckers myself."

Lambrini frowned at her language. Jake grinned. Lambrini didn't mind men cursing, but thought it unladylike for a woman to swear, as if gentlemen and lady were terms that meant much after the apocalypse.

"We'll need everyone to help rebuild the area. Hatch is vital for food production and cattle. You'll have to remain here for the time being. We do a census of survivors, looking for, uh, useful skill sets."

"So I'm kind of an indentured migrant worker," she said.

Jake suppressed a chuckle. Deacon laughed aloud. Jake had heard Lambrini's speech a dozen times over the past year, and Lambrini had gotten no better at delivering it. He sounded like a high school principal at a pep rally trying to drum up team spirit.

Lambrini glared at Deacon. "I thought I told you and Cray to search for the third man."

"Jake asked me to get the keys."

Lambrini continued to stare at him.

"Oaky, okay, I'm moving," Deacon said and left.

Hilda leveled her gaze at Jake. She clearly was not impressed with Lambrini's pep talk.

"What about you? Is Mr. Rogers' Neighborhood here telling the truth?"

Jake smiled at her soubriquet for Lambrini. "He's right about Albuquerque. You'll never make it. There are thousands of zombies and five or six roving gang of bandits on I-25 between here and Albuquerque. Some towns have closed off all the roads in and out and are shooting anyone who comes near. They even took pot shots at an A-10 Warthog sent to photograph the area." He paused. Hilda sounded as though she was eager to leave. He did not blame her. "If you don't like it here, maybe you can hitch a ride to Yuma, Marana, or Maricopa," he suggested. "We've established communities there as well, safe havens. Or if you prefer, the railroad repair crews will reach here in a week or two. You could hitch a ride back with them. That's why we chose Hatch: a railroad, plenty of water from the Rio Grande, arable land, a solar farm, and a wind generator farm. Who knows, you might like it here."

She shook her head. "Fat chance of that. I've had my fill of Hatch. I like to move around." She ran her languid gaze over him appreciatively, taking in his muscle-toned body and his buzz-cut brown hair showing around the edges of his cap, finally ending her visual tour at his face, staring into his green eyes. He felt a pang of embarrassment that he hadn't shaved in three days. "You don't strike me as the stay-at-home type yourself," she said.

Her astute observation struck him deeply. In the beginning, when the Staggers had just hit and the world was going to hell, he had been a loner, a prepper, carefully avoiding people as unnecessary complications. He didn't need other peoples' problems added to his own. He had enough of his own to deal with. Then he had met Jessica, had literally almost ran her over with his jeep as she sprinted across the road just ahead of fast zombies, Lopers. He had rescued her and broken *Jake's Law #4 — Don't bring home more problems than you left with.* Their relationship was as brief and as shaky as his previous encounters with women, but this time she was the one who had said goodbye.

Younger than him by a decade, he supposed Jessica had thrown in with him purely for survival. She had said as much when they first met, but he gradually grew to care about her and thought she cared for him too. Maybe she had at first. She had broken him out of his lonely shell and forced him to rejoin the world of the living. One day when he returned to Marana, she had simply vanished, gone to Yuma leaving only a brief note. Her leaving hurt him deeply, but he couldn't fault her for her actions. He was not an easy man to live with.

"Someone's got to be out there killing zombies and sweeping the human scum off the streets and back into the gutters," he answered. "I got elected by virtue of *Jake's Law #8 — Use the tools you've got.* I'm a killer. That's my tool. That's what I bring to the table. There are only two places for people like me — with the law or against it." He brushed his finger over the tarnished and dented five-pointed star on his chest. "This belonged to my great-great grandfather, one of the original Arizona Rangers. He was a killer too. I guess it runs in my blood."

"Maybe you just give a shit about people," she replied.

"Don't kid yourself," he snapped. He tapped his chest with his fist. "I've got a lot of rage burning inside. I was a survivalist, a prepper, and all my preparations did damn little good in the end. Sometimes it just feels good to kill something. Shooting zombies takes the edge off."

She dribbled water from a bottle into the girl's mouth, but her eyes shifted back and forth between Jake and the girl. Most of it ran down the girl's cheek, but eventually, she swallowed some. Hilda frowned. "What about people like those two low lives?"

"They're a bonus," he said, his voice hard and grim.

She shook her head. "You sound all Billy Badass, but your eyes say you care. I saw the look in them when you saw us. You've got something inside you all right, but I don't think it's rage." She paused, as if afraid to go too far. Finally, she said, "You're carrying around a lot of guilt, Mister Jake Law. I know. I did too for quite a while. It's not worth it. It's a new world out there with new opportunities, and life's too short for what ifs. Each new sunrise brings a brand new chance to start over, but you can't move forward still anchored to the past. I discovered I'm not who I thought I was."

Jake chuckled. "An itinerant philosopher. Do you sing and dance too?"

She blushed. "I've got lots of talents, honey, but none you would want in your new community." She looked around the room. "If you gentlemen don't mind, could you round up some water, preferably hot, so we can wash up? I feel skuzzy." When no one moved, she added, "In private, if you please?"

Lambrini's cheeks reddened. "Uh, uh, of, of course," he sputtered. "I'll get some now."

Lambrini left first, eager to take his absence from the room, especially Hilda, who made him uncomfortable. Jake sighed, wondering if he was making a big mistake, and pulled his .25 caliber holdout piece from his boot. He laid the black Beretta semi-automatic on a table and walked out. Hilda closed the door behind him.

While Lambrini searched the building for a pot large enough to heat water, Jake returned to the room containing the drug stash. He rummaged through the box, finding several vials of opiates — Oxycodone, Methadone, and Fentanyl — and cartons of Ritalin, Amobarbitol, and Nabilone, a powerful hallucinogenic. By the number of empty bottles, the trio had taken no chances on facing reality with clear heads. He wondered what combination of drugs they had given the comatose girl. He didn't find what he was searching for, Actos for his Type 2 diabetes. He kept his condition mostly under control with diet, but he liked to keep Actos handy for an emergency. He did pocket a bottle of Ibuprophen for a tension headache that wouldn't seem to go away. The rest he left where it was. If they established a new infirmary in Hatch, the stash would make a good start on their drug supplies.

He poured a little whisky from the dregs of one bottle into his hand and wiped the cut on his cheek, hoping whoever had left their saliva in the whisky hadn't left a nasty little Staggers surprise behind. Hearing a loud thud in the next room, as if something heavy had fallen and hit the floor, he peeked around the corner, going cold inside when he saw a pair of legs protruding into the hallway from the room next door. He flinched as he recognized Lambrini's ostrich-skin boots. "Damn."

He pulled his Colt revolver and edged along the hall wall. He ducked his head into the room but saw nothing but Lambrini's body lying in a pool of blood.

"The other shooter is inside the building," he whispered into his mic.

He noticed the door to the women's room was open. Just as he sprinted down the hallway, two quick shots rang out inside the room. Seconds later, a man staggered out the door backwards clutching his stomach with both hands. One hand held a bloody knife, the one he had shoved into Lambrini's back, but the knife had not made the hole in his belly. He slammed against the wall moaning, "Sweet Jesus," over and over. Taking no chances, Jake put a round into the man's head. *Jake's Law #1 — Aim high; shoot straight.* The man folded like a house made of straw in a Magnitude 10 earthquake.

Hilda stepped out the door with his .25 caliber Beretta in her hand, smoke drifting from the end of the barrel. She stared at the dead man lying face down on the floor. "Bastard doesn't look so tough now with two holes in him."

Jake holstered his Colt, cursing aloud. Captain Lambrini was dead. He and Lambrini didn't always see eye to eye, but the captain meant well. He deserved a less ignominious death than a knife in the back from some drug-crazed scuzzbucket. Deacon and Cray rushed in, barely glancing at the dead man. They, too, had recognized Lambrini's boots.

"Shit," Deacon yelled, slamming his fist into the wall, "not the captain, too."

"He's dead," Jake told them, though they had already guessed as much. "This guy stabbed him. Hilda shot him."

"Thanks, lady," Deacon said to her. "Nice fucking shooting." He looked at Jake. "I guess that places you in charge, Jake. What do we do?"

Jake swore again, this time quietly under his breath. People always turned to him when the shit hit the fan, as if he wore a sign around his neck that said 'Mr. Wizard.' "We do our job and finish checking out the town. First, one of you go find something to heat some water in for the ladies to bathe. Then, we bury Lambrini right out front and mark his grave as a reminder that an Arizona Ranger died here."

He keyed his mic. "Andrews, Lambrini is down. Third shooter is accounted for and dealt with. Keep an eye open."

Jake suspected that before they restored the southwest to any semblance of its past glory, there would be more Ranger graves dotting the landscape. They weren't fighting renegade Indians and border bandits like his great-great grandfather, but the new enemies were just as deadly, and there were more of them.

"Drag these corpses out of here and burn them in the street with the zombies. I don't think the zombies will mind the company." He turned to Hilda. "I'll see if I can find something for you with a little more knock down power than that .25 caliber."

"Don't bother. Just let me have more ammunition. I don't intend to use it unless I have to, but if I do, it'll be close-up and personal." She smiled at him, but it was a sad smile filled with regret for him. "For a man who claims no ties to humanity and makes up his own rigid set of laws to live by, Mister Jake Law, you seem to take charge awfully easily."

When he replied, he spoke slowly, regretfully, while nodding his head in reluctant agreement with her. "Yeah, that's my problem. When you're good at one thing, people tend to think you're good at everything. People are always looking for a savior. I ain't it."

"You're a complicated man, Jake."

Looking at her standing over a dead man's corpse with his Beretta in her hand, her words struck him as funny. "It's a complicated world, Hilda."

She watched as Deacon and Cray each grabbed a leg and dragged the dead man's body out the front door of the building, leaving a blood smear along the dirty tile floor. "No, it's a simple world now, Jake," she replied. "Kill or be killed. We're like animals." She stared at him. "Will it always be that way?"

"A friend of mine, Alton Reed, doesn't think so. He has faith in mankind's ability to take the punches and bounce back. He talked me into joining the fledgling government's efforts to rebuild the country."

"Sounds like a wise man."

"Maybe he is, but he's paying for it now. He had a little too much faith in his fellow man. He was gunned down approaching a farmhouse full of survivors with his hands raised in the air. He damn near died. Now, he has a busted knee, a bad limp, and a piece of lead in his chest as reminders."

"What did you do?"

Jake's face went rigid at the memory. "I shot all of them down in cold blood, as a reminder to others." It had not been his finest hour, but he had no regrets. As Hilda had remarked, some people didn't deserve to survive.

Hilda had watched him carefully to judge his reaction to her question. She winced at his admission, but said, "Sounds like poetic justice to me."

He grunted, "Humph! Frontier justice. It's all we have for now." He tapped his Ranger star. "This badge makes me judge, jury, and executioner."

"That's a lot of power for one man."

"It's too much power for any man or woman, but someone has to do it."

"And you got elected." It wasn't a recrimination, but it might as well have been for the way her words cut him to the core.

"Right."

"Well, Jake, you just might be a human being after all."

"From my experience, being human isn't all it's cracked up to be." He shuffled his foot on the floor, at a loss for words after his admission. He wasn't sure why he was opening up to this strange woman, but it was a little too much like confessing to a priest. He half-expected her to assign him to say a thousand Hail Marys as penitence. "I'll see you get that hot water and some food. After that ... well, you're—"

"Free, white, and twenty-one?" She chuckled. "Plus a few years. It isn't so politically correct to say that, is it, but I guess no one gives a shit anymore. Zombies come in all colors and religions, and there's no room left for diversity in an apocalyptic world. We're all the same, regardless of sex, the color of our skin, social background, or political affiliation. We're all hanging on by our fingernails, one zombie bite, or a breath of Staggers-laden air away from death. It's a shame it took the end of the world to create real equality, but that just goes to show how hard we fought to be different from one another."

"Damn, you are a philosopher," Jake said.

She laughed. "Honey, I've been called many things, but philosopher hasn't been one of them."

Hilda leaned against the doorframe with her arms clasped under her breasts. For a woman who had endured captivity and physical and mental torture, she was remarkably composed. Jake stared at her for a moment considering possibilities. Hilda was a few years older than him but still a looker. She was tough, brash, and didn't take shit from anyone. She would make a good match for him. He suddenly realized what he was doing and shook his head to dislodge the thought. She was barely out of a bad situation, and he was having lustful thoughts about her. He felt ashamed. She didn't need his problems, and he had already made his quota of women mistakes for a while. He had enough problems to deal with. He was still stinging from Jessica's rejection of him.

Jake's Law #17 — Love isn't just cruel; it's string your guts out on a clothesline to bake in the sun cruel.

As if reading his thoughts, she said, "In case you're wondering, Jake, one of the things I've found out about myself since the ceiling dropped on our heads is that I'm, at most, bisexual, leaning toward lesbian. No offense, but I'm kind of off men right now."

Jake felt his cheeks burn from embarrassment. Had he been so transparent? Was Hilda so astute, or was it an easy guess, something all women learned to see in men. He might as well have been wearing a sign over his crotch saying 'In Service.'

"I ... I'm sorry. I guess I was thinking aloud. I'll ..."

"It's okay, Mister Jake Law. I don't mind your appreciating what I've got to offer, certainly not at my age. You would make a fine catch if you ever decide to become a member of the human race again instead of setting yourself up as its sole protector."

God, she hits the nail on the head. Sole protector. Is that what I am? He was afraid to look at her, fearing she could read his every thought. "I'd better ..."

"Yeah, I'm needed in there." She nodded her head at the room that had so recently been her prison cell.

When Deacon and Cray returned for Lambrini, Deacon shifted his gaze between Hilda and Jake, sensing something had happened between them, but he was too polite to probe. They picked up Lambrini's body and carried it with more dignity than they had his killer. Watching the impromptu funeral procession, Jake felt a lump form in his throat. Lambrini, for all his faults, had been a good man, and the world needed good men. He noticed Andrews standing just outside the front door. His stony face revealed none of what he was thinking, but Jake knew he had to be thinking the same thing he was. Two Rangers were dead. The mission had soured quickly.

Hilda walked back into the room, but before she closed the door, she said, "You might want to check out that old empty building down the street, Jake. Those three yahoos spent a lot of time there. Whatever is in there, they seemed to like it." Then, she closed the door.

Jake stared at it for a moment, and then shook his head. Hilda was a survivor like him. She rolled with the punches life threw at her and came up off the mat before the ten count. There were thousands of people just like her out there, scattered across the country, but for every Hilda, there were thousands more who had no clue; who barely existed, waiting for someone to come along and save them. That was where he came in, and he hated it.

It's a shitty job, but someone's got to do it.

He picked up his Winchester, levered a cartridge into the chamber, slung it over his shoulder, and walked out of the building. His conversation with Hilda had struck too many familiar chords and left him feeling sorry for himself. Maybe he would see what had kept the dead trio so amused in the empty building. *Meth lab? Marijuana?* No, they didn't seem the type to put much effort into anything, especially not when they had a box full of narcotics so handy.

Andrews had laid aside his rifle for a spade, digging a hole for Lambrini in the small patch of gravel and overgrown weeds beside the flagpole in front of the municipal building. He didn't look up at Jake, and Jake offered no greeting in passing. They needed no words to express their frustration at how events had unfolded. Anger ballooned inside his Jake's chest as if someone was pumping too much air into a football bladder. If he didn't release some of the pressure soon, his chest would explode. He bemoaned the fact that there were no zombies to shoot and kicking a garbage can over seemed too juvenile. He was a full-grown irritated bastard and needed a big boy, man-sized target on which to vent his anger.

Why are there no zombies around when you need them?

2

June 10, 2017, 8:30 a.m.   Marana Safe Haven, Marana, AZ —

Alton Reed limped across the street to the new commissary building at Gladden Farms Subdivision, now part of Marana Safe Haven. His right knee barely moved because of the stiff knee brace strapped around it, and he leaned heavily on the cane he probably would depend upon for the rest of his life. A .308 caliber Winchester bullet had shredded ligaments and shattered the patella on the way through from front to back. His knee ached constantly, an incessant dull throb that soared to bouts of ecstatic agony at times, like now. Three tiny metal fragments from a second .308 round, too small to remove from his chest, were reminders of the bullet that had pierced a lobe of his left lung. Only Jake's quick action by getting him to a field hospital had saved his life.

The short journey from his home to the commissary winded him. He refused to give in to the pain and take the pills Doctor Van Ross had prescribed. They were for those extra special days when the pain was so bad he did not want to get out of bed. He already used Millipred for his chronic asthma and kept an inhaler in his pocket for emergencies. A dependency on scarce drugs made things difficult when drug-manufacturing plants no longer existed. He had lost thirty pounds after his surgery. That had helped ease the pressure on his knee and reduce the severity of the pain, but the dull discomfort in his chest served as a reminder of just how close to death he had come.

Jake often pointed out the irony that both he and Alton had chronic medical conditions requiring medication, hardly the likeliest traits for apocalypse survivors. Druggies searching for narcotics and ordinary frightened people seeking a cure or a preventative for the Staggers had looted most pharmacies thoroughly. Physically, Jessica Hubley had been the fittest of the three of them. A former yoga instructor, a health food fanatic, a pacifist, and a strict vegetarian, she had found life after the apocalypse extremely difficult and harrowing. If not for Jake's insistence that she learn to defend herself by teaching her to use a weapon, she probably would be dead.

Alton frowned as he thought of Jessica. He didn't know what had happened between her and Jake, but it saddened him. Jake needed her, even if he didn't want to admit it. Her softness knocked the edges off Jake's rigid exterior. Her serenity countered his contumacy. Her sense of hope balanced his carefully honed cynicism. He still heard from her occasionally through a mutual friend in Yuma, and his work took him there every few months when they had lunch together, but he missed the close-knit bond the three of them had shared. Fate had thrown them together, kept them alive when the odds did not favor their survival. They had become friends, and friends were hard to come by; trustworthy friends even more so.

Jake still had not completely forgiven him for withholding the fact that he had been working with the fledgling provisional territorial government when they had first met. He hadn't lied about being a former high school science teacher in San Manuel. Teaching had been his life before the apocalypse, but he had burned down his former school in a deliberate act of arson to get Jake's attention. The government needed suitable people to help establish safe communities for survivors. As a former Pima County Deputy, Jake had the qualifications they required. Rebuilding the country would be a time-consuming task, and there were far more survivors who needed help than people willing to provide it.

Jake, the ultimate loner, had been reluctant at first, but Jessica slowly broke down his natural distrust of others and put him on the right path, one of service. Jake could not handle the mundane daily problems of community living — complaints about not enough hot water, grumbling about the humdrum choices of food, or the whining about their lot in life — but he did his job his way, Jake style, which was usually noisy and final.

Alton stopped to rest his leg and to catch his breath, sitting on a concrete bench beneath the shade of one of the fifteen-feet-tall Palo Verde trees planted along the sidewalk paralleling the street. A young couple riding by on bicycles waved at him. He threw up his hand in casual greeting. He did not recognize their faces, but the community of six hundred was growing rapidly. The laughter of children drifting from the park down the street lightened his heart. Soon, they would reopen Estes Elementary, and Marana Safe Haven would have a real school.

A black and white Border Patrol SUV driven by an Arizona Ranger drove slowly down the street, patrolling the neighborhood streets. Alton recognized Manuel Avera, a former Phoenix sports shoe retailer, and flagged him down. Ranger Avera rolled down his window.

"Morning, Alton." He pointed his brown hand at Alton's leg. "How's the leg?"

Alton flexed his knee and frowned; then, he held out his hand, almost pasty in comparison to Avera's sun-baked hue, and wiggled it. "So-so. How about you?"

Avera smacked the side of the SUV with his palm and smiled. "Life's good. Heard from Jake?"

"Not since he went to Hatch. He should be back in a day or two."

"Why Hatch? It's a long way from here."

"Hatch is isolated, all right, but it has a railroad, a paved highway, independent sources for generating electricity, water from the Rio Grande for irrigation, and small farm-implement factories—just what we need."

"I hope they don't want me to go there. I like it here. After Phoenix ..." Avera's voice trailed off. Like with many survivors, dredging up old memories raised specters better left buried. "Well, I like it here," he finished. "Do you need a lift to the commissary?"

Alton considered the tempting offer, but replied, "No, I need the exercise. If Doctor Von Ross saw me shirking, he'd blow a gasket."

Avera chuckled. "He's hard-nosed, all right. Well, I'd better make my rounds. Might be a jaywalker somewhere I can ticket."

"If that's the worst of your problems, you're lucky."

"See you later," Avera said, as he rolled up his window and drove away.

It had taken months to round up and eliminate all the zombies in a ten-mile radius of Gladden Farms and the city of Marana. Heavy, chain-link fences and brick walls surrounded the subdivision, and more miles of sturdy fences surrounded the town, the fields, and the former ASARCO copper mine. Twenty-four-hour manned gates guarded the entrances, and armed mobile and foot patrols inspected the fence line daily for stray zombies. Since Jake's epic battle at Split Rock Canyon, his former refuge in the Galiuros Mountains near Oracle, most of the armed gangs and undesirables had retreated to the south side of Tucson or holed up out in the desert. The occasional stray Staggerer or a wanderer looking for a handout was all they had to deal with now. Uniformed security conveyed a sense of law and order in a lawless land.

All civilizations required laws. Their small community was no exception. Their laws were simple and few and required a special breed of men and women to enforce them. Jake was the perfect man for the job, as if he had been born and bred for hard times like a zombie apocalypse. Some people tiptoed through minefields, keeping their gaze focused on the ground at their feet. Jake hit obstacles head on, eyes forward in his famous piercing squint; damn the torpedoes and full-steam ahead.

Despite his hard-nosed attitude and chronic cynicism, Jake was usually right about most things. He had spent years preparing for a doomsday scenario and time had proved him right. He was a difficult man to figure out, not complicated, just difficult. Maybe that was why he liked Jake so much.

Alton's memories of the battle with Levi Comb's band of cutthroats at Jake's ranch in Split Rock Canyon remained somewhat blurred, perhaps a self-defense mechanism imposed by his subconscious mind to suppress the fleeting images of mowing down men with a machine gun. The grim images still popped into his head occasionally like bloodstained panels of a graphic novel and troubled his dreams. He was not proud of his actions, but sometimes life forced decisions upon people they had rather avoid. In the end, Jake had thrown it all away, flooded his entire canyon retreat to save Jessica. He wasn't sure Jake had yet come to terms with his decision.

The commissary was air-conditioned. The cool air bathed Alton's face when he walked inside. He stopped a moment to savor the small feat an air conditioner represented. In a desert, heat was a deadly enemy. In the frigid northern cities, cold was the killer. Heat, cool, water, food—these were the necessities. All else were second-tier concerns. The military had garrisons at the Saguaro Power Plant just up I-10 near Red Rock. Its 2,000-megawatt solar plant and 1.35-megawatt energy plant were capable of supplying all their electrical needs for decades. When up and running again, the ASARCO copper mine, four open pits covering 19,000 acres, would consume much of the power production in its leaching, pumping, and smelting process. The proximity of the power plant, the copper mine, the Marana airport, and the agriculture fields played a part in the decision to establish a safe haven in Marana. Alton was glad. Though he had lived in nearby Oracle, Marana was close enough to call home.

The electric-eye door swooshing open and closed behind him drew him out of his reverie. The commissary, well stocked with food scavenged from area warehouses, represented a huge step forward from the community soup kitchens of early days. Most items were available by chits, a paper script issued by the territorial government as legal currency for assigned work. No one went hungry. That was Rule #1, similar to Jake's Laws. Keeping the few remaining humans alive was not charity: It was a necessity. However, everyone contributed to the community in whatever way they could.

He stopped in the bread aisle and inhaled the hearty aroma of fresh-baked loaves of wheat bread and yeast rolls. Delivered twice a week from a bakery in Summerhaven, an isolated community atop nearby Mount Lemon, fresh bread made the canned potted meats and rough-cured hams used for sandwiches palatable. The eighty-five residents of Summerhaven, safe at 10,000 feet with a single, easily defended winding road up the mountain, chose to keep their independence, but traded freely with the safe havens. Alton hoped that in the future they would join the safe haven conglomerate. Summerhaven had a lot to offer, and every living human being was now a precious part of the human race.

Alton chose a bag of rolls from which he would also toast croutons for salads. His doctor had advised him to cut down on starchy foods, but sometimes living did not seem worth it if he had to forgo simple pleasures.

Few people shopped so early in the morning. Most were at their assigned jobs. As a member of the Council, the community's seven-person governing body, he had the luxury of shopping whenever the mood struck him. He wandered up and down the aisles with his shopping cart, absentmindedly picking up cans and boxes, distracted from what he had come for by thoughts concerning Jake. So much of his life now intertwined with Jake's that his absence left a blank space in his life. He chuckled to himself thinking, *Jake leaves a big hole.*

He missed their lively discussions verging on arguments. From Jake, he had learned to be hard enough to survive in a post-apocalyptic world, and from him, Jake had learned to bend a little. Not everyone could live up to Jake's high standards. He set the bar high for himself and expected others to match his efforts. Most could not. Gradually, Jake was beginning to understand that. The world needed hard people, capable people, to survive the near fatal collapse of civilization, but to rebuild required other qualities, some less tangible. Carpenters, farmers, bakers, and teachers were not enough. Civilization also required artists and musicians; people who dreamed. Dreams made the future possible.

He stopped at one of two large wire bins at the end of one aisle. Damaged cans, cans without labels, and boxes too damaged to read the contents went inside the Food Surprise Basket, and all other items went into the Dry Goods Surprise Basket. Shoppers could choose one item from each basket free on each visit. It was a win-or-lose situation, their version of Vegas. Once, he had won the lottery, opening a can of duck consommé. More often than not, his finds were cans of dog food, canned hash, or moldy underwear. He closed his eyes and chose randomly, letting Fate decide. He glanced in his basket, noting he had taken mostly comfort foods, such as flaked mash potatoes, macaroni and cheese, and Rice-A-Roni, all heavy on starch and low on protein. Maybe his body was trying to tell him something. He debated putting something back and stocking up on canned meats, but gave in to the impulse and added a bag of sugar cookies to his stash. Salvaged from Costco, the two-year-old cookies would be stale, but dunked in coffee, they would serve as a quick, if not nourishing, snack.

The commissary carried few luxury items. They could not spare the salvage crews to search for anything but the necessities. Liquor was always in short supply, as were cigarettes, fresh meat, and electronics. He drew a decent salary, but luxuries were expensive. He tried to secure a bottle of wine or liquor or a few bottles of beer whenever he could, but had learned to do without fresh meat.

The checkout person was a young girl with red hair, maybe sixteen, with freckles, braces, and a dour expression that made her appear older than she was. In the real world, she would have been a Plain Jane, unpopular and chosen last for the Senior Prom. In the New World, she would marry young, start a family, and hope to pass on her Staggers immunity to her offspring. The verdict was still out on that.

The exact mechanism for Staggers immunity was as speculative as its origins. Most believed it an ancient parasite released from its frozen sleep with the thawing permafrost. The first reported cases were among mammoth tusk hunters near the Arctic Circle and Chinese tusk carvers. Staggers had wiped out entire populations of both human and animals before the last ice age. It had been a stroke of mankind's abysmal luck that a period of global warming had unleashed the spores from their centuries of quiet slumber. With modern rapid transportation, the disease had swept through a population ill-equipped to deal with such an ancient pest. Disease and the walking dead were only a small part of the chaos, as first civil, and then military authority broke down. Border wars and regional conflicts broke out all over the world; then, fizzled out as entire armies fell prey to the insidious Staggers Plague.

In the two years since the first reported cases, an estimated 200 million people had died in the U.S. from disease, starvation, lack of shelter, or violence—over sixty percent of the population. Some countries had reported even greater numbers. Colder climates fared better from the plague, but suffered more from weather-related deaths. In the U.S. Southwest, temperature played little part in the spread of the disease. Airborne spores from dust storms, *haboobs*, were a major contributor. With few weather satellites operational, predicting the weather was haphazard, often one city radioing a city downwind that a dust storm was coming. The blaring of weather sirens had replaced tornado warnings.

Everyone hoped and prayed they were immune, but most were simply lucky enough or physically fit enough to delay the inevitable. Globally, with the exceptions of small pockets of closely related individuals, less than ten percent of the population was immune. The possibilities for a natural immunity were numerous—B-cell immunoglobulin, enhanced T-cell lymphocyte coordination, naturally occurring Human Defense Molecules, or Trypanosome Lytic Factor, TLF-1, the High Density Lipid component that humans developed over the millennia against parasites, such as African Sleeping Sickness. Some people went years before succumbing to the airborne and insect vector spores. Some never became infected. However, one thing was certain: Inevitably, a person bitten by an infected person developed the disease. Always. In a few rare cases, normal anti-parasitical medications stopped the spread of the infection, but time was vital. The longer left untreated, the higher the odds of becoming one of the walking dead, a reanimated corpse, as the tiny parasitical worms ate into the brain, changing the host into a living, breathing carrier to further spread the disease.

The girl looked over Alton's items, rolling her eyes at his choice of cookies. He ignored her silent admonition and handed her a handful of chits. She carefully counted them out and wrote a store receipt for the difference, making it legal tender by stamping it with a dated rubber stamp. It was no longer a question of 'paper or plastic.' Both were in too short supply to waste for convenience. He shoved his selections into a well-worn cloth bag, mumbled a polite 'Thank you,' slung the bag over his shoulder, and left.

By the time he opened the door to his house and hobbled inside to collapse on the sofa, panting from the effort, he wished he had given in to the urge to medicate himself for the pain. He allowed himself fifteen minutes to rest; then, after putting away his groceries, he settled for a cup of coffee with a splash of Jim Beam to take the edge off. He eyed the doughnuts wistfully, but made a deviled ham sandwich with mayo and fresh tomato slices and lettuce from the local garden. As an afterthought, he added a thick slice of fresh mozzarella cheese to his yeast roll sandwich. Jake had shown a few people in the community how to make cheese from cow and goat milk. The fresh cheese was a welcomed addition to the often-mediocre diet.

It might have surprised most people that Jake's storehouse of arcane knowledge shifted beyond weaponry. As a prepper, he had turned his grandfather's secluded ranch in Split Rock Canyon into a safe refuge, with a comfortable house built on a high ledge above the canyon floor. A small, dammed pond fed by a seasonal waterfall and a deep well powered by electric pump provided water for drinking and irrigating his vegetable garden. Goats, chickens, and pigs supplied eggs, milk, and meat. Solar panels powered lights, a refrigerator, a freezer, his much-used DVD player, and his small machine shop. A stacked-stone wall with a metal gate across the head of the narrow canyon protected his hideaway from predators, both human and zombie. His retreat had taken him years to build, but he had destroyed it with his own hands rather than allow Levi Combs take it from him. That, more than anything, explained Jake's character. He refused to buckle under any threat. He would turn a blind eye on petty infractions of the law, but he did not tolerate a complete disregard for it. That made him a perfect Ranger.

The deviled ham sandwich tasted bland and unappetizing. He laid the half-eaten sandwich on the table. He did not have much of an appetite anyway. The pain in his knee sapped his energy, leaving him listless and lightheaded. The whiskey helped some, but it would have been nice to take a long nap. Unfortunately, he had work to do. He picked up the spiral notebook on one end of the sofa where he had left it before his trip to the commissary.

Each new recruit to any of the three communities received a thorough evaluation for any pertinent skills and offered a choice of residence and a job in his or her field if available. Right now, they were heavy in clerical personnel and unskilled workers. Some of those candidates he would assign more menial tasks, such as the community vegetable gardens or simple cleaning duties. Classes offered training in much-needed skills — nursing, culinary, mechanical, and electronics. He would like to just once look at a sheet of paper listing personnel skills and match it with a sheet listing community needs. It cost fuel and extra guards to transfer people to other communities. Yuma needed all the farm workers they could get, but few people volunteered to work the fields during the oppressive summer heat.

Maricopa, located between Tucson and Phoenix, was a regional railhead. They needed engineers, railroad workers, steelworkers, and forklift and crane operators. They had a glut of warehouse people. Sometimes Alton wished he could simply place an ad in the local newspaper and sit back to wait on replies. Sadly, it did not work that way. Instead, he had become part diplomat, part enforcer, convincing people to do what they did not want to do by sweet persuasion or by heavy-handed threats, neither of which he was good at. He had rather return to teaching, but like everyone else, he did what was needed.

When the words began spinning on the pages, he closed the notebook and closed his eyes. He could not shake thoughts of Jake from his mind. He had noticed changes in Jake over the past few months, and not good changes. He was as quiet and as reticent to talk about what he was thinking or feeling as ever, but he had become even more morose, his moods darker. In his job, immersed neck deep in the squalid side of life, Jake saw the worst qualities in people, just as he had as a Pima County deputy and as a Squad Weapons Leader in Afghanistan. So much negativity could wear a person down, just as relentlessly as a chronic disease savaged the body.

Jake professed no religious affiliation, but Alton did. However, evidence suggested that God was not as benevolent or as loving as the Bible suggested. He did not doubt the existence of the human soul. If a soul could become tarnished, stained by the death and misery around it, then Jake's surely was.

Jake outwardly shunned power and responsibility; and yet, inevitably assumed it when others failed to do so. A great vacuum created by the zombie apocalypse left millions of people floundering, unable to cope on their own. Many assuming the newly created mantles of responsibility did so for personal gain, often in direct conflict with the needs of their charges. Others, however altruistically motivated, were overwhelmed or ill prepared for the job. The results were often the same. The newly formed Southwestern Territorial Government had all the flaws and resistance to change as did the previous government, but it offered the single best chance at recovery available.

Dramatic shifts in the paradigms of population dispersal after the apocalypse created pockets of civilization scattered throughout a landscape of lawlessness and chaos. The military moved too slowly to provide essential control, seeking instead to hold and expand on current ventures. Jake believed the Arizona Rangers had a more vital role to fill than simply acting as reconnaissance units for the military. Law often came down to one man, a gun, and his willingness to use it, or as Jake so eloquently expressed it in his *Jake's Law #5 — In a lawless land, the biggest gun makes the law.* While intrinsically opposed to the concept of law issued from the barrel of a gun, Alton understood the necessity at times. He had witnessed murder firsthand. He had felt the touch of men such as Levi Coombs, men with no morals. For good people to live their lives in safety, other people had to be willing to sacrifice theirs. Whether he did it for others or for personal reasons, Jake was such a man.

A sudden wave of nausea and pain swept over Alton. His knee began trembling uncontrollably. He gritted his teeth until the spasm passed, and then got up, took two of the pain pills, and washed them down with the cold dregs of coffee and whiskey. Later, when he felt whole again, he might finish his work. Right now, all he wanted to do was clear his mind of everything and sleep.

3

June 10, 2017, 10:30 a.m. Hatch, New Mexico —

Deacon and Cray stood a discrete distance from where Andrews was digging Lambrini's grave, watching the impassive Ranger as his shovel bit into the earth removing spadefuls of sandy soil. Both had offered to help, but Andrews had refused their offer with a shake of his head. Preparing the Ranger captain's final resting place was a burden he alone wished to bear.

Jake motioned for them to follow him as he strode down the street to check out the building Hilda had mentioned. The town was still eerily still. The soft sound of Andrew's shovel slicing into the soil echoed down the silent street. If any survivors were aware that the three men—*two men and a boy, he reminded himself* — were dead, they were playing it close to the vest, remaining behind closed doors until they were sure how things were going. With the three bad guys dead and no zombies at large, others might have basked in the tranquility of the morning, but Jake always expected trouble. His sharp cynicism was a survival tool that kept him alive.

Deacon trotted to catch up with Jake's purposeful long strides. Cray walked more slowly, his head turned to watch Andrews. An expression of dark gloom marred his face.

"What's up?" Deacon asked, as he caught up with Jake.

"Hilda said those three spent a lot of time in that building next to the firehouse. I thought I'd see what they found so fascinating."

Deacon snorted. "Huh. It probably wouldn't take much to amuse them."

Jake said nothing. He did not think much of the trio's sense of humor. For what they had put the three women through, he would have liked to watch them hang. A bullet was too quick. Waiting for the trapdoor's inevitable drop beneath his feet, a momentary sensation of falling, and then the inexorable tightening of the noose around the neck before it snapped like a dried twig, helped a man to understand the error of his ways. Under the former liberal PC culture, the term 'cruel and unusual punishment' had degraded to the point that any punishment was deemed cruel and unusual with federal court cases fought over which lethal drugs states could use. It played into the overriding theme of no personal responsibility. Everything was always someone else's fault went contrary to *Jake's Law #6 — Bad people deserved bad ends.* Those same PC people would consider him a savage, but most of them were dead, and he was alive, so it didn't much matter anymore.

The dilapidated two-story tall building was about one-hundred-fifty-feet long and fifty- feet wide. At one time, perhaps decades ago, it had been white. Now, it was so faded the wood looked like sun-bleached bones. The corrugated steel roof was rusty with three shades of rust red running down the metal like bloodstains. The large windows had been painted black, like empty gaping holes in the side of the building. Jake paused at the door, listening, but heard nothing. He waited for Cray to catch up, and then tried the doorknob. It turned easily. He nodded, and Cray and Deacon once again took covering positions as he pushed the creaking door open with the barrel of his Winchester, his finger on the trigger just in case.

The interior was pitch black. With the windows painted out, the only light entered through the open door, an angry rectangular smear of light across the floor that the hungry shadows eagerly swallowed. The door's rusty hinges creaked loudly, echoing from the cavernous room's bare walls. A small, wooden table beside the door held two empty whisky bottles and a half-filled kerosene lantern. Jake struck a match to the wick and turned it up. He held the lantern out in front of him for a better view.

The large open space had no rooms or dividers. It contained no furniture or shelving. There was no second floor or attic. The bare walls rose to meet the pitched roof twenty feet overhead. A latticework of wooden rafters supporting the roof crisscrossed the ceiling.

"Empty," he said after a brief scan, "but stay on your toes."

The space was not completely empty. Deep inside the room, barely visible in the shadows, a graffiti-covered, gray metal storage container sat near two large, sliding wooden doors in the rear wall. The container was suspiciously incongruous in the otherwise empty building. Moving the lantern around, he saw rising like a guard tower in the center of the room, two metal scaffolds bolted together to form a platform. A ten-foot metal ladder leaned against its side, secured at the top by a loop of chain.

"What were these boys up to?" Deacon asked, scratching his head in wonder.

"What's all that?" Cray asked, pointing to streaks of various colors along the bare wooden floor and marking the wooden support beams thrusting upwards from the floor. "Looks like paint."

"It is paint," Jake replied. He stared at the streaks and splotches of orange, white, red, and blue paint splattered across the entire floor of the building. What at first he had mistaken for graffiti were streaks of paint on the side of the storage container.

"Do you think they were wannabe artists?" Cray asked. He glanced at the platform. "Maybe they threw paint balloons at the floor from there, like that Pollack fellow."

Deacon laughed. "Those three? More likely they would sniff the paint fumes."

His curiosity aroused, Jake climbed the ladder. He was surprised to find three paintball guns and boxes of paintballs on top of the makeshift platform. The platform swayed, as Deacon climbed up to join him.

"Paintball!" he chuckled when he saw the paintball guns. "They were playing paintball warriors."

The setup had Jake mystified. "It doesn't make sense," he said, as he studied an assortment of pulleys secured to the rafters and the array of ropes crossing the ceiling from one corner of the platform to the storage container. "They look like dog leash runs. Targets?" he asked Deacon who shrugged noncommittally.

"Why go to so much trouble?" Cray yelled up from the floor. "Although that would explain the absence of stray dogs. Any bastard that would shoot stray dogs ought to be shot."

Cray spotted a pair of heavy-duty truck batteries sitting on the floor beneath one of the scaffolds and began examining them. Jumper cables connected the two batteries. Wires ran into the darkness. One wire connected to the negative post of one battery. The second wire ended in a spring-operated clamp and lay on the floor beside the second battery.

"What's this?" he asked, as he connected the clamp to the positive post.

Dozens of strings of Christmas lights suspended from the ceiling flickered on, casting a multi-hued aura over the floor, driving back but not quite dispelling the deeper shadows. In the center of the room, dangling from a chain, a kaleidoscopic disco ball began to rotate slowly, scattering dancing shards of light across the floor.

Deacon slapped his knee and laughed with delight. Jake shook his head in confusion. Paintball and a disco light show—what other surprises did the trio have in store?

"It's pretty," Cray said. "Kinda like a discotheque. All we need is music."

"Keep your eyes open," Jake snapped. He scanned the room, but his gaze kept returning to the storage container. The three men had gone to a lot of effort to set the room up, and moving the heavy storage container inside had been a considerable task, even if they had used a forklift or a tractor for the heavy work.

"There's a lever attached to one of the wooden posts supporting the roof," Cray informed them. "It's got a rope running from it up over a pulley in the ceiling, and then on across the roof. I wonder what it's for."

"Don't touch anything else," Jake warned.

"Yeah," Deacon snorted. "Maybe it drops a tub of water over you, like Jennifer Beals in *Flashdance*. I'd pay to see that."

"Maybe it's for the music," Cray said, and reached for the lever. "You can't have a discotheque without music."

That familiar itch hit Jake between the shoulder blades again, but before he could stop him, Cray pulled the lever. The rope tightened, pulling a pin from the top of the storage container door with a loud snap. All three men froze at the sound with rifles ready. At first, nothing happened, but then the door sprang open, and ten zombies lurched from inside. Each one wore a rope collar around its neck with a second rope connecting it to a sliding metal ring that was threaded onto one of the horizontal ropes in the ceiling. Each creature wore a collage of various colors of paint on their tattered clothing and on their exposed flesh, making them resemble gruesome carnival clowns. They spread out quickly across the room, making soft mewling sounds, but their dead faces were masks of ravenous hunger. Noses thrust high into the air, they did not need light to detect food; their enhanced sense of smell served as a natural radar. They knew prey was nearby and were eager to rend flesh.

In the soft glow of the multi-colored lights, with the spinning disco ball throwing specks of scintillating light around the room, the parade of painted zombies looked surreal. It would have been comical if not for the deadly seriousness of the danger the creatures represented.

"Get out of here!" Jake yelled at Cray, but too many zombies now lumbered between him and the front door. Jake noticed the slight hesitation, as Cray decided to rush the tower. Jake knew he would never make it. He sighted his rifle on one zombie nearest Cray and fired. The zombie staggered; then fell. Beside him, Deacon had shaken off his initial amusement turned to shock and was busily taking out zombies with his weapon. The report of their rifles thundered in the cavernous space.

Cray rushed forward, and then retreated as two zombies cut him off from the ladder. He raised his rifle and shot one of the creatures, but the bullet only grazed its shoulder, spinning it careening into the second creature. The pair ricocheted like two billiard balls with bad English. Jake put a bullet into one's head, but the second was invisible deep in the shadows.

Cray backpedaled out of reach, but slipped in a pool of zombie blood and went down. He recovered quickly, but he had lost time, and the zombies had gained ground. They ignored the invisible shooters atop the platform and focused their animal attention on Cray. Now, most of the zombies and Cray were beneath the platform. They were all three cut off from the building's only exit. Jake hoped forgetting *Jake's Law #9 — Always have an exit strategy*—didn't kill them.

"Screw this!" Deacon shouted. "I can't see anything from up here. I'm going down to help him."

"No, wait!" Jake yelled. He had no clear shot at any of the zombies because of the platform's wooden floor, and their stumbling against the rickety platform spoiled what little aim he could manage. He couldn't shoot them, and climbing down would put him in the middle of the danger. He only had one slim chance of saving Cray. It was a serious move and one he hesitated to make, but his curiosity and lapse of mission protocol had placed Cray, all of them, in danger. Cray's frenzied cry urged him into action.

"Hell," he groaned and laid his rifle down on the platform. As Deacon looked on in stunned horror, he took a deep breath and leaped over the side of the platform. His goal was not to reach the ground, but rather to grab onto a handful of ropes dangling just within reach. *I hope*, he thought without amusement. If he missed, he would wind up on the floor with a broken leg and become an easy meal for zombies.

The fingers of his right hand touched hemp, and he grabbed frantically at the rope, finally snagging it with one hand just a few feet above the floor. As he hoped, his weight and momentum on the ropes attached to the zombie collars snatched them back toward the open container, but now, he was on the ground armed only with his Colt revolver—six shots. He drew and fired from the hip at the zombies threatening Cray, not taking time to aim. He simply wanted to get their attention.

Deacon took advantage of Jake's desperate maneuver, picking off creatures Jake had yanked away as fast as he could cock his rifle, keeping them off Jake's back. Jake shot one creature whose rope he had missed. It's red and white face exploded, adding more crimson to the grisly paint marking its flesh and clothing. Cray's panicked yells grew more frenzied. One large zombie, half a head taller than Jake with shoulders as broad as a Volkswagen minibus, had Cray pinned against the base of the platform. Cray held his rifle crosswise against the creature's massive chest to keep it at bay, but he was losing the shoving match with the much heavier zombie.

With no clear shot, Jake pulled his K-Bar knife from its sheath and raced at the creature. He leaped into the air and came down on the creature's back, plunging the nine-and-a-half-inch blade into the zombie's neck just below its occipital ridge, and hung on. The giant reared backwards, almost throwing him off its back. He grabbed the zombie's belt with one hand for support and shoved harder on the knife with the other. When he felt the metal blade strike bone, he twisted the handle counterclockwise. The zombie collapsed, its cervical vertebrae severed.

He rolled away from the massive creature before it landed on top of him and came up on one knee, searching the room, but he saw no more movement. At a groan from Cray, he looked over, and to his horror, saw Cray clamping his hand over a bloody wound on his forearm. He looked up at Jake almost in tears.

"Son of a bitch," he moaned through clenched teeth. "The bastard almost bit my arm off."

"Let me see how bad it is," Jake said and reached for Cray's arm. He hoped it was a mere scratch that Cray was exaggerating. If so, a good scrubbing and disinfecting with alcohol might save him.

Cray jerked his arm back. Even in the dim, multihued light, his eyes were haunted, filled with despair. "Forget it, Jake. Bastard got me good. I'm fucked and you know it."

"We can try," Jake said, but without conviction. He knew Cray was right.

The Staggers spores thrived in zombie blood and saliva. Any bite delivered millions of active spores into the bloodstream, where they quickly began to grow and spread. If they had been near a hospital or a medical facility with access to a wide variety of anti-parasitical drugs, he might have stood a chance, but they were hours from anywhere. There was nothing anyone could do. In a few hours, Cray would become feverish. In days, he would fall into a deep coma. Hours after that, he would either die, a blessing in Jake's opinion, or reawaken as a zombie Staggerer-driven to spread the disease.

Deacon climbed down the ladder, saw Cray, and kicked the battery over, disconnecting the lights. The room once again became a shadowed cavern enveloping a small circle of light cast by the lantern on top of the platform.

"Damn it, Gerald!" Deacon growled. "Why did you have to be so damn stupid?"

"Just a natural born idiot I guess," Cray replied, trying to smile, but the pain in his arm and the knowledge of the certainty of his death quickly erased the brief flicker from his lips.

Deacon raised his clenched fist in the air. "I want to burn this goddamned town to the ground," he shouted at the ceiling.

"We need it," Jake reminded him.

Deacon waved his other hand at Cray's arm. "Not this damn bad!"

Cray shook his head. "Estes, the captain, and now me — what a FUBAR operation." He began to sob; then, he stopped and stared at Deacon. "Damn it, Deacon, I don't want to die, not this way."

Realizing at what Cray was hinting, Deacon turned pale and backed away. "Un uh. No way. Not me. I'm not doing it."

Cray focused his haunted gaze at Jake. "What about you, Jake?" he pleaded. "I know you've got the *cajones*. One quick shot." He touched the center of his forehead with his finger, leaving a bloody dot as a target. "That's all I ask."

A lead weight settled in Jake's stomach. Killing zombies, hardened criminals, or someone trying to kill him was one thing, but someone he knew—that was lowering the bar even for him. *No, that's not it,* he admitted to himself. *I don't want to do it because I'm the one who's killed him.*

"I, I ..." Jake's voice faltered as the first twinges of guilt gripped him. His curiosity had led them into the building. He had let his guard down, and Cray was paying the price for his mistake. He would not let Cray suffer the agony of the Staggers. He certainly could not allow him to become a zombie. He took a deep breath to clear his head and calm his racing heart. "Yeah, I'll do it," he agreed with bitter reluctance, "but not here." He glanced around the gloomy room. "Not now. Out in the light of day."

Cray moaned and clamped his arm to his chest. "I don't want to wait. I might—"

The shot drowned out whatever Cray was going to say next. Cray's head exploded, splattering both Jake and Deacon with his blood. He dropped to the floor between them in a pool of blood.

"What the hell!" Deacon cried, backpedaling away from Cray's corpse, as the echo of the shot reverberated through the cavernous empty space. He stared down at the fingers of blood trailing across the uneven floor toward his feet and stepped aside.

Jake wiped spatters of blood from his face with the back of his sleeve and looked toward the open door. Mitch Andrews stood in the doorway. His expression was difficult to read.

"I heard," Andrews said. His soft voice conveyed pity but no regrets, but it also held a touch of recrimination aimed at Jake and Deacon. "I figured it might be better if he didn't see it coming."

Deacon was livid. "He might have wanted to see the sun again, or write a note, or something!" he yelled at Andrews.

Andrews' countenance remained impassive. "It's the way I would have wanted it. He knew what was coming. He wanted it." He stared at Deacon. "Would you have shot him?"

Jake sympathized with Deacon. He and Cray were close friends, but Deacon knew as well as anyone what had to happen. Cray was a dead man the moment he was bitten. He was surprised at Andrews' actions, but not disappointed. He knew Andrews was capable of administering a coup de grâce; he had just not expected it. He was relieved that the burden of killing Cray had slipped from his shoulders, but his hesitation in doing the job had only added to his burden of guilt.

Andrews was one of the perpetually saddest men he knew. Jake didn't know his whole story, just the bits Andrews had chosen to reveal, but being an African-American, a minority even among the Native American minorities in Arizona, placed him in a class by himself. In the two years since the plague, Jake had seen less than a score of African-Americans among the survivors. He felt Andrews was always on guard, desperately trying to represent his race in the best possible fashion. There was no need. As Hilda had said, the apocalypse had erased all social and ethnic barriers. No one had the time to be prejudiced anymore. Everyone was in the same boat, a survivor hanging on by his or her fingernails.

"Let's go," he said and began walking toward the door.

"What about Gerald?" Deacon asked.

Jake did not slow down. He wanted to be away from the dismal room. "We'll come back for his body later."

Andrews turned around and began walking away from the building. Deacon lingered for a few moments, staring down at Cray's body, and then followed.

Before, the summer sun had been sweltering, a reminder of what an Arizona summer can feel like. Now, it could not dispel the chill that had enveloped Jake like an icy cloak. The sun shone just as brightly, but the cloudless day seemed filled with invisible dark clouds blocking the sun, just as the universe with filled with invisible Dark Matter soaking up the light and heat of Creation. He and Cray had not been particularly close, but he had been a comrade-in-arms, a fellow Arizona Ranger. He had seen friends die before, more than he cared to remember, but because of its bizarre nature, Cray's senseless death insinuated itself under his skin, which, it seemed, was not as thick as he had imagined. Christmas lights, revolving disco balls, and paint-splattered zombies made for a peculiar death. He wondered how it would look on his report.

For a moment, Jake could not remember what day of the week it was. The days seemed to run together, bleed into one another like the layers of blood on his uniform. Wednesday, he remembered. *It feels like a Monday.* He made up a new law on the spot, *Jake's Law #20 — If the day sucks, call it Monday, and start your week there.*

Cray had been right about one thing; the mission had definitely been FUBAR. They should have waited to go in after the delay, but they hadn't. Estes should have been more cautious, but he wasn't. He should have ignored the empty building until the town was secure, but his curiosity had gotten the better of him. Now, Captain Lambrini, Estes, and Cray were dead—half of the recon team. Three dead bad guys. Three dead rangers. It did not come out even.

Estes, Cray, and Lambrini were the seventh, eighth, and ninth Rangers they had lost in the past seven months. Things had to change. The Rangers were not strictly law enforcement, and they weren't exactly military. They were something in between, a new breed of paramilitary lawmen—judge, jury, and executioners. They were the only thing standing between civilization and total chaos. They could ill afford to sacrifice more lives uselessly. If the law meant anything in a lawless land, it had to be above petty squabbles and politics. If people did not fear the law, they did not respect it.

As things presently stood, the laws only applied in situations that directly affected the building of new communities, the safe havens. The rest of the country was in a state of total lawlessness, fair game for armed gangs, petty land barons, or militias, many worse than the zombie threat against which they offered protection at a high price.

Being safe from zombies was not enough. Unless people felt safe wherever they were, their only chance for security was a safe haven, and they were slow in coming. He, like many people, shunned close-knit groups. Some preferred living on their own, but defending against zombies as well as roving bands of outlaws was just too much for an individual. He knew. He had tried and almost failed.

He had an idea of which the military might approve. After all, they saw things in terms of black and white, friend or foe. That was closer to the new reality than street cops walking a beat, however large the beat was. Something like the movie, *Judge Dredd*. Civilians would object, of course. Under normal circumstances, he would too, but the blood of the guilty had to stain someone's hands, or the blood of the innocent would stain everyone's.

He glanced back at the empty building, now not so empty. In it lay an Arizona Ranger. He intended to see that no more died on his watch.

4

June 12, 2017, 4:15 p.m.   Marana Safe Haven, Marana, AZ —
"They'll never go for it," Alton told Jake.

The two of them were eating a late lunch in Alton's home. Jake had returned earlier in the day after two days in Hatch waiting for the military to arrive and take over. He was exhausted from a week in the field, but too keyed up to rest. He had just confided in Alton his proposal to the territorial governor.

"They don't have much choice," Jake insisted. "Rangers are the face of the law. Using us to scout out towns is more than a waste; it's a betrayal. Sending a handful of men into potential danger, while the military sits on its ass isn't working. The military can do the job quicker."

"It's matter of diplomacy, Jake," Alton explained. "When people see the military come bursting into town, armed to the teeth, they get nervous. It reminds them of jackboots and brown shirts. The Rangers are something with which they're familiar. The Rangers represent civilian authority."

Jake pointed a finger at Alton and nodded. "My point exactly, except we're under military authority. Look, Alton, what it boils down to is this: Either we're going to have military rule or civilian law. I can live with either, but the pretense of civilian authority in the guise of Arizona Rangers is a slap in the face to the idea that spawned the Rangers. When Captain James Henry Tevis formed the Arizona Rangers in 1860, he did so to protect the territory. During the Civil War, they were disbanded, and the Confederate government controlled the territory, but during the height of the Apache Wars in 1880, the Rangers reformed to keep the border safe. They delivered swift and sure justice from the back of a horse. They were more than a just symbol, but by God they were a symbol believed in."

Jake rose from his seat and paced around the kitchen, too wound up to sit still. The fire of his conviction burned hot inside him, stoked by the deaths of Lambrini, Estes, and Cray. If he could not convince Alton of the need for a free and independent Arizona Rangers, he would never convince the territorial governor or the military authorities. He became passionate about few things, but this was one of them. His great-great grandfather had risked his life to keep the territory safe. Jake felt a generational need to do likewise. He wore his ancestor's tarnished and dented badge on his chest to keep that memory alive. It's what he had been doing all his life—protecting and serving. Some people, even Alton, found it difficult to reconcile his seeming lack of empathy with people with his passion for the law. To Jake, it was simple: The law was an ideal that people usually fell short of. Most people paid lip service to the law, but ignored it when it suited them.

The law was the thread with which the tapestry of human civilization was woven. Changing morals shifted certain aspects of the law about like pieces on a chessboard, but the backbone of the law did not change. It was irrefutable, based on thousands of years of civilizations' rises and falls. Often called the Golden Rule, the basic tenet of the law stated that each person deserved the same respect, and that no one was entitled to take from another his or her freedom or the fruits of their labors. Jake held these basic laws inviolate.

He stopped pacing and stared out the window at a group of people in the fields clearing weeds. Without asking, he could never guess at their previous occupations. Some could have been used car dealers or preachers. They could have been schoolteachers or strippers, pizza makers or landscapers. Whatever their past, they were there not because of a desire to chop weeds in the hot sun but because they yearned for the freedom to rebuild their lives in safety. They deserved that small comfort that security brought them.

He took another sip of the iced tea Alton had prepared for them. Tea, like coffee and chocolate, was difficult to come by. Very little international trade existed, and rare items brought exorbitant prices. Once the warehoused supplies became exhausted, tea and coffee would become relics of the past. *Like me*, he thought wryly.

"At the rate we're going, it might take years, decades, to spread throughout the country one town at a time restoring civil order. What about the suffering that occurs during that time? The land swarms with zombies and human scum. People don't know if the next dust storm or the next fleabite will turn them into a zombie. They wonder if the next time they enter a store or an abandoned building searching for food or with the next knock on their door someone will shoot them because they feel their need for the food is greater than anyone else's right to it.

"Establishing safe havens like this is all well and good and necessary, but it takes time. It's a slow, tedious process. Even you admit that. Since you recruited me into this speculative venture," he cast a recriminating glance at Alton, "we've started three. Three communities! Hatch is the fourth, but it will take months to establish. Each community, except maybe Marana and Maricopa, is isolated and vulnerable. Any interruption in the highway or railway service could cut them off from essential supplies and assistance. They could easily slide back into savagery. If we can't offer people a new world, the least we can do is offer them the idea that the law is there for them. Rangers can't walk beats like cops, or prevent robberies or murders, but we can track down and apprehend or execute the perpetrators. If people understand that justice is sure and swift, not just some lofty ideal instilled in a marble blindfolded woman bearing a set of scales, they'll believe that there is hope for the future, that change is possible. They will believe that their lives, their futures matter."

Alton waved his hands in the air, indicating his annoyance. Jake knew he could infuriate anyone, even his friend Alton, but Jake believed Alton's frustration stemmed from the fact that at least a small part of him knew that Jake was right.

"All that is well and good, Jake, but what you're proposing is a group of ... of ... mercenaries is the only word I can apply to it, running around meting out gun-barrel justice. What about the right to trial by a jury of peers, *habeas corpus*, or rules of evidence? We don't have access to DNA tests, not for a while. What if you're wrong and an innocent person dies?"

Jake nodded. It was a valid point, one that he had considered often without a solution. It had always been the main objection to the death penalty — better a hundred criminals go free than execute one innocent person. Unfortunately, those hundred criminals took more than a single life. As with most things, it all came down to numbers.

"Innocent people die every day. Do you believe that more, or less, innocent blood will be spilled by bringing about law and order?"

"It's ... it's anathema to what made our country great."

Jake smacked his palm down on the kitchen counter with a suddenness that made Alton wince. "No, what made our country great was the concept of justice for the victim and speedy punishment for the guilty. Once justice and punishment became subject to manipulation by lawyers and judges, it became pointless. Justice became a commodity sold to the highest bidder. A guilty rich person or corporation could outlast a poor person or a small business through years of costly, drawn-out appeals. Money talked and criminals walked. Justice has to be pure to be effective. Punishment has to be swift and commiserate with the crime." He brushed his hand through his hair; then, massaged his throbbing temple. "The death penalty was never about serving as an example, though it makes a damn good one. It was about justice. A fine for ruining hundreds of lives was as unjust as a short sentence and time served for murder. There's a reason Lady Justice wears a blindfold. She doesn't want to see the faces of the innocents that inevitably pay for the crimes of the guilty and for the leniency of the law."

"I'm not convinced."

Jake laughed. "I didn't expect you to be. You're too good for the times, Alton. You still cling to the notion that all people are fundamentally good in spite of the evidence to the contrary." He glanced meaningfully at Alton's cane lying on the counter. "I just returned from Hatch. There were three men. What they did to three women we found ..." He paused as the raw emotion of what he had witnessed bled through. "Their guilt was evident. There were no extenuating circumstances. If they hadn't tried to kill me, I still would have killed them as surely as the sun rises in the east. Such people have used up their last chance. They don't deserve mercy."

He did not mention that one of the women, Hilda, had killed the third msn. He had left that part out of the report to save her any possible repercussions. As far as he was concerned, she did the right thing.

"All men deserve mercy," Alton replied.

"You earn mercy like bonus mileage points on a credit card by doing something deserving of mercy."

"Mercy is a God-given right," Alton countered.

Exasperated by his friend's descent into religious dogma, he replied, "Then let God grant it. When it becomes one person's word against another's, the law must weigh the character of the two people into its decision. You can't compromise by claiming they are both half-right. The law can afford to be wrong. It can't afford to be indecisive."

"Jake, you were a cop, a deputy sheriff. You believed in a code of laws."

He was disappointed that Alton did not understand him. He had thought them closer than that, knew each other better. Like many people, Alton confused the legal code with the *Law*. Men, mostly lawyers who allowed wiggle room for their brother lawyers, wrote the one, and the other was the crux of the matter; what was right, and what was wrong.

"I did, and I saw laws subverted every day. Rules of evidence became so rigid that a video of someone committing a crime would not be admissible if the prosecution didn't dot every 'I' and cross every 'T,' because it might prejudice the jury. Do you believe that? The letter of the law became more important than the meaning of the law. We can't afford that same mistake. Not now. The stakes are too high."

Alton sighed. Jake knew he hadn't changed the former teacher's mind. He had just given up on the argument. "Even if the governor agrees, will the military?"

Jake shrugged. "I don't know. No one likes to concede authority, but even they realize they can't be everywhere. Their weakness is a rigid chain of command. No one wants to make a decision. The governor wants the Rangers to succeed, but he may be afraid to buck the military. They keep him in power. I'll find out in two days. The governor has agreed to come here and listen to my spiel."

Alton motioned to Jake's chair. "Please sit down. You're making me nervous." While waiting for Jake to sit, he finished his iced tea. "I'm afraid for you, Jake."

Jake raised an eyebrow. He hadn't expected such an admission from Alton. "Why?"

"Because you, too, are a good person. I believe you think you can do what you say, but I'm afraid the weight of authority will crush you. Good men have succumbed to power before. I don't think you will allow it to go to your head. Instead, I think you'll question every decision you make, wondering if you were right. That doubt, however small, will grow like a cancer until it consumes you. I don't want to see that happen to you."

Alton's concern touched him, and his perception amazed him. It was something he had been mulling over in his mind as well. He was glad to see that Alton understood he did not seek power for power's sake. If anything, he was afraid of what he was proposing. If he knew of someone more fitting, more able to succeed, he would gladly step aside. Unfortunately, for the plan to work as he hoped, he would have to be the one in the captain's seat.

"Let me ask you something, Alton. If in the certain knowledge that you would be shot, would you still have walked up to that farmhouse that day?"

Alton's look of surprise turned to one of deep concentration, but Jake could see that his friend had asked himself that same question, perhaps more than once. "I think so. I believe in what I'm doing. Sometimes you have to accept the risks."

"This might break me. I agree with you. I don't propose such a thing lightly. The other Rangers in the field with equal power will face the same doubts and struggles with their consciences that I do, but the men I lead will have no such doubts. They will know that I accept all blame, all responsibility for both their and my actions. They will do their jobs with a clear conscience, and if heads roll, it'll be mine." He paused. "Maybe they can sleep at night."

Alton blinked several times and shook his head slowly. "My God, Jake. I didn't know you felt so deeply about this. At first, I thought that, just maybe, you were looking for an excuse to separate yourself from your fellow man, but were too ... too dedicated simply to walk off into the wilderness alone. You really feel this is the only solution, don't you?"

Jake sighed. "It's the only one for now. Later, things can change, but for a while, someone has to be the bad guy. Alton, you think you know me. Maybe you know me better than anyone else left alive, but I've got so much blood on my hands that a little more won't make a difference. If I can atone for some of that blood by spilling a little more, I'll take the risk. If you're right and there is a God, someday I'll stand before him in judgment. From what I've read, he knows the difference between murder and killing. I hope he takes my intent into account."

Alton leaned back in his chair, as if Jake's admission had been too heavy to bear. He glanced around the room, biting his lower lip as he formulated his thoughts, a thing Jake had often seen him do. Unlike many hasty men who later regretted their decisions, Alton was methodical. He could usually wade into the muddy puddle of argument and pick up the shiny stone of truth. To Jake, the fact that he was no longer arguing was a good sign. The ticking clock on the wall behind him punctuated his thoughts, as if counting down to a decision. After almost two minutes, as Jake waited patiently, he spoke.

"I don't know if what you propose is noble or the last refuge of a desperate man, but I can't fault you for stepping into the fire. The difference between even-handed justice and retribution is in the hand of the dispenser. I trust you, Jake. As my friend, I wish you wouldn't do this, but if such a thing is necessary, I believe you're the man to pull it off."

The cold, hard knot in Jake's stomach relaxed, not all the way, but it no longer gnawed at his intestines like a hungry animal. "I've got to try. It's the only way I know to stay sane."

Alton nodded. "I know you do. First, however, let me prepare a nice meal. I have a can of beef and gravy, a few potatoes, a handful of carrots, an onion, and a can of mushroom soup. With a little imagination and some salt and pepper, we can put them in the oven and pretend it's a Yankee pot roast. I have a bottle of red wine, but I know you prefer beer. Well, I've been saving a couple of *Dos Equis* for some special occasion. This will do as well as any."

Jake smiled. One of Alton's better attributes was his ability to move quickly beyond the decision he had just made. The onus fell on him now, right or wrong. The meal was Alton's way of showing support.

He remembered the first time he and Alton had met, at the burning school in San Manuel where Alton had trapped dozens of zombies, many former students of his, and was offering them mercy. At the time, he had not known that the fire was a ruse to bring the two of them together. Alton had offered him a meal of canned beef stew. In a time of famine, the sharing of a meal was an act of friendship, but above all, it was a demonstration of trust. Displaying what you had to strangers could lead to dire consequences. Alton trusted him. That meant a lot to him.

"That sounds good. I've been eating off a campfire for almost a week. Beans and bacon always sounded good in the westerns, but it gets old real quick."

"Was it rough in Hatch?"

Jake's mind shifted gears from the present, to the future, and back to the past. "Pretty bad. I'll tell you about it later, after dinner." He rubbed his hand across his scraggly face. "Do you mind if I shave and shower? If I go back to the Ranger barracks, I'll have to file my report. I'm not ready for that yet."

Alton smiled, "Mi *casa es su casa.*"

Jake returned the smile. He knew Alton really meant it.

* * * *

June 14, 2017, 8:45 a.m.   Marana Safe Haven Community Center —

Jake was nervous when the territorial governor, Alexander Lapaige, walked in, followed by two hulking bodyguards wearing Kevlar vests over black T-shirts, black jeans, and Glock G22 .40 caliber semi-automatics slung under their armpits. Both men were professional and took their responsibilities seriously. They quickly scanned the room, saw that it was empty, and focused on him sitting on an uncomfortable metal folding chair in front of the desk. He had left his weapons in his room and felt naked beneath their cold, appraising gaze. They took up positions beside the door, one facing the door, the other facing him. Lapaige scurried across the room like a man in a great hurry and plopped down in the upholstered office chair behind the desk like a man who immediately took ownership of any room he entered.

He wasted no time. He focused his gaze on Jake and frowned. "What is this matter you wish to discuss with me?" he asked.

Jake took the time to look him over. He had seen the governor once or twice, but only at a distance. Up close, he looked less imposing, more like a CPA than a head of state. His freshly pressed blue suit made Jake feel like a tramp in his blue jeans and wrinkled T-shirt. Lapaige wore a tie, but he wore it loose at the open collar of his white shirt. He was shorter than Jake had thought, 5'6'' or 5'7'', and a little on the thin side. His brown hair was thin as well and combed self-consciously over a growing bald spot on the left side of his pate. His heavy, large-rimmed glasses sat low on his nose, revealing his intense, gray eyes. His unfaltering, focused gaze added to his strength of character. He was not a mealy-mouthed politician thrust into power over the corpses of his protégés. Lapaige had been the CEO of a major electronics firm before the apocalypse, and he knew how to wield power.

"You read my report and suggestions?" Jake asked.

"I read it," Lapaige answered, frowning. "It was very detailed and very disturbing."

"We lost three good men in Hatch that we could not afford to lose."

"I agree, yet you propose placing Rangers in even greater danger."

Jake tried not to sound defensive. The governor was trying to hem him in, force him to answer questions instead of making his proposal. "We're Arizona Rangers, Governor. We represent law and order. Danger goes with the badge. The military is using us for recon missions, grunt work. We're just bodies with guns. That's a waste of skilled manpower. Let the military do its own dirty work.

Our job should be to protect the people, everywhere, not just in the safe havens."

Lapaige leaned forward on the desk, folding his arms on the desktop. He squinted at Jake through his thick glasses, making his eyes appear larger and more intimidating. "How do you propose we do that?"

"Give the Rangers *carte blanche*. Invest us with the power to enforce warrants, determine guilt or innocence on the spot if necessary, and mete out swift justice so people can see we're serious."

Lapaige eyed Jake for a long, uncomfortable moment, and then leaned back in his seat. "Let's be clear. You're proposing I grant you the power of life and death."

Jake nodded. "That's what it boils down to, yes. We're not risking our lives to bring in criminals just to watch them beat the law or sit in jail consuming valuable resources to which their victims don't have access. Otherwise, we'll need judges, juries, jails, prisons, guards … all the things it takes to keep a prison system operating. We don't need another bureaucracy; we need quick results." He paused to make his next point sink in. "What percentage of our limited resources do you want to invest in criminals awaiting punishment? Who goes without so that we can feed and house murderers?"

"Hmm. Good point, but the people might not be so forgiving. They tend to frown on endowing supreme authority in the police. Police States have usually not been good for democracy."

"The military and the police, Rangers in this instance, are two separate and unequal entities. Once people see that justice is blind and that the guilty receive swift punishment regardless of who they are, they'll start to appreciate the Rangers."

"You're assuming people now are like people were in the Wild West."

"It's like the 1860s in some areas out there. People are living hand to mouth, no electricity, and no running water. There's no law and no hope. We have to offer them hope while they're waiting on us to get around to them. The least we can do is offer them law and order."

"I spoke with General Langston about your proposal." He paused and lifted his hands. "He doesn't approve."

Jake suppressed a chuckle. He noticed a glint of approval in Lapaige's eye, as if he and the general did not always see eye to eye. "I didn't think he would. He gets to use the Rangers to ferret out zombies, while his men come in later to finish the job." Jake shifted tactics. "Martial Law gives him authority over even you, Governor."

The governor wrinkled his brow and scowled. *Yes, definitely some conflict between them.* "Hmm. That has always bothered me," he said.

"We can call this a test case, an easing from military to civilian authority. He might not balk at that."

"He probably will, but what can he do about it? He never leaves Luke Air Force Base. He can use his troops to reconnoiter new safe haven sites and to patrol the highways and railways. It will save time and resources. I have one question. What about non-capital murder cases? What do you propose we do with them, hang them?"

Jake was certain the governor had read those two paragraphs of his proposal. Lapaige wanted to hear the words from his mouth. "If the crime warrants it, then they can pay for their crimes by making restitution, in this case to the community through a fine that entails physical labor. They work the fields, do the cleaning, move boxes, tote bales – whatever we require of them, though no more than we require of others. Make it clear that if they escape, the next time we apprehend them will warrant the maximum sentence."

Lapaige nodded. "Hard labor. Good, that frees others for more important jobs."

Jake smiled. "You're not as opposed to this as you pretend."

"Son, believe it or not, I want what's good for the country. We don't have time for mistakes, and we've made plenty of those both before and after the Apocalypse." He smiled. "Besides, if things go south, I'll have you to hang from the nearest flagpole."

Jake frowned. "There is that."

Lapaige rose from his seat, pushing up swiftly and rounding the desk in short quick steps. "Let me handle the general. We speak the same language. I'll issue a *quo warranto* for the Rangers as proof of your legal authority." He jabbed a finger at Jake. "You'll be in tentative charge of the operation. You select the men you think capable of being Chief Rangers, set up teams, and assign areas. I'll see if you can take the heat, Major Blakely. There'll be plenty of it for both of us." He began striding across the room. Jake rose to follow, but Lapaige waved him back down. "I want hard evidence on each case. No vigilante justice. If we're going to have law, it'll be real law. I'll appoint a territorial judge to issue warrants and handle the caseload. You'll have to prove to him you did everything properly and by the book, or you'll get a taste of the law yourself, and as you said, we don't have the resources to coddle prisoners."

One bodyguard opened the door and stepped outside to check the grounds. He then nodded for the governor to follow him. The second bodyguard kept his eye on Jake, but he had a slight smile on his face.

"You think I'm screwing myself, don't you?" Jake asked the bodyguard.

"I wouldn't want to be in your shoes, Major Blakely. All I have to worry about is taking a bullet for the governor."

"Yeah, you may be right."

"Good luck, major," he said as he left the room.

Major. He would have to get used to that. He sat there running the conversation over in his mind. Had he missed something, or had the governor given him everything he wanted? It had been too easy. He had expected to plead his case, get shot down, and plead some more, settling on what he could get. He heard the twin turboshaft engines of the governor's HH 60G Pave Hawk helicopter revving up to take off and smiled. The governor took no chances on his personal safety, traveling with two armed bodyguards and a four-man crew in the heavily armed Pave Hawk. It might look like overkill, but it was the act of a prudent man. The governor did not like to take chances. That made Jake wonder even more who had gotten the better end of the deal.

5

June 25, 2017, 10:00 p.m.   South Tucson, AZ —

Jake had barely assumed command when his first opportunity to show the governor what he had in mind for the Arizona Rangers arose. Most of Tucson was still a city of the dead. Only Davis-Monthan Air Force Base, the Union Pacific rail yard on Aviation Parkway, and the Sundt power plant on S. Irvington Road were of any immediate concern to the military or the territorial government. Even these received only cursory patrols by the small garrison at Marana.

However, the Air Force base had weapons and the boxcars on sidings at the UP rail yard contained tons of freight, both tempting targets for gangs of looters or enterprising individuals. When a report of looters at the rail yard arrived at the Ranger station, Jake called on Deacon and newcomer Adrian Grossman to investigate.

Grossman had trained at Maricopa and had transferred to Marana with high recommendations, but he was new to Jake. At thirty-five and a former Phoenix cop, Jake had hopes that he might prove valuable enough to promote to Chief Ranger. First, he had to see him in action.

He had offered the position of Chief Ranger to both Deacon and Andrews. Andrews, as he had expected, turned him down flat. Deacon had not been as blunt, but made it clear that he felt he wasn't ready for the job. Jake hoped that at some point both or either man changed their minds. He needed experienced men.

They had arrived at the rail yard just after dark and took positions to keep an eye on the cars the looters seemed to favor.

The shipping container on one flatcar car contained machine parts, which the thieves had ignored. However, they had half stripped a container of canned goods. Such a find would keep the safe haven in food for a month. He made a mental note to suggest a thorough examination of the sidelined cars. He was betting the looters would return to finish the job tonight, fearing others would discover their cache and beat them to it.

His ear bud squealed as someone keyed the mic of their squad com unit. "Jake, how long do we keep this up? I think a pack of coyotes was sleeping in this shed. I've got fleas."

Jake smiled at Deacon's complaint. "I'll send you a flea collar, Deacon. Hold tight. If they're coming, it'll be soon. They'll want to finish the job before dawn."

Jake scanned the area through his Pulsar N550 Digisight attached to his rifle. In spite of the moonless night, he would have no difficulty seeing anyone approaching. As he swung the scope off to his right, he noticed a tall figure cutting across the rails. At first, Jake thought it was a zombie, but the person was not shambling or moving furtively as a zombie would. Nor was he skulking or moving stealthily as would someone bent on breaking the law. In fact, he moved as if he were out for an evening stroll. The man was painfully thin, but his long legs did not falter as he leaped over rails and climbed between flatcars. He watched the man for a full five minutes, urging him to leave the area and not frighten away their quarry.

A second figure appeared near the man's path. This one was unmistakably a zombie. It moved with a jerking motion, first traveling in one direction, and then suddenly changing directions in an unfathomable random manner.

"Watch out," Jake muttered to the man, wanting to call out a warning, but he could not without giving away his position. Just when he decided catching looters wasn't worth the life of a man, to his astonishment, the tall, thin figure saw the zombie. He stopped for a moment, but instead of moving away, continued on his direct path across the rail yard. Jake did not want to watch the man die, even if he deserved it for his ignorance. In a moment of weakness, he flicked on the laser sight of his rifle and pointed it at the ground in front of the man, moving it rapidly in a circle.

The man noticed the moving red dot, scanned the area until he saw Jake kneeling atop a boxcar, and stared in his direction as if he could see him clearly. Jake could barely make out his features in the green glow of the night vision scope, but the gaunt figure's eyes seemed to glow as they zeroed in on Jake's. A dark-knitted stocking cap covered his head. He nodded as if to thank Jake, held out a book in one hand, and then made the sign of the cross in the air with the other hand. The large gold cross and Holy Bible imprinted on the cover stood out as if blazing. Then he continued walking in the direction he had been heading, toward the zombie.

"Thanks for the blessing, old man, but you're gonna die," Jake whispered, shaking his head in disbelief. "If you're going to be foolish, I'm not saving you."

As the two figures neared, Jake expected the zombie to smell the old man and attack. Instead, the zombie stopped as if waiting. The gaunt man walked past the zombie as if it was not there, and in turn, the zombie ignored him.

"What the fu…?" Jake croaked in disbelief.

He watched the old man disappear behind a row of boxcars, wondering what he had just witnessed. The zombie continued its shambling as if nothing had happened. "He must be the luckiest bastard in the world." As Jake pondered the bizarre episode, Grossman announced over the comm, "I see a truck coming this way, lights off."

Jake switched to professional mode. "How many people?" he asked.

"Two in the front. I can't see the back. No, wait, one I think."

"Both of you stay low and don't spook them," he warned. "We have to catch them red-handed. No shooting unless they fire first."

"Hell, if nothing else, I'll inflict my fleas on them," Deacon said.

Sure enough, the flatbed truck stopped beside the opened cargo container. Three men emerged, two from the front and one from the rear. The one from the back of the truck carried either a rifle or a crowbar. Jake was taking no chances. He waited until the trio began ferrying boxes from the container to the truck before making his move.

"Okay, move in slowly, but be quiet about it."

Jake saw Deacon emerge from the shed scratching his chest and grinned. Grossman was closest to the three men, sitting on the edge of a flatcar. He slid to the ground and crawled under the car to come up from the opposite side of the men. From his position atop a boxcar two rails over, Jake covered both men his M2010 rifle as they crept closer. In spite of the moonless night, the images of all five men stood out against the shadowy background in the night vision scope.

"Grossman, be careful crossing the open space between the rails. Take your time."

"Roger," came Grossman's reply.

"His name's Jake," Deacon added.

"Enough humor," Jake chided Deacon. "One may have a rifle. Act as though all three are armed."

He didn't know if they were just three men desperate for food for their families or part of one of the dangerous gangs behind the thriving black market in the area. People were willing to pay anything to keep themselves or their families alive. That often included bartering themselves off as slave labor for the gang or become a sex slave. Jake could not blame people for trying to survive, but he could stop those who preyed on the weakness of others.

"I'm in position," Deacon reported. Jake could see him waving from behind a row of fifty-five gallon drums near the three men.

"Almost there," Grossman said.

Jake watched him cross the open space and climb over the coupling between cars two cars down from the three men.

"I'm set," he called out.

"Okay, I have you covered. Deacon, give them a warning."

Deacon raised the bullhorn to his mouth. "This is the Arizona Rangers! You are under arrest. We have you surrounded. Drop any weapons you may have and raise your arms where we can see them."

The bullhorn pierced the night and echoed through the still rail yard. For a few seconds, everything remained silent and still. Then, "Screw you!" came from one of the three men.

A shot rang out. Jake spotted the man with the pistol kneeling and pointing it toward where he thought the voice was coming from. The echo made it difficult, so he began shooting all around where Deacon was standing.

"Give him another warning," Jake said.

"Last chance!" Deacon called out. "Drop your weapons."

This time, the man with the pistol focused on the bullhorn. A bullet struck a drum less than five feet from Deacon. That one, at least, did not want to be taken alive. Jake would oblige him. He aimed his rifle and adjusted the night scope until the crosshairs aligned on the shooter's skull; then, gently squeezed the trigger. The man's head shot backwards as the bullet struck. He fell in a fetal position.

The other two bolted, leaving their dead companion and the truck.

"They're running your way," Jake informed Grossman. "Deacon, move to your left. They're not in my visual range. I'll come down and join you."

If the three men had simply fled, he would not have pursued them. Looting did not warrant a death sentence. Putting the fear of the law in them might shake their confidence and put a stop to their looting. However, shooting at an Arizona Ranger after he had properly identified himself required that he catch the two men. They would stand trial as accessories at attempted murder.

"I see them," Grossman yelled. Jake saw him break from the shadows and race down the side of the train in pursuit, and then climb up on an empty flatcar.

Jake ran to join him with Deacon moving in from his left. The sound of a scuffle drew him like a beacon. He found Grossman sitting on top of one man with his pistol pointed at the other.

"Good job, Grossman." Jake was pleased that Grossman showed such potential.

"Get off me," the man beneath him yelled.

Grossman bounced on his back. "Shut up. Didn't I just tell you that you had the right to remain silent? Now, use it."

"We didn't do anything," the second man complained. "Will was the one who took a shot at you. We just wanted to take off."

"This one was carrying this," Grossman said, holding up an M4A1, the Air Force variant of the M16. "I think these three were

part of the gang that broke into the barracks at Davis-Monthan."
He held the rifle to his nose. "It still smells of cosmoline."

"I found that," the man argued.

Grossman rapped him on top of the head. "I said shut up."

"Get him up and tie their hands. We'll deliver them to the judge."

Deacon smiled and started to say something, but Jake stopped him. That the governor had appointed Alton a territorial judge was still a sore spot with him. "Don't go there."

Grossman lifted the man to his feet and pushed him to where his companion was standing. "Hands behind your back."

As he removed a plastic tie from his pocket with one hand, the man he was holding turned and grabbed him around the neck. "Get him, Varga!" he yelled.

Varga produced a knife from his pocket and stabbed Grossman in the chest. Grossman groaned and grabbed at the man holding him, but the blade had punctured his lung. He began coughing up blood. The man released him, and he fell to his knees. The pair began running. Just as one scrambled beneath one of the cars, Jake shot him in the leg. The man screamed and began moaning while holding his leg. Deacon stopped the other one by firing a shot at his feet.

"Next one goes in your head," he warned.

Jake ignored the man he had just shot and went to Grossman. Grossman looked up at him.

"Damn, I can't believe I let the bastard get the jump on me. Ten years a cop and I let some greaser knife me."

"We'll get you to the doc," Jake said. "He'll fix you up."

Grossman shook his head. Blood dripped from his mouth. "Fat chance of that," he said and fell over.

Jake checked his pulse but did not find one. "He's dead," he told Deacon.

Deacon stepped closer to Varga and jammed his rifle in his belly. "I say we shoot this bastard right now."

Jake shook his head. "No, I have a better idea. Bring him here."

While Deacon covered him with his rifle, Jake bound Varga's hands behind his back. Then he walked over to the other man and pulled him from beneath the train by his good leg. He kicked and screamed, but Jake held on. He rolled him onto his belly and tied his hands with the plastic tie Grossman was going to use.

"By virtue of the authority of the Territory of Arizona as granted by the 2016 charter of the Arizona Rangers under the jurisdiction of the territorial military, you have been found guilty of murder. The sentence is death."

Varga's face paled. "You can't do that, man. We get a trial."

"This is your trial. We're Arizona Rangers with the authority to apprehend and punish criminals. Your guilt is not in question. We have two living witnesses." He nodded at Grossman's body. "And a third over there."

"What are going to do?" the injured man asked. "You got to fix my leg. You can't let me bled to death."

"You won't bleed to death. You won't have time." He allowed that to sink in before saying, "I'm going to hang you." He pointed to a signal tower over the tracks just a few yards away. "From that."

"You can't."

"Oh, I can. The governor gave me the authority."

"You sure about this, Jake," Deacon asked. "I'd shoot the bastard right now if you say so, but hanging? That's …"

"A horrible way to go," Jake finished, staring at Varga. "Yeah, I think so too. So does the governor. That's why he authorized it." He understood Deacon's squeamishness, even sympathized with him, but shooting them would be too quick. He wanted the men to feel something of the terror Grossman must have felt as his life's blood dripped away. He would have preferred a public hanging as a warning, but their bodies hanging from the signal tower would serve just as well.

"We got rights!" Varga sputtered. "I ain't no illegal. I was born here, right here in Tucson."

"Your rights ended the moment you killed an Arizona Ranger. You'll hang as an example for anyone else considering it. You'll make a better deterrent than you did a human being." He turned to Deacon. "Deacon, I need you as a witness, but you're to take no part in this execution. Got it?"

Deacon swallowed hard. "If you say so, Jake."

He remembered the governor's warning. If anything happened, he wanted Deacon to have no culpability in the incident. It was what he had promised Alton. "This is all on me."

Deacon guarded the two men while he retrieved a length of nylon rope from the back of the SUV. In front of his prisoners, he measure two lengths and fashioned nooses at one end of each. It had been surprising how many old books he had found detailing the proper way to hang a person, including weight charts, length of rope according to humidity charts, length of drop, and various knots. Hanging had once been more of an art than a science.

It was difficult hauling the two men up the steps to the signal platform by himself. Both men whimpered and moaned the entire time, but the fight had gone out of them. He tossed the ropes over the signal arm and tied one end to the railing. He then placed the nooses around the men's necks. The injured one refused to stand.

"Do you want to die on your knees or standing like a man?" Jake asked.

"For God's sake quit whining, Peters," Varga snapped. "Don't give this bastard the satisfaction of watching you cry like a baby."

Peters stood, leaning to one side to take the weight off his injured leg. "I hope someday someone guts you like a fish, Ranger. I wish I could watch you squirm."

"We all die, Peters. Today's your day. Mine will come later."

He stepped back and faced the men. "By the power vested in me as Major of the Arizona Rangers by the governor of the territory, I hereby carry out the sentence of the court. May God have mercy on your souls."

He shoved both men off the platform. They dropped six feet before the rope snapped taut with a popping sound, breaking their necks instantly, just as he had planned. His worst fear had been that he had calculated wrong and that they would dangle until they slowly choked. He wanted to execute them, not torture them. He had spared them that.

As he climbed down, he noticed his hands were shaking. He felt no thrill of revenge or sense of *fait accompli* at the pair's death. He felt numb, as if the entire episode had been some sort of vivid dream. He glanced back at the dangling corpses, and the full impact of what he had done hit him in the stomach like a sidekick by a Muay Thai kickboxer. He had performed his first hanging, and he had not enjoyed it.

"What do we do with the bodies?" Deacon asked. "Take them back with us?"

"No, we leave them here. Let the zombies finish them off."

Deacon nodded and went to Grossman's body. "Too bad. I liked him." He looked at Jake. "I'm glad the bastards that did it are dead."

Jake read Deacon's expression. "But you don't like what I did."

"It's not that ... It's... I guess I'll get used to it."

"I hope you don't. Go get the SUV and we'll take Grossman back to bury. He deserves that."

"Yeah. Yeah, he does."

As Deacon trekked back to the SUV, Jake let the turmoil inside wash over him. He had done what was necessary, but he did not like it. He had killed men before in war and after the apocalypse. He had stared into their eyes as he did so, watched the life fade away, and felt nothing. However, this time the bile rose in his throat like the mercury in a barometer marking every death he had caused. He doubled over on the ground and threw up. He continued retching until his empty stomach ached from the effort.

He sought to placate his raw emotions by repeating *Jake's Law #6 — Bad people deserve bad ends*, but *Law #10* kept popping into his mind — *Serve revenge in big doses*. Had he hung the men in revenge for Grossman's death, or was had he been acting as a major in the Arizona Rangers? *The latter,* he concluded. *Revenge wouldn't make me sick to his stomach.*

6

June 30, 2017, 2:15 p.m.   Chiuli Shaik, Tohono O'odham Reservation, AZ —

Aden Ortega checked outside carefully with the door slightly ajar before fully opening the door of the two-bedroom adobe home he shared with his grandfather. Standing just outside the door, shielding his eyes against the blazing sun, his dark eyes scanned the terrain around the house. Finally, satisfied that he was alone, he relaxed. Barely seventeen, Aden was tall for his age, standing almost 5'11". His long black ponytail, as dark as a raven's wing, was held in place with a broken and oft-retied rubber band. A sweat-stained straw hat covered his head. Jeans, a white T-shirt, and hiking books made up the rest of his apparel.

He was not eager to leave his ailing grandfather alone, but food was running low. He would have to walk into Sells, a distance of a little over twelve miles. His father's old Chevrolet S-10 pickup had finally given up the ghost. He could perform most of the repairs necessary to keep it running, but the cracked rear axle was beyond his capabilities. Even if he found a replacement, he could never drag it home, and the repair was a two-man job. Carrying supplies in his backpack was difficult enough. Small loads did not last long and required numerous foraging trips. Each outing was dangerous and becoming more so.

It was not his first foray into Sells on foot. The neighboring houses, of which there were few, had already been looted by him and others. Chiuli Shaik was not big, a dozen government-built homes and cheap mobile homes scattered along a winding dirt road halfway between Sells and Baboquivari Peak. Its distance from populated areas had kept it relatively safe from zombies, but he was now venturing farther and farther from home for supplies.

He cast a quick glance east toward Baboquivari Peak, home of *I'itoi*, creator of the Papago people, the Tohono O'odham. His people held the 7,730-foot mountain, called *Waw Kiwulik* in their language, sacred, but that did not stop it from becoming a popular hiking and climbing destination for tourists. He mumbled a short prayer. His belief or lack of belief in the old legends was secondary to the comfort the prayer gave him. His eighty-five-year-old grandfather, Mateo, was growing weaker every day. His Type 2 diabetes, the predominant disease of the Tohono O'odham, second only to the Staggers, was winning the battle for his life.

He needed proper medical attention, more than Aden could provide, but none was available. The clinic in Sells, abandoned during the first months of the plague, was now a blackened, gutted ruin, as were many buildings in the town. Like the plagues of yore, people considered fire a way of cleansing infected buildings. The flicker of blazes on the horizon had illuminated the night sky for months. No longer. Most of Sell's 2,500 residents had either fled or succumbed to the disease.

Aden readjusted the scabbard for his Buck knife that rested on one hip. His Gator machete rested on the other. The 18-inch blade had seen much use, more than he cared to remember. He kept both weapons well honed. He slung his handmade leather quiver filled with homemade arrows over his shoulder, followed by his 68-inch-long white ash bow. He was a crack shot with his grandfather's old Marlin hunting rifle, but they had only a few rounds of ammunition left, and he preferred to save it for a real emergency.

The machete and the bow were excellent weapons for dispatching zombies—silent and effective. He had long ago run out of store-bought arrows. He now manufactured them on a small hand lathe from walnut limbs gathered on the higher slopes of the Baboquivari Mountains. He hand knapped points from flint found in abundant deposits in the area. The feathers were from birds, mostly quail, he snared for food, dyed a bright yellow so that he could easily reclaim any arrows.

Aden worried for his grandfather. Since his mother had died ten years ago and his father had disappeared during the initial outbreak of the plague, he and the old man had kept each other company. His grandfather had taught him the old ways of the Tohono O'odham. Now, he seemed to be wasting away daily. He seldom moved from his bed, and often went days without eating. It was as if he wanted to die, to join the spirits of his ancestors. Aden wasn't quite as ready. He did not want to be left alone.

That was the hardest part, the solitude. In school, he was popular, a freshman tight end for the varsity football team, the Warriors, ranked number 20 in the state. He dated several local girls and enjoyed a normal, fifteen-year-old's life. All of that had disappeared almost overnight with the Staggers Plague. It had been months since he had spoken to another human being other than his grandfather, and he could not remember the last girl he had seen that had not been a raging, flesh-eating zombie.

He sighed and shook his head. Feeling sorry for himself got him nowhere. He had a long trek ahead of him. He faced the sun, already edging toward the western horizon, and headed cross-country, avoiding the roads and any houses. Once, a man had shot at him for walking through his back yard. The house was now long silent, its trigger-happy occupant either dead or gone, but others were out there equally as cautious and frightened. Once, early during the plague outbreak, a gang of older Tohono O'odham men from across the Mexican border had swept through the area, attacking the helpless, stealing, looting, and killing. He found it difficult to believe their own kind would prey on them, but hard times brought the worst in people, even him.

He had killed, and not just zombies. He was not proud of it, but it had been a case of kill or be killed. The man, he did not know his name, had tried to break into their home during the night. Repeated shouted warnings did not discourage the man, who was drunk on looted alcohol. Firing a warning shot in the darkness with a bow was useless. He steeled himself for what he had to do and let an arrow fly. His first arrow had found the man's heart as he kicked in the front door. The man had a pistol stuck down the front of his pants. Aden did not know if the man would have used it, but he did not regret his decision to protect his grandfather. The man lay buried on a nearby rise, along with half a dozen zombies Aden had killed.

He followed each taking of a life with a cleansing ceremony, a ritual upon which his grandfather had insisted.

"Why not just burn the bodies?" Aden had asked.

"The cleansing ceremony is to purify your soul," he had said, "not theirs. They were once human. Perhaps some small part of them still is. Taking a life is a bad thing, done only out of necessity. It cannot be done without thinking, without remembering."

He wasn't sure he understood fully the significance of the ritual, but under his grandfather's guidance, he had performed all the necessary steps and buried the bodies, keeping nothing he found on the dead, not even the pistol.

"We do not take an enemy's possessions," his grandfather explained.

Sometimes his grandfather's mind wandered, remembering old events as if they occurred yesterday, but on these two things, he did not waver. Aden accepted them as part of his heritage and tried to adhere to them.

Aden lifted the brim of his straw cowboy hat and wiped the sweat from his brow with his hand. The day was scorching, the sun beating down on him as it were a fiery hammer and the earth an anvil with him a piece of iron waiting to be shaped into something new, something different. He had wanted to leave with the coolness of first light, but his grandfather had needed tending to, and wood gathered for the fireplace. The air was humid, ripe with early monsoon moisture, but the only clouds in the azure sky heralded wind not rain. Wind stirred the dust, and dust carried the Staggers spores. He had escaped the disease so far, but that did not mean he was immune. He would have to hurry to beat the wind.

The sun-baked dirt crunched beneath his boots as he leaped across a narrow dry wash. The stench of a recently killed animal enveloped him mid-leap. A young javelina lay dead in the wash, its throat ripped open by some predator. Several sets of coyote tracks tore up the nearby soil. Oddly, the coyotes had not eaten the javelina. Something had frightened away the killers. He became instantly alert. In the desert, predators did not kill and abandon scarce food without reason. Only three things could frighten a pack of hungry coyotes—a puma, a man, or a zombie. A puma would have claimed its prize. That left man or zombie.

He had seen more zombies in the area lately during his salvage excursions. Some wandered in from Tucson, but most were arriving from the Mexican state of Sonora just across the border. He was not sure what had set them on their northward trek, but their numbers were growing weekly. He had avoided most of them, but it was becoming more difficult to move about unseen or unchallenged.

He paused beside a twenty-foot-tall saguaro, careful to avoid the sharp quills, using its meager shade to conceal his outline from any observers. He scanned the area, but he was on a flood plain of winding washes and arroyos, capable of hiding from view anything only yards away. He listened but heard only the wind and the sound of his own breathing. He silenced his breathing and opened his senses to what was around him, as his grandfather had taught him. He detected the scratching of a Collared Lizard as it dug a hole in the hard clay of the wash bank to escape the afternoon heat. The soft flutter of a hummingbird's wings came from the vicinity of a blooming agave as it fed on sweet nectar.

In the distance, the sound thud of a jackrabbit's rhythmic hops, as it moved; then, stopped to check its surroundings, reached his attuned ears. He would have liked catching the rabbit for the dinner pot, but his grandfather needed more than stew. He needed vitamins and minerals sorely lacking in their bland, unvarying diet. He would trade all his possessions, as meager as they were, for a single bottle of multi-vitamins.

Then, he heard it, the shuffle of feet in sand. He dropped his bow from his shoulder, placed the nock of an arrow against the string, and drew the arrow back slightly to tension the bow. He took a deep breath and stepped from behind the saguaro, facing the direction of the sound. The decaying zombie, dressed in tattered, filthy underwear and nothing else, was a mass of cuts and scratches, most of which oozed a foul ichor. Cactus thorns protruded from its naked legs. It stumbled along the wash with its mouth open, issuing a mewling sound, as if its inability to climb the steep sides of the wash confused it. Aden raised his bow, sighted along the shaft, and released the arrow, all within the space of a single heartbeat.

The string barely made a sound as the arrow left the bow. The arrow, carefully balanced on the lathe, flew straight and true, striking the zombie in its open mouth. The yellow quail-feather fletching protruded from the creature's mouth like a New Year's Eve horn, quivering from the impact. The finely knapped flint broadhead penetrated flesh, bone, and teeth, slicing deep into the creature's medulla oblongata, severing the lower brain from the spinal cord. Its heart and lungs, kept functioning in the decaying body by enzymes released by the Staggers parasitic worms, immediately ceased functioning. The zombie made no sound as it collapsed to the sand. He waited a few moments to make sure it was alone, and then continued his journey.

Sells was a small city, but the largest on the reservation. It had few restaurants or grocery stores. Looters had already ransacked most businesses and homes. Several, like the Jack-in-a-Box and the Desert Rain Café, were now piles of blackened rubble. The Baboquivari High School cafeteria had earlier yielded him a few cases of canned vegetables and soup, and the small nurse's room a handful of first-aid supplies. However, on his last visit, even the vending machines were empty. He hoped to find food and perhaps medicine for his grandfather at the sports complex. Athletes always received injuries during hard practice or a game. He had seen bandages, pain medication, and vitamin supplements in the coach's office and in the locker room. Even stale tortilla chips and cans of nacho cheese sauce from the vendor's storage room would be a welcome addition to the rabbit and wild vegetable stews they currently depended on. It was unlikely the locker room first-aid cabinets would contain anything for diabetes, but it was worth the risk to check.

He crossed Ajo Highway warily, fully exposed to any zombies or anyone intent on doing him harm. A few dozen of the starving skeletal creatures ambled along the side of the highway or shuffled aimlessly in parking lots, but only one noticed him. He dispatched it with his bow before it could alert others. He tried not to look at the occasional picked-clean skeletons in wrecked autos and littering the streets, or stare too closely at the fifteen skeletons in an overturned school bus. In a school with less than three hundred students, he knew all of the dead in the bus. Seeing the bones of an old friend would be more than he could endure.

He reached the football field without incident, but as he slid open the metal gate, the rusted hinges screamed out in frozen agony. The shrill screech echoed across the empty field and through the covered walkway. He cursed himself for being a fool and froze. After almost a full minute, he relaxed, believing nothing had heard him. His luck did not hold for long. Five creatures, drawn by the sharp sound, drifted in from Main Street. Twice that number exited the stadium bleachers in twos and threes.

He could not kill them all even if he had enough arrows in his quiver. If he continued, they would trap him inside the stadium. He had no choice but to retreat and try another location. He managed to avoid most of the slow-moving zombies, but a few were fresher, less decomposed, and moved quickly, keeping pace with him. He shot two of them, but used three arrows doing so. As he passed a small shopping center, a mob of zombies poured from two of the buildings and joined the pursuit. He could still get away, but he would have to go straight through them, moving quickly and without stopping before they surrounded him. He had no time for his bow. He slung it back over his shoulder and drew his machete. He would have to fight his way through, hacking and slicing at the creatures.

He yelled a war cry that would have done his ancestors proud and rushed the nearest concentration of creatures with the machete raised high in the air. The sun glinting from the polished steel blade drew the attention of one zombie. It was still staring at it mesmerized, as the sharp blade detached its head from its body. A two-handed sideways slash opened up one's chest from side to side. A third quickly lost an outstretched arm before he stabbed it straight through the neck. However, now the zombies were bunching closer together around him. It looked as if every zombie in town was converging on him. He could not protect his back and fight his way through the mob of creatures at the same time.

He eyed a flatbed trailer parked along the edge of the road. At one time, it had held bales of hay for sale, but a fire had destroyed the hay, the cab, and most of the trailer. As meager as it was, it offered the only refuge within reach. He vaulted atop the trailer and skidded to a stop just before rolling off the other side. His hat tumbled off his head. One zombie seeing the movement lunged at it thinking it food and came away disappointed that it was not. The frenzied crowd of zombies careened against the trailer, clawing for him. He stayed away from the edge and the large hole burned through the trailer's bottom. Any creature that seemed close to climbing onto the trailer received a slashing blow from his machete. He split one creature's head open from the top of its skull to its jaw.

The grunts and groans became more frenzied, as the zombies packed tightly against the sides of the trailer. With nowhere to go, he climbed on top of the cab and sat down to wait until they lost interest, if they ever did. Starving zombies could be determinedly single minded. He watched the creatures as they milled around the trailer for half an hour before one of them stumbled atop the back of a fallen comrade and used it to climb onto the trailer bed. Aden hopped down onto the trailer and sliced off its head with his machete. The severed head landed at the feet of the other zombies, kicked about like a soccer ball until it finally disappeared beneath the trailer. By now, the others were following its lead, clambering all over each other in their eagerness to clamber onto the trailer bed and eat him.

The next three creatures were not difficult to kill. He took them out one at a time, but then they started clambering up in small groups. He replaced his machete with his bow and fired arrows as quickly as he could reload, but they relentlessly forced him back against the truck's cab. For the first time since the beginning of the outbreak when he had faced and killed his first zombie, a neighbor, Aden was afraid for his life. More than that, he was afraid he would be bitten and change into one of the hideous creatures. What would become of his grandfather then?

When the top of the nearest zombie's head exploded, Aden could not spot the shooter. The muffled report of the shot reached him a second later. Moments after that, a second zombie tumbled dead from the trailer. Aden thanked his unseen mysterious benefactor and used the confusion among the zombies to his advantage. He climbed back atop the semi's cab, used the hood as a springboard, and, pretending they were linemen of the opposing team, leaped over the heads of the nearest zombies. He hit the ground running, swinging his bow wildly to deflect attacking zombies. He plunged one arrow into a zombie's face with his hand.

He ran blindly in the general direction of his home, all thoughts of supplies erased by his encounter.

"This way, kid!" someone shouted.

Aden altered his course slightly toward a distant figure dressed in black wearing a black cowboy hat. The figure killed two zombies closing in on him with a Winchester .30/30. Movement atop a roof revealed a second shooter, this one armed with a high-powered rifle. He used it well, aiming and firing almost as quickly as Aden could fire arrows, but his shots were more effective and much quieter than the .30/30.

Aden was out of breath by the time he reached the man in black.

"Hop in," the man said, and waved his hand at a nearby Arizona Ranger black and white SUV.

Aden did as directed, collapsing onto the back seat amid a pile of backpacks and extra weapons and ammunition. The man climbed into the front driver's seat seconds later and cranked the vehicle. He drove straight through the oncoming zombies, crushing several beneath the tires and sending others flying through the air. Blood splattered the dirty windshield. He slid to a stop beneath the roof bearing the second shooter. The second man dropped down onto the roof with a thud and slid inside through the open window opposite Aden. He grinned broadly, as he collapsed the folding stock of his rifle and laid it across his knees.

"Thought you might like some help," he said.

Aden quickly took in the strange black rifle equipped with 30X scope. He did not think they had come specifically to rescue him. He had just been fortuitous to be in the right place at the right time. Nevertheless, he was grateful. "Thank you."

"Headed anyplace special, or just out sightseeing?"

"Chiuli Shaik. I live in Chiuli Shaik a few miles from here."

"Never heard of it," the driver said over his shoulder. "Point the way."

Aden, still confused by the sudden nick-of-time appearance of the two men, pointed south. The driver swerved to avoid a wrecked vehicle and floored it. The SUV fishtailed in the loose gravel, but the driver kept the vehicle under control and used the controlled spin to point the nose of the SUV south into the desert.

"Who are you guys?" Aden asked.

"Arizona Rangers," the man beside him with the sniper rifle answered. "The man behind the wheel is Deacon. My name's Jake."

Deacon drove straight across the desert, avoiding deep washes and dodging the larger cacti. He ploughed through the smaller ones. Aden wished he had fastened his seatbelt, when the SUV became airborne as it dove into a wide wash and bounced him around like a pair of dice in a crapshooter's cup.

"You're a good shot," he said to Jake.

Jake nodded and rubbed the rifle affectionately. "I have a good weapon. This is a .30 caliber Remington M2010 ESR, an Enhanced Sniper Rifle. It has fifty percent farther range than the old M24 SWS. It can drop a zombie at 1300 yards, 1500 if there's no wind. The Black Earth suppressor avoids drawing unwanted attention." He stared at Aden. "You're pretty good with that long bow. I know. I had a Parker compound bow I was good with also."

The SUV hit the dirt road leading to his house, leaving a cloud of dust. "Who are you guys, really?"

Jake pointed to the tarnished five-point star on his chest. "We're honest to God Arizona Rangers."

"What are you doing here on the Rez?"

Jake frowned and narrowed his eyes. Aden saw such intensity in the man's gaze that it frightened him. "We're tracking a couple of murderers. They stopped a vehicle, and robbed and killed the driver and his wife. We're here to dispense justice."

Detecting the edge of bitterness in Jake's voice, Aden nodded at the sniper rifle. "With that?"

"It's the only kind of justice some people need."

"Are you guys legit?"

"Too legit to quit," Deacon replied from the driver's seat, rapping his words like lyrics while tapping the steering wheel.

Jake ignored him. "The Rangers are working with the territorial government to bring the law to the land."

"White Man's law?" Aden asked. His peoples' history was awash with tales of White Man's justice.

"The Law," Jake replied. "It's a one-size-fits-all kind of law. Justice is swift and punishment is final." He tapped the M2010 grimly. "This is my warrant, my Mirandizer, and the court of appeals."

Jake's somber tone raised a chill specter inside Aden that the heat of the day could not dispel. Then, thinking of his grandfather, he asked, "Do you know a doctor? My grandfather is ill."

Jake's face softened with concern. "What's wrong with him?"

Guessing what Jake was thinking, Aden replied quickly, "No, not the Staggers. He has Type 2 diabetes. He needs medicine."

Jake's expression relaxed. He patted his shirt pocket where he kept his Actos. "I'm somewhat familiar with Type 2 diabetes, kid. I think I can help him for now. After we find our quarry and administer justice, we can take him to the infirmary in Marana. You can both join our little safe haven if you want, or after he's seen the doctor, someone can bring you back here."

It was too much for Aden to take in all at once. Arizona Rangers, the law, medicine, doctors, a safe haven—it was like a dream. He was afraid to pinch himself. He nodded. "Uh, yeah, we'd like that." He pointed to his house. "That's it."

Deacon did not slam on the brakes. Instead, he hit the clutch, downshifted into second, released the clutch, and spun the wheel. The SUV reared onto two tires, slid sideways across the front yard, and came to a stop beside the front door facing toward the road. The vehicle settled back down on all four tires.

"I love to do that," Deacon said, grinning.

Two crazy-ass White Men, Aden thought, but he was glad he had run into them. For the first time in two years, he felt safe.

7

June 30, 2017, 5:00 p.m.   Sells, AZ —

Jake followed the boy, Aden—*young man,* he reminded himself. *No mere boy could survive among zombies or use a bow like a pro*—inside his house, while Deacon remained outside on guard. Aden rushed straight for one of the two bedrooms where an old man, painfully thin and pallid, lay in his bed. Except for the long white hair and Native American complexion, Jake thought he looked a lot like his grandfather as he lay dying in his hospital bed at eighty-three. He wondered what his grandfather would have thought of today's zombie-ridden world. Jake checked his pulse, which was weak, and examined his swollen hands and feet. He pinched his foot experimentally.

"Does that hurt?"

The old man was barely responsive, but he did shake his head.

Aden looked worried. "Grandfather, are you all right?" He stared at Jake, as Jake opened his med-kit and removed a disposable lancet and a vial of glucose test strips. "What are you doing?"

Jake jabbed the lancet into the old man's thumb. The old man jerked but did not cry out. Then he touched the end of the test strip to the drop of blood. It immediately turned dark blue. "Over 200. He's hyperglycemic." He handed Aden an alcohol swab. "Hold this over his thumb for a minute or two."

Because of his Type 2 diabetes, Jake always carried a vial of insulin in his kit for an emergency. It was a myth that it needed to be refrigerated, but he had wrapped it carefully in an insulated sleeve to protect it from the heat. He had never needed it. His diet and exercise kept his diabetes under control, but he felt safer knowing it was handy. He drew 100 units of insulin into a syringe and injected it subcutaneously in the old man's belly. Without knowing the old man's physical condition, he was afraid to try a higher dosage. One hundred units should be enough to bring down his sugar, but his long-term chronic diabetes could have wreaked havoc with his organs. He didn't want to put more strain on the old man.

He tried to keep his face from displaying his skepticism, as he said, "There, that should help. Do you have water?"

Aden nodded.

"When he rouses, make him drink a couple of liters. He's badly dehydrated."

Aden watched Jake put away his med-kit. "Are you a doctor?"

Jake laughed. "Hardly. I just know a little about diabetes." He frowned down at the old man. "He's pretty anemic and just generally worn out, but he looks like a fighter. He needs his daily dose of oral medication."

"He was taking *Precose*, but we ran out a few weeks ago."

"I have some *Actos* I could leave with you, but your grandfather needs real medical help to get him back on his feet. You should come back with us to Marana."

Aden looked at his grandfather and nodded his head. "All right."

"I'll wait around to see how he responds to the insulin, but I still have some justice to administer."

"The two men you're after … What are they driving?"

Jake arched an eyebrow at Aden wondering what the boy knew. "A late-model white Ford van with no side mirrors and a cracked windshield. Do you know them?"

"No, but two men live in a trailer just outside of town. They're dangerous. I've seen them around a few times. I try to stay out of their way. They drive around in a van like that shooting zombies for fun."

"Later, you can show me." He glanced around the house. It was surprisingly neat and tidy. He eyed a Marlin 336 lever-action rifle hanging in a gun rack on the wall. The .30 caliber rifle was old and the wooden stock worn smooth from much use, but it was in good condition for a forty-year-old rifle. "Yours?"

"Grandfather's. I only have a few shells left."

"I can leave you a box. Can you shoot it?"

"I'm a good shot, but I prefer my bow. It's quieter."

Aden showed him his bedroom, converted into a mini-workshop where he manufactured arrows and flint points. A pile of lathed walnut blanks lay in a pile awaiting tips and fletching. Quail feathers, yellow dye, and a bottle of Elmer's Glue sat on a table. It reminded Jake of his gun workshop in Split Falls Canyon, now a pile of flood-deposited debris scattered along the washes of the Galiuro Mountains north of Oracle.

"Did your grandfather teach you this?"

"He insisted. He said he saw bad times coming where the old ways would save us."

"He was right. You used quite a few arrows today."

Aden nodded. "On my next trip into town, I'll try to recover as many as I can. The trip into the mountains for more hardwood is getting too dangerous." He grinned. "Maybe I'll find my hat, too."

Jake studied the wooden shutters covering the windows. Slits let in light and would allow the boy to fire arrows or the rifle through them. The shutters were well built and mounted on the inside of the window where an intruder could not rip them off.

"Did your grandfather make these?'

"No, I did, but Grandfather taught me to use a hammer and a saw when I was ten."

"You're good with your hands."

Aden shrugged, embarrassed by the praise. "He was a good teacher."

When the boy's grandfather had recovered sufficiently enough that Jake felt safe in leaving him, he and Deacon prepared to finish the job they had set out to do. It would soon be dark, and he preferred confronting the two murderers in daylight. He left Aden to pack what he and his grandfather would need to return with him and Deacon to Marana. Aden drew a crude map of the location of the two men he and Deacon were after. They located the trailer and parked the SUV down the road out of site. The white Ford van with missing side mirrors and a broken windshield that a witness had described was sitting in the front yard amid a clutter of rusting automobiles, motorcycles, and trailers. Jake took a position behind a tree about fifty yards from the trailer, while Deacon picked a spot with a clear view of both the front and rear doors.

Jake tried to quell the rising trepidation in his chest. It was never easy confronting armed men. You never knew how they would react. Some turned passive and cooperated, while others went berserk. Though he would not hesitate to burn them out if necessary, he would give them the chance to surrender quietly.

"You! In the trailer!" he yelled. "Arizona Rangers. Come out and identify yourselves."

A curtain brushed aside and a rifle barrel poked through the window screen. Jake ducked behind the tree, but the bullet struck ten feet away. The men might have been deadly with a pistol at close range, but they couldn't hit the side of a barn at fifty yards.

"Last chance!" he called out, sliding a round into his rifle.

A second shot got a little closer, kicking up the dirt at the base of the tree behind which he stood. Jake raised his rifle and fired three shots slowly through the thin aluminum walls of the trailer, evenly spacing them on each side of the window with the last one right through the window. A startled yelp from inside told him one of his bullets had struck his mark. The rear door opened, and Deacon peppered it with shots from his 30/30.

"I'm coming out!" someone yelled from the trailer.

A few seconds later, a man walked out the door and down the steps with his hands in the air. He was overweight with a scraggly beard and long, unkempt hair. He kept looking back at the trailer. "You killed my brother."

"He shouldn't have fired at us."

"We didn't do nothing. We didn't know who you were."

Jake motioned Deacon to check out the trailer. Deacon moved cautiously in case the other brother was still alive. "We announced ourselves loud enough, and witnesses say otherwise. Sit on the ground with your hands behind your back."

He complied. Jake searched him for weapons, found nothing, and cuffed him with a plastic tie. He checked the man's wallet, bulging with cash and stolen credit cards, and read aloud from his driver's license, "Lester Leon Manson, age 37, of Taos, New Mexico. Welcome to Arizona, Lester."

Deacon emerged a few minutes later. "Just the pair of them. The other one's dead."

"We didn't do nothing," the man repeated. "You murdered him in cold blood."

"What did you find?" Jake asked Deacon.

Deacon stared down contemptuously at their prisoner. "Two pistols, a dozen rifles, drugs, booze, and an assortment of purses and wallets from about a dozen different people." He held out a plastic bag with a wallet and two driver's licenses. "The Hernandez's included."

"We found those."

"I just bet you did," Jake shot at him. He hated cold-blooded killers, but he hated buffoons worse. "It's bad enough you steal from others, but murdering people for their money is just plain stupid. What did you expect to do with it, Lester?"

"It'll be good again someday." Realizing he was confessing, he said, "I'm not saying anything more until I talk to a lawyer."

Deacon burst out laughing. "Lawyer? You've got to be kidding me. The last lawyer I saw was shambling down Fourth Avenue carrying someone's foot in his hands."

"I got rights." Lester's voice started out self-assured, but as he looked at Jake's cold, hard mien, he faltered. "I mean, you got to prove it, right?"

"This isn't *CSI*, Lester. We have witnesses, evidence in the form of stolen items from the victims, and you tried to kill us. That's all the proof we need."

Lester was beginning to fidget nervously. "What do you mean? What are you going to do?"

"Lester Manson, by virtue of the authority of the Territory of Arizona as granted by the 2016 charter of the Arizona Rangers under the jurisdiction of the territorial military, you have been found guilty of murder. The sentence is death."

Lester's face paled. He tried to stand, but Deacon shoved him back down with his foot.

"You can't kill me. Don't I get a trial? Take me to jail."

"We don't house and feed murderers. We hang them."

"You can't do this," Lester protested. "There's no more law. It's survival of the fittest."

"And you think you're the fittest?"

"I've got the right to survive."

"Your right doesn't supersede anyone else's right." He yanked Lester off the ground. "I think the tree at the end of the road will do nicely. People will see your rotting corpse and think twice about murder."

Lester screamed an incomprehensible obscenity, knocked Jake aside, and began running into the desert. Deacon started to chase him, but Jake called him back. He allowed Lester get a couple of hundred yards away, sighted him in the crosshairs of his scope, and gently squeezed the trigger. Lester somersaulted forward from the impact and lay face down in the dirt.

"Sentence carried out," Jake said.

"We should have chased the bastard down and hanged him."

As far as Jake was concerned, it wouldn't have bothered him to tie a rope around Lester's neck and drag him behind the SUV until his head popped off, but a shot to the head was cleaner and quicker. He had performed only one hanging since getting the go-ahead by the governor to change the scope of the Rangers, and he had found it a gruesome business. A bullet was cleaner.

"He made his choice. Tag the evidence and mark the warrant served. Take a photo of the van and of both bodies. We need to go pick up the boy and his grandfather and head back to Marana."

Deacon stared at him. "You looking to adopt him?"

"I intend to make a Ranger out of him."

* * * *

June 30, 2017, 9:00 p.m.   Marana Safe Haven, Marana, AZ —

Jake sat across from Alton Reed, the new territorial judge Governor Lapaige had appointed. Jake didn't know if it was a joke on him by the governor or if he thought Alton the best man for the job. Whatever the reason behind the governor's decision, Alton did not enjoy his new position as Judge Alton Reed. Jake believed the only reason Alton had accepted the appointment was to keep him in line.

Alton leafed through the slim file folder on his desk, barely glancing at the photos of the dead men. "You announced yourself?" he asked.

"Loudly and clearly. That's when they started shooting."

"The one you captured, Lester Manson, how did he manage to escape?"

Jake had been expecting the question. "I told him we were going to hang him. He went crazy, knocked me down, and ran."

"Cuffed? You didn't pursue him?"

Jake stared at Alton. He knew what Alton was thinking, and he might be right. He could have chased his prisoner down if he had desired to. "So I could turn around and hang him?"

Alton lowered his head and looked crestfallen. "I suppose shooting was more merciful."

"Maybe, but that's not why I shot him. Mercy wasn't on my mind."

Alton jerked his head up and glared at Jake. "So I gathered."

"He was guilty of murder, Alton, er, Judge Reed. They both were. From the evidence we found at the scene, several murders. Hanging would send a stronger message, but I don't enjoy putting a rope around someone's neck even if they deserve it. It may be necessary, but I don't ever want to enjoy it."

Alton's accusatory mien softened to one of embarrassment. "I'm sorry, Jake. I'm not sure why the governor appointed me judge. I don't know the law. I'm a science teacher." He pointed to a stack of law books on the floor beside his desk with dozens of Post-It note page markers sticking out from different sections. "I need a legal dictionary just to understand half of the terminology. All I know about the law I learned from watching television."

Jake felt sorry for his friend. The responsibility the governor dropped on him was a heavy one, and Alton took everything he did seriously. Jake was glad he did not have Alton's problem. It was all cut and dry for him. He had a judge-issued legal warrant, he made an ID, and he dispensed justice. He didn't need to know more law than he remembered from his days as a deputy. He just had to be fast with a gun and willing to use it.

"You'll grow into the job. People like me need people like you keeping watch over us. Like you said — too much power."

"Now, I've got the power. I'm not sure I like it."

"When you start to like it, that's when you need to worry."

Alton changed the subject, as if he was still uncomfortable talking about himself. "What about that Tohono O'odham boy and his grandfather you brought in? What do you want to do with them?"

"The old man needs medical attention. He's old, diabetic, and skinny as a rail. His grandson is tough though, the kind of person we need in the Rangers."

Alton was flabbergasted. "He's only a boy," he protested

"He's a tough seventeen year old. Kids are maturing early nowadays. They have to. Seventeen was old enough for the original Rangers." To Alton's look of horror, he added, "I agree he's too young now to go out on missions, but he can help out around the office, learn the ropes. He's good with his hands. He can help out in the motor pool." He shrugged. "Who knows, he and his grandfather might just want to go back home."

"I'll see that his grandfather gets the medical attention he needs. The boy can bunk with me for a while."

Jake nodded and smiled. "I see you didn't suggest he stay with me in the barracks."

"You're still a loner, Jake."

He knew Alton meant it as matter of fact and not as an insult, but it still stung. "You're right."

"I have a report that the military have moved into Hatch, a full company. They've located sixty-two survivors in town and in the surrounding farms. One of them, Hilda, said to tell you hello."

Jake smiled. Hilda was another tough one. If the country managed to survive the Staggers and pull itself back together, it would be a stronger, tougher nation because of people like her. "What about the Mexican girl? How is she doing?"

Alton frowned and shook his head slowly. "Not good. We can deal with her physical problems, but her mental state is quite another matter. We don't have enough psychologists available. The ones we do have are doing double duty as medical doctors. She's in for a long recovery."

Jake nodded. He had not expected her to come out of her horrible ordeal all bright, shiny, and eager for company. He had seen strong people suffer less and fold like a cheap lawn chair under a 300-pound man. There were hundreds, if not thousands, of people like her spread out just in the Southwest, each one wondering when help was going to come. If word spread that the Rangers were active, it might give them just enough hope to hang on.

"Is Hilda moving on? She seemed eager to get out of Hatch."

"No. In fact, she decided to help the medical team set up an infirmary. I think she'll prove very valuable."

Jake smiled. "Maybe I could hook you up with her. She might change your outlook on life." He had not told Alton that Hilda was a lesbian.

Alton's cheeks reddened. He stuttered in his nervousness. "I'm, I'm too busy for hook ups, thank you. Besides, she seemed very interested in you."

Jake shook his head, trying to suppress a chuckle. "Me and women are like water and oil."

"I'll be visiting Yuma in a few days." With Alton's sudden change in direction of the conversation, Jake knew what was coming, but it still hit him hard. "Do you want me to say anything to Jessica?"

She was still a sore point between them. He knew Alton held him responsible for driving her away, and for the most part, he was right. She had never hidden the fact that she had stayed with him out of necessity, sex for security—an even trade. They had been mutually attracted for a while, maybe a little more on his part, but he had been afraid to allow her too deep into his life because of his doubt about her emotional involvement. Things cooled quickly after they moved to Gladden Farms. Amid the unaccustomed security, his doubts about her need for him grew stronger. At the same time, he became restless among so many people. Perhaps she had interpreted his volunteering to scout out safe haven sites as abandoning her. Perhaps she had not been too far off the mark. He couldn't blame her for his inadequacies. He missed her, but knew their brief time together was over. It was time to move on. He wished Alton would.

However, Alton wouldn't. He knew Alton had been secretly infatuated with her and enjoyed being around her, even in Jake's long shadow. Now, she was gone and both of them were alone.

Jake shrugged. "What's to say? I wish her well. I don't blame her for running away. Hell, I would run away from me if I could."

Alton shook his head. "You're too hard on yourself, Jake."

Getting too morbid in here. He nodded at a stack of manila folders on Alton's desk. "New cases?"

Alton looked relieved to drop the touchy subject. "Six new cases—four murders, an attack on a military food convoy, and a bizarre report of a lunatic wandering the countryside yelling out texts from the Bible and claiming the devil is coming north for us all."

Jake sighed. "Forget the convoy. Let the military deal with it." He did not feel like hanging another man so quickly after the first. "I'll send a couple of teams out to search for and serve warrants on the murders. What about this crazy man? He sounds interesting."

Alton shrugged. "Not much to go on, really. Just another poor psycho. I only mention him because he's armed and potentially dangerous."

"Aren't we all? Well, he's not too far off on the devil claim. The past couple of years have been hell on Earth. If there is a Boogey Man, a dapper dude in a red suit, it wouldn't surprise me to see him walking around town with a sly smile on his face."

"He could be harmless. He was last spotted near Orange Grove and I-10 headed in our direction."

Jake stretched his right leg, moaning as he massaged his cramped knee, but noticed Alton watching him and stopped, a little self-conscious about complaining about a slight cramp in light of Alton's condition.

"I'll swing down that way and take a look. Like you said, he's probably harmless, just another lunatic on a mission from God." He paused. "But then again, there may be something to his claim."

"Jake, don't tell me you're beginning to believe in the Bible?"

"Except for Jesus returning, the Book of Revelations wasn't far off the mark. No, it's the bit about the devil coming north. Deacon and I encountered a lot more zombs on our way to Sells than we should have. They seem to be moving north, like this Preacher Man said."

Alton pursed his lips and frowned. "Yuma reported an unusually large number of zombies along the Colorado River over the last few days. Nothing they can't handle, but if the trend continues ..." His voice trailed off in thought as he looked at Jake and recognized his look of intense concentration. "Do you foresee a problem?"

"I always see problems. You know that. If the border fence is down, we could get an influx of Mexican zombies. When's the last time anyone checked it?"

"I don't know. I suppose we could ask the military to do an aerial reconnaissance."

Jake shook his head. "A few photos taken from 10,000 feet won't tell us much. We need eyes on the border."

"Are you volunteering? I thought you were out of the recon business."

"One last time into the breach. Besides, I'm curious."

"Good. You can accompany me to Yuma in a few days," Alton suggested.

Seeing the direction Alton's conversation was headed, Jake sighed. "She's moved on, Alton. We had our thing, but she needed something more than I could give her. Hell, she's still a kid, practically."

Alton spread his hands. "I won't bring it up again. Still, Yuma is a good place to start. You're safer traveling in a convoy, and I would enjoy the company. Besides," he added, nodding at the stack of folders on his desk, "one of the warrants I issued is for three men near Yuma. They broke into a farmhouse, murdered the owner and his wife, and looted it. The dead man worked for our farmer's co-op in Yuma. We take care of our own."

Jake stared at Alton's slight smile and decided to give up. His friend was determined to get him to Yuma one way or another. "Okay, I'll go with you to Yuma, but meeting Jessica is not on my list of priorities. I'll serve the warrant and check out the Staggerers situation."

Alton acknowledged Jake's concession with a slight nod of his head. "That's all I ask."

Jake snorted. "Yeah, sure."

Jake only half-listened as Alton rambled on about legal procedures, his plans for Yuma's future, and gossip he had overheard around Marana Safe Haven. He was trying not to focus his mind on Jessica. It was like ignoring an itch. To see her again would be tempting, but would probably only cause more pain for both of them. It was better to focus on his job.

The Preacher Man intrigued him, not because he was a loony on a mission from God, but because he might be closer to the truth than any of them was willing to admit. Building fences to keep out the zombies and the bad guys made them feel safe, but it could not protect them from a massive wave of zombie invaders. It would only take a few hours to find the Preacher Man, learn out what if anything he knew, and perhaps bring him back to the safe haven before someone felt threatened enough by him to shoot him.

Sounds like a cinch.

8

July 1, 2017, 7:00 a.m.   Tucson, AZ —

Hollis Boudreaux rose unsteadily from his bedroll when the sun stabbed into his eyes. He massaged his legs to ease his aching muscles, and then said a quick prayer of thanks for another day on Earth. He relieved his bladder in a corner of the building, used a handful of water from his canteen to wash the sleep from his eyes, and ate his usual meager breakfast. The handful of pecans he had picked from a nearby orchard and pan roasted over his campfire did little to assuage the gnawing hunger in his belly. He eyed the package of stale crackers in his pack, but he reserved them for their salt, a necessity in the desert heat. The inescapable heat, like his near fast, was something else he never thought he would get used to. He washed his meal down with a few sips of tepid water.

As he ate his paltry ration, he stared out the window of the slab yard in which he had taken refuge for the night. The large granite and marble slabs were mostly for counters, not graveyard markers, but the word slab brought to mind the uncountable graves he had seen along his journey. He had slept very little. A train passing during the night awakened him. At first, he had thought it was the chariot of God coming for him, but then he heard the train's mournful whistle. Still, the unexpected reminder that all of mankind's mechanical marvels had not vanished disturbed his thoughts and would not allow sleep to come. The area around Thornydale Road and Orange Grove had been mostly commercial and therefore largely abandoned during the height of the Staggers Plague, but he spotted a couple of God's chosen creatures shambling across a parking lot. He wondered if any of who they had once been remained within the decaying bodies, or if they were simply parasite-driven animals in human shells. Perhaps they were demons incarnate in the flesh of men. God had not yet revealed the secrets of their origin to him or their ultimate purpose, but the Almighty had not put them here on the Earth for extermination like vermin.

Not that he felt any great love for them. He had almost become a zombie himself. Stricken with the Staggers Plague, he had thought his life was over. The fever, the chills, the nightmares had all finally faded as his ravaged body gave up the fight, and he sank into dark oblivion. However, he awakened, arisen from the darkness a new man, free of the Staggers. Weakened by his illness and abandoned by all those who professed to love him, he had struggled back to health a changed man, touched by God.

He packed his few possessions, a few days' supply of food and water, a waterproof poncho, an extra shirt, and his Bible. Then he pulled the knitted stocking cap over his bald head to protect it from the sun. Lastly, he shoved the sickle he had carried from Mississippi through his belt. His load was light to ease his steps. His path from Biloxi, Mississippi to Tucson, Arizona had been a winding one, wandering uncounted miles along the Gulf Coast and through the swamps of Louisiana, up and down the state of Texas, and across the deserts of New Mexico and southern Arizona. There had been many lean, hungry days during his two-year sojourn, but people along the way, even amidst their own scarcity of food, had felt compelled to feed him and offer him a place to sleep in exchange for the word of God.

Now, his hunger was self-imposed. In the beginning, like so many prophets of the Bible, he had hoped fasting would bring clarity to his scattered thoughts, bring him closer to God. After four days of nothing but water, he had almost died of sunstroke. Now, he allowed himself a few precious bites each day to prevent his starved body from consuming his muscles.

At first, his wanderings had been random, a search for a God he thought had abandoned him, but one night in a barn outside Odessa, Texas, he had come face to face with three zombies. Instead of devouring him as he expected, they had stood and stared at him as if waiting for something. He had taken out the sickle he carried for protection to end their suffering, but God had stayed his hand. The three creatures eventually wandered away, as if sensing in him a kindred spirit, leaving him unmolested. He knew then that God had a purpose for the zombies and for him. Nothing happened without His knowledge or consent.

The day was already uncomfortably warm. Soon, it would become unbearably hot, like every other day in the desert. He thought back on days before the apocalypse, of air conditioning and iced drinks, of languid, humid evenings on the front porch, and of the sound of waves lapping on the beach. All of Arizona was a beach. All it needed was water. He watched the two zombies for a while until they disappeared down the street. Then, slinging his pack over his back, he went out to greet the day.

He had wandered the streets of Tucson for over a week, bringing the word of God to those who would listen and waiting for some sign to tell him which direction he must travel—north to Phoenix or west to California. Something would happen that day, something grand. He could feel it coming as he could feel the air change before a storm, his skin tingling as the tiny hairs stood on end. He did not know if it would signal the end of his journey or simply another signpost along the way. God worked in mysterious ways, and where it concerned his mission, Hollis felt as if he were traveling blindfolded.

One cannot argue with God.

He inhaled a lungful of hot, dry, flinty air and frowned at the bitter taste it left on his tongue. The relentless sun and the parched landscape had wrung all the moisture from the air, and the constant desert dust particles rode the wind like an avenging demon bent on turning the lining of his lungs into concrete. He did not allow his mind to dwell on the tiny Staggers spores clinging to the dust particles. God had spared him so far, and He would continue to do so until He had no further need of him. Hollis missed the soft offshore breezes of Mississippi tasting of the salt of the sea and the heady fragrance of magnolia and lilac. He was a long way from home and felt certain he would never see the white, sandy beaches again.

It was difficult not to be bitter. He wondered if Moses had been bitter. Certainly, he had fought against God's call to free the

Hebrews, and in the end, after forty years of wandering, did not get to enter the Promised Land. Jonah had tried to run away from God's mission, and a giant fish had swallowed him. Had he been bitter at his experience?

Hollis shook his head and said, "God guides my footsteps and sets the path before me. I may not see the end of my journey, but God knows." The sound of his own voice surprised him. He often went days and weeks without speaking aloud. His once deep, resonant, Southern Baptist preaching voice sounded weak and reedy.

It's the damn dust. It gets everywhere. Something else Moses and I have in common, a desert.

He set out on his journey by passing beneath the railroad bridge on Orange Grove Road next to I-10. The interstate led north to Phoenix and west to California. Somewhere along the way, he would discover the true purpose of his sojourn. He had seen a Costco sign down the street and briefly considered a stop to replenish his supplies, but God hurried his footsteps. Around him, the sights, sounds, and odors of an abandoned city fought to distract him. He ignored the forlorn skeletal remains, the foul, dark pools of stagnant rainwater collected in the plugged drains, and the miasma of smells wafting from decaying corpses and mysterious bubbles rising from the depths of the puddles. However, he could not ignore the stench emanating from the gravel pit half a few hundred yards away on opposite side of the expressway. The early morning breeze was light, but it carried with it the foul odor of the unburied dead.

Early on during the plague, the gravel pit had become a dumping ground for the tens of thousands of Tucson cadavers overpowering the city's ability to bury or properly cremate them. Bulldozers had hastily pushed sand and gravel over layers of half-burned bodies, but even that had proven too slow. Someone had come up with the bright idea of placing explosives in one wall of the pit to bring it down over the corpses, but the attempt had failed, leaving thousands of bodies exposed to the elements and the ravages of scavengers, such as coyotes, wild dogs, and vultures. Rainwater had collected in the low end, creating a noxious, toxic organic soup poisoning the area. Even the plants had become stunted and spectral in appearance.

Hollis had passed the pit near sunset the previous evening and had stared down into the unholy chasm of the dead with a sense of loss that overwhelmed him. It was not his first glimpse of wholesale carnage, but the sight still troubled his soul. He knew none of the people carelessly deposited there, but each had friends, family, and loved ones to lament their deaths. The litter of corpses represented how far mankind had fallen from the grace of God. For a moment, as the dying sun sent dark shadows scurrying across the pit, it looked as if the corpses were moving, trying to rise from their graves. He had not been certain if it was real or a hallucination caused by his fasting. He had experienced several haunting phantasms and disconcerting mirages, most of them in the past few days. He considered them ominous signs heralding a coming event, but it could as easily have been a warning that he had pushed his beleaguered body near its limits. He had no desire to look upon their dead, forlorn corpses again this morning. One glimpse into the depths of Hell was enough. He said a brief prayer for their souls and continued his journey.

The muscle memory of many miles of walking quickly reinstated itself in his rhythm. For months, his pace had not varied rain or shine, paved road or desert, hale or sick. His walking tempo had been as constant as the ticking of an antique grandfather clock or the uplifting melody of a Broadman Hymnal. It had not always been so. When he had first set out on his pilgrimage what seemed a lifetime ago, his muscles had rebelled at what he required of them. He had spent many nights in tears from the agony of protesting muscles and cramps he could not massage away. He had not been as eager to answer God's call then. He had wanted nothing more than to find a safe place to live out his remaining days, or even a brief respite from the damnation around him.

God had worked with clay more reluctant to shaping than him many times in the past. Day by day, his heart had yielded to God's will. He was to be a witness to the end times, a chronicler of events, and a messenger for the remainder of mankind.

Born to poor white trash in southern Mississippi, he had flirted with the law most of his young life until joining the Navy at seventeen. There, he had learned to work with his hands, tearing down and rebuilding engines. He had traveled the world, learning that it was a much larger place than his small corner of rural Mississippi. He had found God at the late age of twenty-five during a tent revival in Pearl, Mississippi, listening to an old wheezing, red-faced revivalist mix visions of Paradise with the threat of fire and damnation. He knew his calling, to become a lay preacher and spread the word or God. His steps had not faltered.

Today, his steps faltered often, as if the earth itself, the very ground he trod, wished to tarry him. He had plodded through rain-engorged muck in Louisiana and Texas clay the consistency of wet cement, but neither had impeded his progress like the hard-packed soil on the side of the interstate. Finally, with a weary sigh, he dropped his pack and sat down on the ground.

"If it is your will, God, I will not fight it."

Then, he waited.

9

July 1, 2017, 9:30 a.m.   Tucson, AZ —

Normally, Jake rose each morning just after dawn's first light dispelled the night shadows, but sleep had not found him until the early morning hours. Alton's insistence on bringing up Jessica had dredged up old memories that bothered him more than they should have, though in truth he could not place all the blame on Alton. He had never buried his confused feelings for Jessica deeply enough to dispel the disquieting emotions memories of her evoked. Tossing a few spadefuls of metaphorical dirt over the open grave her departure had left in his soul, and then proclaiming her dead and buried had fooled no one, him least of all. His fear of losing her had inevitably driven her away, and losing her had haunted all his fears since. It was a vicious circle, a ghost serpent biting its own tail.

He could not heal the wound between them, but he should not have allowed it to fester. He would look her up when he reached Yuma and see what, if anything, he could do to make things right, or at least more right than they presently were. He smiled at the thought that that was exactly what Alton, torn between their friendships, had been hoping for.

Sly devil.

Jake had no appetite. The turmoil in his mind has spilled into his stomach. He did not want to see anyone, especially Alton, until he had time to sort through his emotional baggage. It was already after eight o'clock before he dropped by the Rangers HQ to pick up one of the ATVs from the motor pool. The economical two-seater Yamaha Wolverine burned less fuel than an SUV or truck, and fuel was precious. It was also four-wheel drive, and he might have to go off road in his search for the Preacher Man. He topped off the fuel tank, dropped his pack and extra water in the rear cargo box, and laid his .30 caliber Remington M2010 ESR between the seats. In addition to his Colt revolver in his holster and his Enhanced Sniper Rifle, he brought his Browning A5 12-gauge shotgun. He jammed it into the space between his seat and the door for easy access. The double-ought buckshot, 3.5-inch magnum shells could cut a wide swath through zombies if they crowded the ATV. The ESR was for distance shots.

He had retrofitted the Wolverine with a fold-down Plexiglas windscreen and 18-gauge steel wire mesh for doors and over the fiberglass roof. Braced with half-inch metal pipes, the mesh was strong enough to keep zombies at bay, but not the dust or rain.

He cursed his luck as he saw Deacon walking from the main building towards the garage. With his appointment as the new Chief Ranger and his promotion to major came responsibilities Jake did not enjoy. He now had to interact with his Rangers more intimately than he was comfortable with, but with leadership came compromise. He had gotten what he wanted. Now he had to pay the piper. He was certain Alton was enjoying the irony of his dilemma, trading being a loner for being a leader. He knew he should have checked in with the office before setting out, but today of all days, he just wanted to slink away quietly.

No such luck.

Deacon's long legs covered the distance between the main building and the garage quickly. He wore a big grin on his face, but his eyes were cloudy with questions. After Cray's death, Jake had become his new best friend. Of all the Rangers under his supervision, he could tolerate Deacon most, but a little Deacon went a long way.

"Where you headed?" Deacon asked, watching Jake prepping the ATV.

Wiping an imaginary spot of dirt from the ATV's five-pointed star decal bearing the words *Arizona Rangers* with the side of his fist, he said, "Taking a little spin south."

"Need some company?"

By his hanged-dog expression, he judged Deacon had become bored with the paperwork that came along with the job. "Not this trip. I'm looking for someone. If I find him, I'll need the extra seat."

Deacon frowned. "You serving a warrant alone? That's not smart."

"No. No warrant. I'm looking for a wanderer they call the Preacher Man."

"Preacher Man? That sound like a CB handle. What do you want him for?"

"Judge Reed thinks he's harmless, but he's afraid someone might take a shot at him. I'm going to see if he wants to come here."

Deacon chuckled. "Judge Reed. Ain't that a kicker? How are you dealing with that?"

How indeed? "I'm coping. He just wants the paperwork nice and tidy."

Deacon scratched his head. "Yeah. Been all morning on the stuff. I type like a chicken pecking corn." He wiggled his fingers in the air and sighed. "Well, if you don't need me, I guess I'll see if I can get this report finished before bedtime. Stay frosty out there. Oh, you might need this."

He pulled a hand-held radio from his back pocket and handed it to Jake. Jake was chagrined that he had forgotten it. One of his first official decrees had been an upgrade in the VHF base station and antenna for longer range, more reliable communications, and that all Rangers carried radios, as well squad-com gear when working as a tactical unit.

He took the radio, checked to see that the battery was fully charged, and replied, "Yeah, thanks."

He watched Deacon as he sauntered back into the building, envying his air-conditioned environment, if not his mountains of paperwork. He hoped Aden would stick around and lend a hand. He had been a senior in high school when the shit hit the fan, smart enough to handle the paperwork while he learned what the Rangers were about. They needed new blood. Aden had the skills to become a good Ranger, but suspected a lot depended on his grandfather. The bond between the two was strong. Part of Jake wanted the old man's recovery to be a long one to keep him at Gladden Farms, but even that degree of selfishness made him uneasy. Aden could decide for himself if he wanted to stay. Pushing would not help.

He wiped the sweat from his brow with his handkerchief and glanced up at the sun hanging in the sky like a 300-watt interrogation lamp hovering over a suspect's head cooking out a confession. The morning had the makings of a scorcher building to medium-broil by mid-afternoon. The ATV had no A/C, just the hot wind blowing through the wire mesh to keep him from suffocating in the stifling heat. He wished he could throw on a pair of shorts, a T-shirt, and sandals, but the uniform, as hot as it was, represented the law as much as the badge or the emblem on the vehicle.

Satisfied he had forgotten nothing else, he climbed into the driver's seat and strapped in. He drove slowly through the neighborhood just now beginning to stir, and threw a wave to the security guard at the main gate. He opened the ATV up as he climbed the ramp onto I-10, maxing out the vehicle's 708cc engine at 51 mph. Once on the expressway, he dropped the speed to a less noisy 40 mph and headed south.

The last report had placed the Preacher Man somewhere near I-10 and Ajo Highway. He could head east into the Tohono O'odham Reservation or south to Mexico, but Jake had a hunch he was moving north toward Phoenix. The first obstacle he faced was that he wasn't sure how to find the Preacher Man if he did not want to be found. He couldn't drive around with a bullhorn calling his name or set up a roadblock. He would have to trust to luck and his hunch.

The last thing Jake expected was to find the Preacher Man sitting by the side of the road as if he were waiting for Jake's arrival. At first, he thought it was just another emaciated Staggerer and considered shooting it, but zombies did not normally sit and stare as this one did. Jake slowed the ATV and edged off the asphalt onto the gravel shoulder, keeping one hand on the shotgun beside him. The tall, gaunt figure was as emaciated as most zombies, but he was clearly a living human. He stood, brushed off the seat of his pants, placed the Bible he had been reading back in his pack, and walked toward the ATV. Jake recognized the knitted stocking cap the man wore and the Bible and remembered the strange gaunt figure the night he had hanged the two men at the rail yard. Then he saw the sickle thrust through the man's belt and cocked the shotgun.

"Are you the Preacher Man?' he yelled out.

The man stopped walking and chuckled. "Some have called me that. My name is Hollis Boudreaux. Are you the law?"

Jake nodded. "Arizona Rangers. I'm Jake."

Jake noticed how weary Preacher Man looked. He was a thin as a scarecrow and as pale as a ghost in spite of his time spent beneath the sun.

"I felt God's call this morning, telling me to wait for you. Am I under arrest?" There was a playful crinkle in Preacher Man's eyes as he asked, but Jake suspected he had not found many things humorous in a long time.

"No, we received reports about you and thought you might need a safe place to rest or even sanctuary."

"Sanctuary? The word sounds Godly, doesn't it?" He shook his head. "God will not allow me to abandon my journey, officer, put perhaps He will not deny me a few hours of rest and a bit of conversation." He stared at Jake, and Jake felt as if Preacher Man were seeing deep into his soul. The scrutiny made him uncomfortable. "Have we met before?" he asked Jake. "You seem familiar."

"We haven't met, but I think we saw one another. A week ago in the rail yard?"

"Oh, the man on the boxcar. Thank you for warning me."

"What did … how did …?" He wasn't sure how to ask if what he had seen that night was real.

"God protects me."

Jake decided to let it slide for the time being. He noticed movement near the Mike Jacobs Sports Park separated from the interstate by a small gravel median strip and a dilapidated fence. Two zombies, roused by the noise of the ATV's engine, ambled toward the road. "We had better get a move on. We've got company." He nodded toward the zombies and picked up his Winchester.

Preacher Man frowned. "They will not bother me, my son, but rather than have you kill God's creatures, let us leave this place."

The Preacher Man's defense of zombies mystified him, but he lowered his rifle. "I kill zombies, Preacher Man. That's what I do. You got a problem with that?"

Preacher Man nodded. "I understand. I do not fault you for your conviction, but please do not question mine."

Preacher Man dropped his pack behind the seat and climbed in, wearily, Jake noticed. "Fair enough," he replied. "Buckle up." His passenger's hands trembled as they snapped the seat belt. "You look like you could use a good meal."

Preacher Man leaned back and closed his eyes. "Perhaps, but fasting clarifies my thoughts so that God may speak to me more clearly."

"Fasting in this climate is a quick way to see God up close and personal. You had better have our doctor look you over. Maybe a few vitamins will perk you up."

Preacher Man smiled. "Perhaps God would not frown on vitamins." He opened his eyes suddenly and stared at Jake. "Do you have orange juice?"

Taken off guard by the question, Jake slewed the ATV sideways as he got back on the road. "Orange juice? Sure. Fresh. We have an orange grove."

Preacher Man closed his eyes, but a smile flickered across his lips. "That would be nice."

* * * *

Preacher Man was not asleep, but he seemed to be beyond the present, in a waking dream, as he remained in the seat after Jake pulled up in front of the infirmary. His breathing was even, but his hands jerked slightly, like a puppy running in its sleep. Jake reached over to grab his shoulder. Preacher Man's eyelids snapped open like jerking on the draw strings of Venetian blinds. He blinked rapidly several times, and then looked at Jake.

"God was speaking to me," he said in a whisper.

Jake stared at Preacher Man. *Loony Tunes, all right.* "Yeah, right. We're here."

Jake's noncommittal reply did not offend him. "It's not necessary that you believe me. God told me that our paths crossed for a purpose. You are about to embark on a journey of your own."

It was not a question but a statement. "Yes, Yuma."

Preacher Man nodded. "It is important that I accompany you."

Jake shook his head. "I don't think so. It could be dangerous. Besides, you're in no shape to travel."

"Each day is dangerous in this Brave New World we have wrought for ourselves. He informed me to break my fast and to prepare for the journey and the battle."

Alarmed, Jake asked, "Battle?"

Preacher Man shook his head. "I do not understand either, but battle was the word He chose, so it must mean something. I am no warrior, so perhaps he meant a spiritual battle. Regardless, I must be there."

Jake walked around and opened the passenger door. "First, we get you checked out. Later, we can talk."

Preacher Man followed meekly, as Jake escorted him to the infirmary with his arm around Preacher Man's waist to support him. Inside, the infirmary was empty except for Edward Van Ross, their only real doctor. He sat behind his desk reading a well-thumbed magazine. He glanced up over the rims of his reading glasses, saw the condition of Jake's charge, dropped the magazine and his glasses on the desk, and rushed to help. Jake navigated Preacher Man to one of the three treatment rooms and laid him on the bed.

"Is he injured?" Van Ross asked, as he examined his new patient's arms; then, pulled up his pants legs to check his legs. He frowned when he saw the sickle thrust through Preacher Man's belt. He removed it with three fingers, as if afraid to touch the bloodstained blade, and deposited it on a metal tray on a table beside the bed; then, after a moment's consideration, moved the tray out of reach.

Jake laid Preacher Man's well-worn backpack on the floor beside the bed and nodded to his charge. "Ask him. Except for fasting and too many road miles, he seems pretty coherent to me."

"If you have some orange juice and perhaps some fruit, I would be grateful," Preacher Man said. Lying on the white sheets of the bed, he looked even paler and frailer than when Jake had first seen him.

Van Ross crossed his arms over his chest and tapped his left cheek with the forefinger of his right hand as he spoke, "First, I'm going to hook up a saline solution for dehydration and check your blood. A 5% Dextrose ringers IV will help give you some strength. Then, you can eat a little solid food."

"I am in your capable hands, physician. Heal me."

Jake glanced into the other two rooms, but both were empty. "Where is the old Indian?"

Van Ross stepped out of Preacher Man's room and smiled. "You mean Chief Mateo?"

Stunned, Jake repeated, "Chief?"

"He was once, long ago. Now, he's just a sick old man."

"The question stands, Doc."

"I moved him to the room in the back that I sometimes use when I stay overnight. It's much quieter. His grandson is staying with Judge Reed." He smiled when he said the title. "You saved his life with the insulin injection, you know. His diabetes is presently under control. We have no *Precose*, so I have him on *Actos*. I have a large supply of it on hand, as you know. He's remarkably healthy for his age. His mind is sharp. He needs rest and a healthy diet." He glared at Jake. "The same could be said of you."

"I took my *Actos* this morning," he lied, "and I'm trying to stay away from unhealthy fatty fast foods. I haven't had french fries in two years."

Van Ross put his hands on his hips and fixed Jake with his dark brown eyes. He stood six inches shorter than Jake, was slightly overweight, and looked as if he had never seen the inside of a gym, but he was nevertheless an imposing figure. There was no humor in his voice when he said, "Very funny. Your prescription should have been refilled five days ago, so don't try to convince me you're taking it regularly."

Jake realized Van Ross had caught him red-handed. "I've been busy, Doc."

Van Ross sighed heavily. "If your diabetes progresses to Type 1, you'll probably die. We don't have the facilities to store large quantities of insulin, and I don't know how to install an insulin pump if I could find one. I can't start chopping off pieces of your body if they become gangrenous. I was an Eye, Ear, Nose, and Throat specialist at the VA Hospital, not a surgeon."

The same dark thoughts had crossed Jake's mind when he first learned of the diabetes that ended his army career. He had read medical journals about diabetes, had seen the photos of running sores and amputated limbs, and felt helpless. Then, focusing on the fact that his diabetes was mild and controllable, he had decided to get on with his life and became a Pima County deputy.

"I'll have to take my chances. An apocalypse is a helluva time to be drug dependent. In my line of work, diabetes is the least of my worries."

Van Ross removed a bag of .9 % saline from the cabinet in the hallway, rolled a wheeled IV rack to the side of the bed, and suspended the saline from one of its arms. He used an alcohol sponge to wipe away the accumulated grime from Preacher Man's scrawny left arm, wrinkling his nose at the strong odor of perspiration wafting from his patient. He hit the vein with the needle on the first try and thumbed the valve open. He watched the saline flow carefully for a couple of minutes to time the drips; then, satisfied, he secured the needle to Preacher Man's arm with tape.

He went to the refrigerator for the orange juice his patient had requested. Out of sight of his patient, he broke open two capsules, poured the contents into the juice, and sloshed the juice around to mix it. He handed the juice to Preacher Man.

After his first sip, Preacher Man grimaced. "Did you put something in here?" he asked.

"Just an antibiotic. I'm going to add some vitamins to the IV drip. You're malnourished. That's why I want a Dextrose ringer drip later."

Preacher Man glared at him. "No sedatives."

"If you insist, but you must try to rest. You're running on sheer will power. Frankly, I'm surprised you're still alive."

He downed the rest of his juice and settled down in the bed. "God is not through with me yet."

Van Ross cast a sideways glance at Jake, who shrugged his shoulders. "Whatever he wants with you can wait a couple of days, surely."

He glanced at Jake. "That depends on the lawman. He and I have a mission."

"Mission?" Van Ross asked, but Preacher Man was already asleep, snoring softly. He drew the blanket over him and slid the curtain to the room closed as he left. In a soft voice, he asked Jake, "Are you taking him somewhere? I must object. He's in no shape to—"

"Relax, Doc. I'm not taking him anywhere." He tapped his forehead with his finger. "I think he's been out in the sun too long."

Van Ross stared at him long enough to make him uncomfortable before saying, "You look like you could use some vitamins, too."

Jake tensed. "Don't start with me, Doc."

Van Ross raised his hands in the air in mock surrender. "Okay. Okay. You're a grown man. Just don't work too actively to kill yourself."

Jake snorted. "I'll try to die in slow stages. Look, I've got to tell Alton I found Preacher Man. Try to keep him from wandering off."

Van Ross smiled. "He won't be going anywhere soon. Only one of the pills I put in his juice was an antibiotic. The other was *Nembutal*. He'll be out for hours."

Jake shook his head. "Don't ever try any of your little tricks on me, Doc." He patted his holster. "I'd hate to shoot our only doctor."

The color drained from Van Ross's face. "You wouldn't dare."

Jake smiled. "No, I wouldn't. I was just yanking your chain." He looked at the supply cabinet. "As long as I'm here." He grabbed a vial of insulin and a few items to replenish his first-aid kit.

"You need to sign for those, you know."

"200 ccs of insulin, a box of medium bandages, a tube of Neomycin ointment, and a dozen alcohol swabs," he called out over his shoulder, as he stuffed the items in his pockets. "Log it for me, will you?"

Van Ross huffed in irritation. "Sure, Jake. I have nothing better to do."

"Thanks," Jake replied as he walked out the door.

He liked Van Ross, but self-doubts plagued the forty-year-old VA Eye, Ear, Nose, and Throat specialist about his ability to be the all-round physician the safe haven needed. That made him doubly cautious in his treatments, and made Jake nervous when he was on the receiving end of those treatments. He tried to avoid the infirmary as much as possible, but someone had to stitch up the wounds he couldn't reach.

Marana Safe Haven was lucky to have him. Most often exposed to people infected with the Staggers, the plague had hit doctors, nurses, caregivers, and pharmacists especially hard. Out of the nearly two thousand survivors involved in the three safe havens, they had only Van Ross, one general practitioner, an ex-Navy corpsman, three RNs, three veterinarians, and a retired oral surgeon to tend to their healthcare needs. A small but rapidly growing school in Yuma taught by a former surgical scrub nurse and the Navy corpsman trained twenty students in the basics of healthcare. Van Ross went to Yuma twice a month to lecture at the school. Jake imagined him sweating bullets standing in front of so many eager faces and grinned.

Something about Preacher Man bothered Jake. It was almost certain he was ill and a little touched in the head, but his steadfast conviction in his cause lent an air of credence to his words. He was insistent that he needed to be wherever Jake was going. Jake was tempted to postpone his Yuma trip for an additional day and see if Preacher Man was well enough to travel. That would not please Alton, which in itself was reason enough to wait. After all, what difference could one day make?

10

July 1, 2017, 1:00 p.m. U.S.-Mexican Border, Yuma, AZ —

Corporal Vince Diluna slid the jeep to a stop on the dirt road and waited for the cloud of dust the tires had kicked up to catch up. He closed his eyes and mouth as the dust enveloped the open jeep.

"Damn it, Corporal, did ya have to raise such a sandstorm?" Davers groaned, flailing his hands at the cloud of dust swirling around his face.

Diluna grinned. He enjoyed antagonizing Davers almost as much as he hated listening to Davers slow, southern drawl. Before his promotion to corporal, Davers had been an irritating thorn in his side, constantly reminding him, an Arizona native for three generations, that the Confederates had controlled the Arizona Territory during the Civil War. Now, he was getting some payback. He and Private Chris Davers were making their daily rounds along the U.S.-Mexican border south of Yuma. It was a boring job, but someone had to report any damage to the border fence. The flimsy fence was all that stood between Yuma and 10,000 Mexican zombies in San Luis Rio Colorado across the border.

"Quit bitching, Private, and hand me those glasses."

Davers handed him the binoculars. Watching the mass of zombies milling around less than a hundred yards away made him uneasy.

"Why can't the Mexicans do something about the damn zombies?" Davers complained. "We did."

"Maybe there isn't much of an army left, Davers. Did you think of that? The Citizen's Committee has sent a group to meet with the Mexican officials to discuss the problem."

"Maybe they'll let us cross the border for some target practice." Davers raised his rifle and sighted along the barrel.

"Drop that weapon, Private. We don't need to start a border war, and I sure as hell don't want any zombies around here to come calling."

Davers frowned but lowered the rifle. Diluna did not hold out much hope of any cooperation from Mexico. During the height of the plague, the U.S. had slammed shut the border and threw away the key. Anyone, living or dead, caught crossing was shot by patrolling choppers or drones. It had created a lot of conflict and tension, but neither country had the means or the military to do anything about it.

Diluna eyed the dark storm clouds brewing to the southwest, a low-pressure center moving out of the Sea of Cortez. Flashes of lightning made filigree lines in the roiling mass. He had been caught in a *haboob* once a few years earlier. He did not want to be out in the open when the sandstorm preceding the storm struck. Echoes of distant thunder rolled across the countryside, sounding much closer than the storm looked.

"We'd better head back to base."

"I see trucks along the fence."

Diluna raised the binoculars again and checked in the direction Davers pointed. Two military trucks were driving along the fence, stopping every hundred feet or so, and then moving on twenty or thirty seconds later.

"They must be checking the fence," he replied, but something in their hurried movements bothered him. Of course, they might be as afraid of zombies as he was. Even as he watched, a machinegun opened up on a group of zombies getting too close to the trucks. A few minutes later, both trucks turned south and disappeared. "Whatever they were doing, they're through now."

"I wish we were," Davers moaned. "I'm burning up out here. Why the hell would someone want to live in this Godforsaken desert?"

He pulled his collar away from his neck to emphasize his discomfort. Diluna expected to see a visible red ring denoting Davers status as a true Alabama redneck hillbilly. His slow drawl made him sound dumber than he really was, but then Davers was not the brightest bulb in the lamp. A series of explosions along the fence stopped Diluna before he could answer.

"What the hell?"

Diluna got out of the jeep and walked to the nearest rise for a better view. Ten columns of smoke and dust billowed into the air along a thousand-foot-long section of fence. Slowly, like an accordion, the entire fence began collapsing. Hundreds of zombies began moving toward the sound of the explosions.

"Oh, shit," Diluna moaned, "they're blowing the fence."

A few minutes later, the unmistakable pop of mortars firing rose above the constant groans of the walking dead. A new series of explosions erupted in the center of the town. As he watched, the explosions marched north as the mortar men changed the elevation of their mortars.

"Son of a bitch," he groaned as he saw what was happening.

"What? What?" Davers yelled from the jeep. Then, he, too, saw the thousands of zombies, forced northwards by the concentrated mortar fire, moving toward the gap in the fence. "Oh, fuck."

"They're deliberately herding them across the border. Bastards!" He turned to Davers. "That wasn't thunder we were hearing. They're demolishing the entire fence."

"Why?"

"It's cheaper and quicker than killing off the zombies themselves. They drive them north and make us do it for them."

"God damned Mexicans," Davers said, spitting over the side of the jeep.

"We've got to warn the base what's happening. Bring me the radio."

The ground around him suddenly shoved up against the soles of his boots, sending him flying through the air. Simultaneously, the sound of the explosion thundered in his ears. He landed hard ten yards away. He looked back through the dust and saw the wreckage of the jeep. Davers smoking body lay beside it. His mind reeled from the explosion, but he realized what had happened. The

Mexicans had spotted the jeep and aimed their mortars at them to prevent them from reporting what they had seen.

He rose to his feet, but fell back as his leg gave way. Then he saw the long gash in the side of his thigh, a piece of shrapnel still protruding from the wound. Seven miles from base with no jeep or radio and an injured leg, Diluna knew he was going nowhere. The first wave of zombies was already climbing the side of the rise toward him. His M16 had been in the jeep. He had his 9mm pistol, but knew it would not do him much good against the zombie army headed toward Yuma. It looked as though they were on their own.

As the first zombie reached for him, he looked down at the pistol in his hand. They might eat him, but he didn't have to suffer first. He placed the barrel of the pistol in his mouth and pulled the trigger. The first zombies on the scene claimed their prize. The others kept moving north toward an unsuspecting Yuma.

* * * *

July 1, 2017, 4:00 p.m.   Mirada Del Sol Safe Haven, Yuma, AZ—

Lauren Street examined the blisters on her hands and grimaced. Her hands throbbed from gripping the hoe, and a couple of the blisters had already split open. She knew she should have worn work gloves, but she had been so eager to get away from the crowds and tend to her garden before the heat became unbearable she had forgotten. *At least the weeds are gone,* she thought with bittersweet satisfaction. She picked one of the red tomatoes protruding through the screen mesh she had erected to protect them from the birds. Several tomatoes bore holes pecked by birds. She worried that in spite of her fences and scarecrows, the birds and rabbits would probably benefit more from her garden than she would.

She held the tomato in her hand for a moment, admiring its perfect symmetry and beauty. It was not quite ripe, but she had created it, grown it from seeds, nourished, and protected it. She felt a sense of accomplishment. She wiped off the dust and bit into it. The juice squirted down her chin. She wiped the juice from her chin with her hand, enjoying the sweet, slightly acidic flavor. She leaned on her hoe and stared with pride at the rows of tomatoes, okra, green beans, carrots, and lettuce. It was her first garden, and she was proud of it. The garden work gave her something to do besides driving a forklift in the warehouse.

The community vegetable gardens were located at the western edge of the large fields of corn, squash, and cauliflower the safe haven grew for their own use and for trade with other communities. Each person had an assigned garden space, a thousand square feet, the size of an average two-car garage, or slightly larger than a two-bedroom apartment in New York City, but many who worked in the commercial fields chose not to work a garden. She had bartered guitar lessons for an extra lot, but she was finding the amount of labor necessary to maintain it intimidating. However, she would endure. She had endured much worse living in Phoenix during the height of the Staggers Plague.

She shuffled her feet uneasily. *No, I won't go there again*, she whispered to herself.

The Mirada Del Sol subdivision in Yuma just north of I-8 was undergoing extensive renovations to make it a model safe haven. It would be completely zombie proof, with a ten-foot-high reinforced brick wall surrounding the entire subdivision, a metal entry gate, and four guard towers securing the perimeter. In the meantime, the six-hundred-fifty residents lived temporarily in the Holiday Inn and the adjacent Springhill Suites across the road from the subdivision. While her second-floor room was comfortable with hot water, electricity, and air conditioning, Lauren dreamed of her own home away from the communal cafeterias and overcrowded lounges. Normally gregarious in nature, when faced with forced intimacy, her community spirit was running thin.

Because of the proximity of the Colorado and Gila Rivers, like the Imperial Valley just across the state line in California, Yuma, Arizona, had boasted a vast expanse of fields under cultivation wrested from the surrounding desert by irrigation. Agricultural and select cottage industries were the keys to development in a growing new nation, just as they had been to Colonial America. In some ways, the new America more resembled Eighteenth Century America than its Twenty-First Century predecessor. To Lauren, that was not a bad thing. Perhaps they could get it right this time.

Just north of Mirada Del Sol, Lee Pate Industrial Park, where she worked on the warehouse dock, acted as transportation hub for agricultural produce and manufactured goods from the numerous nearby small metal-fabricating shops, clothes factories, and electronics factories. Once the Mirada Del Sol Safe Haven was complete, the inns and hotels presently in use would serve as dormitories for temporary workers brought in at harvest time and to accommodate new citizens as the Safe haven expanded to other neighborhoods. On the books, the official name was Yuma Safe Haven, but most of the residents preferred the name Mirada Del Sol. So did she.

The sound of gunfire broke the illusion of tranquility she had woven over the fabric of harsh reality and jerked her from her reverie. Squads of heavily armed militia had eliminated most of the tens of thousands of zombies in the area, but more appeared every few days from overlooked buildings or wandered in from the surrounding desert. She was always on the alert, but there had been no major zombie incursions in months.

Until lately. Almost as if someone had left open a gate, scores of zombies now wandered north from San Luis Rio Colorado and east from Ejido Merida and Ciudad Morelos in Mexico, funneled by the Colorado River basin straight into Yuma. The surge grew daily, requiring constant patrols. If it continued, all the effort placed in cleansing Yuma of its zombie threat would be for nothing.

More shots rang out, heavier automatic weapons this time. Although no true gun enthusiast, by necessity she had learned how to shoot and recognized the rapid pop-pop sound of an M240B machinegun with a noise suppressor. A young Marine had once allowed her to fire the 7.6mm machinegun after she had shown some interest in it, but the large weapon had jarred her so badly her teeth ached. She glanced around and saw how exposed she was in the open field. Though armed guards protected workers in the fields, she was alone. She decided she had done enough gardening for the day. As always when outside the safe perimeter, she wore her Smith and Wesson M&P .45 caliber pistol in the holster on her hip. She hardly noticed its weight anymore. With a ten-round magazine plus one in the chamber and two extra magazines in the holster, the .45 semi-automatic would keep her safe enough from most danger either human or zombie, but an open field was no place to face a zombie horde.

She moved her long legs as fast as she could, leaping rows cabbages and squash and plowing straight through rows of corn. The gunfire was becoming more widespread throughout the city and was drawing closer. When she burst through the doors of the Holiday Inn where she lived, the lobby was full of frightened people. The harried young man who served as their representative in the Citizens Council, Lawrence McNamara, was under verbal assault by questions and demands faster than he could respond. The intimidating throng of people had pushed him against a wall. Lawrence's panicked eyes searched for a way out.

Feeling sorry for him, Lauren tried to get the crowd's attention, but the din was too loud for her soft voice. In desperation, she pulled her .45 and fired a shot into a potted tree beside the door. The wooden planter box burst open, spilling dirt onto the floor. The room went instantly silent. Now, she had their attention. Fifty pairs of eyes stared at her.

"Calm down. Let him speak."

They stared at the gun in her hand with trepidation but made enough room for Lawrence to move to stand behind the reservation desk. With a solid counter between him and the crowd, he relaxed. He threw her a quick smile of gratitude and faced the crowd.

"There is no need to panic. A large number of zombies have moved into the area, but the military has the situation under control. The gunfire you hear is them eliminating the problem." People in the crowd began speaking to each other, drowning him out. "However," he shouted, "as a precaution, the field workers have been brought back in to the residences."

Gunshots punctuated his speech. With each outburst of gunfire, his assurances became less believable. One gentleman wearing tan shorts and a lime green, short-sleeved shirt asked, "Are you sure they're zombies? I keep hearing about the Mexicans trying to move north."

Lawrence held up his hands to stop people from speaking over one another. "While there have been reports of units of the Mexican Army gathering south of the border, they are simply doing what we are doing here, clearing out zombies from the farmlands. They need food as direly as we do."

"But what about the zombies?" the man insisted.

"Some of the zombies are fleeing the army's advance and entering the U.S. through unattended or otherwise ineffective border crossings. The Council has sent representatives to Mexico to work out a cooperative effort in eliminating the zombies from both sides of the border. We will find a solution. In the meantime, there will be occasional incursions, but nothing we cannot handle."

"How long do we have to remain here?" a woman asked. She wore the dirty work clothes of a field worker and her hair tied back in a bandana.

"Until we hear the warning siren," Lawrence replied.

"Why didn't it sound when the zombies appeared? Isn't that what it's for?" another person asked from the crowd.

"We thought it best to warn everyone in person rather than sound the general alarm, which would create a panic and draw the zombies in our direction."

While the siren would indeed draw zombies toward the safe haven, it would also bunch them closer together, making them easier to kill rather than search the entire city for them. To Lauren, it sounded more like someone falling down on their job. Most of those gathered in the lobby accepted his explanation, and she saw no reason to burst their bubble by asking more probing questions to which he probably did not know the answer. The crowd began to break up with most of them heading back to their rooms, thankful for the rest of the day off. Her back ached and her hands cramped from her morning exertion in the garden, but sitting around in her room reading or staring out the window until the all clear sounded did not appeal to her.

She decided she needed a long hot shower to wash the sweat and grime from her body. She rushed up the stairs before everyone else had the same idea and overloaded the hotel's aging hot water heater. She shed her dirty clothes at the door, freed her long auburn hair from the ponytail she wore while working, and strode across the room naked. She stopped before the mirror, not to admire her lithe figure, which she thought was a little too broad in the hip and sparse in the breast department, but to check for any wounds. Open wounds or sores invited germs and infection, and in a world with few doctors and fewer medicines, infections could be fatal. She believed she was immune to the Staggers, as were a pitifully small percentage of the population, but she did not wish to put that theory to the test. On windy, dusty days, she wore a mask over her nose and mouth just to be safe. Other than her blisters and a few scratches on her legs, she was all right.

In spite of a twinge of guilt for using too much water, she let the hot water massage away the soreness in her neck and shoulders before lathering her body and scrubbing away the dirt. After rinsing and toweling herself dry, she changed into jeans and a T-shirt. As she tended to her blisters with a dab of burn gel to soothe the pain and a few Band-Aids to cover them, she thought of what she wanted to do. She stared at the four walls of her room, feeling them pressing in on her. The sound of gunfire continued outside. She detested not knowing what was happening and decided to see for herself.

She strapped her holster around her waist and threaded her way through the smaller but still overly nervous crowd lingering in the lobby and the small lounge. They stared at her with curiosity as she removed her Charge Cooker Maxi Fat Bike from the bike rack outside the front door. Though it looked strange for a bicycle, the Fat Bike's 4-inch wide, low-pressure tires made riding in sand and on rough, potholed streets easier than a regular bicycle with narrow, thin rubber tires. There was less chance of a flat and the 10-speed gearbox allowed her to travel fast. She tucked her hair up inside the safety helmet, clipped her water bottle to the frame, and pedaled off. She had no particular destination. She just wanted to get away from the maddening crowd for a while. So many people whining and complaining annoyed her.

It had been almost an hour since the first shots had sent her scurrying back to the hotel, and the all-clear siren still had not sounded. Something was not right. She realized she had seen no helicopters in the air all morning. Usually, at least one of the Marine UH-1Y Venoms or AH-1Z Vipers patrolled the perimeter of the city twice each day. The base had two of each; all equipped with 20mm Gatling cannons or .50 BMG Gau-16/A Gatling guns.

If the zombie incursion was so bad, why were there no helicopters flying?

Most of the small arms fire came from west of her near the East Main Canal that divided the city, followed by a large explosion that shook the ground. A plume of dark billowing smoke climbed into the air. Her alarm climbed another notch higher, as a second explosion occurred less than a minute later. A normal person would have turned around and returned to the safety of the hotel, but Lauren continued riding toward the explosions. Like many in the Mirada Del Sol, she had attended several mandatory first-aid classes. She could bandage a wound or suture a wound. If there were any injuries, she might be able to help.

She pedaled west on 24th Street toward the canal. As she neared the bridge over the canal, she saw that the smoke was pouring from a burning building across the canal. She skidded to a stop when she noticed a group of soldiers racing across the bridge toward her, firing into a crowd of zombies pouring onto the bridge behind them.

One soldier saw her in the middle of the street and yelled a warning. "Go back! Go back! There are too many of them!"

The sight of the rampaging zombies sent fear coursing through her veins. She had killed zombies before out of necessity, but she had never gotten used to their inhuman, single-minded focus on killing. The urgent panic in the soldier's voice convinced her to heed his advice. She turned around to flee, but to her horror, she saw more zombies filing across 24th Street behind her headed north, in effect cutting off her retreat. She quickly thought of alternative routes. If the zombies had crossed the canal at the 32nd Street Bridge south of her as they had here, they were threatening the Marine Corp base adjacent to the Yuma International Airport. That explained the heavier gunfire she had heard earlier

The soldiers held their ground valiantly, but ten men could not stop an army of crazed Staggerers. Most were gaunt, starving creatures, but a large number of the zombies had fed recently and were fast and dangerous. She tried not to think about what they had fed on. As she watched, one of the soldiers stumbled and fell. Two more following on his heels tripped over him, and all three wound up in a heap. A pack of zombies leading the horde pounced on them. The soldiers' dying screams chilled her to her core. Another soldier stopped just long enough to toss a grenade in their direction, killing the zombies and ending his comrades' suffering. His life ended seconds later, as two zombies took him to the ground.

The remaining six soldiers fled toward two Humvees forming a roadblock across the bridge. One soldier leaped into the back of one of the Humvees and manned the machinegun mounted above the cab. The .30 caliber cleared a path for the others, cutting down zombies like harvesting wheat, but it quickly ran out of ammunition. Before he could reload, the remaining zombies, undaunted by the deaths of their fellow creatures, surged across the bridge and overwhelmed the hapless soldiers. They tore into the soldiers with teeth and claws like a pack of wild animals. Blood spurted from severed arteries, spraying the zombies and driving them even madder.

Witnessing the ghastly horror, the soldier in the Humvee abandoned the machinegun and dropped back down inside the vehicle into the driver's seat, but he had no chance to crank it. A zombie dragged him kicking and screaming from the vehicle into the reaching arms of a dozen more of the creatures. The soldier's screams snapped the icy grip of fear that had frozen her to the spot. She quickly looked around, searching for a way to escape, but to her horror, saw none. Zombies were west, north, and east of her in numbers far greater than she could expect to fight her way through. That left only one direction—south.

She was certain more zombies lay between her and the Marine base. With the absence of helicopters in the air, for all she knew they may have already overrun the base. Still, the canal would be on her right, offering a little protection in that direction. She briefly considered jumping into the canal, but then dismissed it. Zombies could not swim, but the water was barely chest deep.

The leading edge of zombies finally noticed her. She could delay no longer. For once in her life, she was glad of her long legs. She had always thought them too long for her torso, but now she put them to good use, pumping the pedals of the bicycle as fast as she could. Shifting through the gears smoothly in spite of the fear gripping her and urging her to rush, she quickly opened a lead between her and the zombies. As her lead increased, she forced her runaway heartbeat to slow and gear-shifted down to an easier pace. She passed the Yuma Regional Medical laboratories and had just reached Ray Smucker Park along the canal, when her hopes of escaping faded as she spied hundreds of zombies moving north along both sides of the canal and through the streets and alleys of the medical buildings to her left. Her heart sank as realization set in.

"Damn!" she whispered. "Don't let it end like this."

She had nowhere left to go. Her ride was over. She jammed on the brakes, slid the bike to a stop, and dropped it to the ground. She could not pedal and shoot at the same time, and the Smith and Wesson was more useful to her than the bicycle. She drew her weapon, thumbed off the safety, and waited. If her aim was true and her courage held, her three magazines could account for thirty zombies, but she doubted they would be considerate enough to come at her single file. She expected she could count her remaining life in minutes rather than years.

She tried not to let the snarling and growling affect her, but watching the horde of hungry zombies approaching without running away was akin to watching a charging rhino hoping to pet its snout. She waited until the first creatures were within range before firing. She took a deep breath, held it, and gently squeezed the trigger. The first zombie stumbled and fell, but dozens of others shuffled over its body. She began pulling the trigger as quickly as she could aim, holding the gun with both hands to steady it. Her shots were effective but hardly made a dent in the crowd of creatures. She discarded the empty magazine, reloaded, and continued firing until it, to, was empty. She slid in her last magazine. The zombies were now less than twenty yards away. To her surprise, her fear had become extraneous; something of which she was aware in a vague manner, but it did not affect her. The outcome was not in doubt. She was in a no-win situation.

She had expected death at any moment since the beginning of the Staggers Plague. As others died all around her and she lived, her fear had become manageable but had never abated completely. When a squad of army troops had rescued her from a dangerous situation by and brought her to Mirada Del Sol Safe Haven, she had even come to believe she might survive after all.

So much for wishes and dreams.

She was down to her last three rounds, and the number of zombies seemed to increase, drawn by the sound of gunfire. She did not intend to become a quick snack for Staggerers. The gruesome thought of the creatures tearing at her flesh while she was still alive gave her the courage she needed. One bullet would be for her.

Deafened by the noise of her pistol, she did not notice the rising thumping sound coming closer until the leading zombies fell dead, riddled by gunfire from overhead. Then the wash of air and dust swept over her. She looked up and saw the underbelly of a helicopter hovering over her, its twin turboshaft engines creating a dust devil around her. One of the crew leaned out of the open door and pointed toward the canal, while a second crewmember fired his 7.62mm minigun into the zombies. Hot shell casings dropped on her, but she ignored them. She sobbed in relief.

She turned and raced for the canal. Without stopping on the bank, she leaped in and swam to the center of the canal. The HH 60G Pave Hawk swung around and came toward her. A hoist cable dropped from the helicopter to the water. Then, two miniguns began dropping zombies by the score, but a few pushed through the dying and jumped in the canal after her. More zombies entered the water from the other side of the canal. As soon as the hoist cable slicing through the water reached her, she leaped up, grabbed it with both hands, and clamped her thighs around it. She had no time to secure the safety belt around her. The crew in the helicopter didn't bother with the winch. The pilot pushed the helicopter forward straight down the canal, dragging her through the water, almost drowning her, until it lifted into the air.

Now, they used the winch as she dangled swaying a hundred feet above the ground. If she fell, she would be as dead as if the zombies had gotten her. As the cable brought her up, a beefy hand reached down and grabbed hers. A large man holding a Glock G22 in his other hand pulled her aboard the helicopter. She looked up into a face she recognized from the leaflets dropped around the city urging people to come to the safe haven.

"Governor Lapaige," she said, as the bodyguard who had helped her up and a second bodyguard took up positions on each side of him. "It's good to see you. Your timing couldn't have been better."

"Glad we could help, young lady. I was supposed to stop by to review the plans for the safe haven expansion, but I'm afraid my plans will have to change."

The governor's steely gray eyes were ablaze as they darted past her and swept out the door. She followed his gaze and saw thousands of zombies moving north as if a herd of migrating caribou, and her heart climbed her throat. It was the stuff of nightmares. "What's happened?"

"It seems our meeting with the Mexicans failed. They're forcing the zombies north across the border. They overran the Marine base and airport before we were aware what was happening."

"What about Mirada Del Sol?" she gasped.

"The people should be safe enough for the time being. The Holiday Inn and the Springhill Suites are both under lockdown, and the field workers reached the warehouse safely, but I'm afraid the city is under siege."

She noticed the helicopter turning east, flying over and away from Yuma. "Where are we going?"

"To Luke Air Base outside Phoenix. It's going to take everything we've got to stem the tide of zombies crossing the border and relieve the city." His hardened his face and his lips compressed. "Then we'll have to deal with the Mexican Army. This is an invasion by proxy. They will regret their action."

Exhausted, she lay back on the vibrating deck of the helicopter and hoped the dreams of a series of safe havens were not coming to a bitter end.

11

July 1, 2017, 5:15 p.m. Marana Safe Haven, Marana, AZ —

Jake had just stepped out of the shower when Alton burst into the bathroom. The Ranger barracks were in a converted office building adjacent to the headquarters. It was a large communal shower and Jake was accustomed to people walking in unannounced. No one bothered locking the door. He wasn't even sure if it had a lock. However, it was obvious that Alton did not want to take a shower. The long walk from the administration building had flushed his face, and he looked as if someone had just punched him in the gut.

"We just received a message from Yuma. They are under siege by an army of zombies."

Jake shook his head to remove any water from his ears. He was certain he had misheard Alton. "A zombie army?"

Alton glanced away uncomfortably to avoid staring at Jake's naked body. He had seen the scars on Jake's back and chest before, but they reminded him of the scars from his wounds.

"Several hundred, if not thousands. The Mexican Army drove them across the border. No one saw them approaching until it was too late."

"God damn it!" Jake yelled. "Somebody screwed up royally. What about the air patrols?" He walked across the room to his locker, leaving a trail of water on the floor.

"The helicopters were late getting airborne due to some last minute maintenance issues. They posted squads at the bridges across the canals, but there were just too many of them. The zombies were on the base before they knew what was happening."

He opened his locker and removed a fresh uniform, glancing only briefly at the pieces of tape that had once held a photo of Jessica on the inside face of the door. He laid his uniform on the wooden bench in front of the wall of lockers. He then grabbed a pair of underwear, socks, and his boots.

"Casualties?"

He could see Alton trying to keep his emotions under control, as he replied, "About thirty so far, possibly more. We don't know. Most were soldiers. The Marine base, the airport, and the dormitories are surrounded and under siege."

Jake stood there, dripping wet and naked, seething with a mixture of dismay and indignation that such a thing could happen despite all the planning and procedures for just such an occurrence. He wanted to ask about Jessica, but Alton would have told him if anything had happened to her. He quickly toweled dry and got dressed.

"The governor was on his way to Yuma for a meeting. He was in the air when it happened. He returned to Luke Air Base to confer with General Langston."

Jake swore as he laced his boots. "It will take General Langston too damned long to come to a decision. He's a paper shuffler with an amalgamate army. He'll send a reconnaissance fly-over before he commits to anything. In the meantime, people will die."

"What do you suggest?"

"First, we'll gather up every able-bodied person who can fire a weapon, including the military attachment, and then drive all the trucks we have to Yuma as fast as we can. You contact Maricopa and ask them to dispatch a train to Yuma—one with real boxcars, not flatbed container cars." He stood and slipped on his shirt, then buckled on his holster. "We'll clear a corridor between the hotels they're using for dorms and the nearest section of track; then, we'll use the trucks to convoy people to the train and get them out of there. Afterwards, General Langston can come in and level the place if he wants to."

Alton looked startled. Jake didn't blame him. A lot of man-hours and resources had gone into developing the Yuma Safe Haven. It would be a shame to lose it, but the people came first. The rest was just buildings.

"Can we get them all out?" Alton asked.

Jake didn't lie. "No. We have maybe fifteen trucks available, plus what we might find there. We can pack a dozen people in each truck while leaving room for our armed men. It will take at least four trips to ferry almost seven hundred people to the train. I don't think we can make four round trips through hundreds of zombies. Don't forget they're in two separate buildings," he added.

"We can't leave anyone, Jake."

Jake hated to dash Alton's hopes, but it was best if he understood the harsh reality of the situation. "It all comes down to numbers, Alton. If we can manage three trips before zombies surround the train, we'll be damned lucky. The train will have to leave before that happens regardless of how many are aboard. A moving train has a lot of momentum, but trying to gain speed through a horde of zombies is like plowing through deep snow. We can load anyone else remaining into the trucks and head west out into the desert until the military gets things under control." He glanced at his watch and grimaced. "It's going to be dark by the time we reach Yuma. That's going to complicate things. If things fall apart, we may have to go for Plan B and fortify one of the hotels."

"Isn't that the safest option?"

"When the military starts dropping munitions, they're not going to be too particular where it lands. A living person looks too much like a zombie from the air. I don't want to become a friendly fire casualty. Dead is dead, no matter whose fault it is."

Alton stared at him incredulously at that, but finally nodded his head. "You may be right. You know more about these things than I do. Can you do it?"

Jake sighed. In theory, his plan was plausible. Real life applications never went as smoothly as planned. The logistics of such an operation were daunting. In this case, he was going in with minimal intel. There was no best-case scenario. "We can try, but we have to move now."

"I'll alert everyone as to what we're doing and ask for volunteers."

"No one goes unless they can fire a weapon with some degree of accuracy. I don't want bystanders or cheerleaders. This could go south real fast."

"I'll go to the switchboard and issue an alert while you commandeer the vehicles."

Jake nodded. One of the things he was proud of was Marana Safe Haven's local phone service. Channeled through an automated switchboard in the administrative office, it offered unlimited local connections between households and offices, but its main purpose was to serve as a rapid and effective method for making announcements and broadcasting warnings and alerts. Someday, it would expand to include regular phone service to the other safe havens, but for now, the radio served that purpose.

After Alton left, Jake went to the Ranger headquarters. Word had already reached them, and the place was abuzz with activity. Deacon saw him come in and rushed over.

"I called back any teams not already in the field, but that's just seven Rangers, including me. Everyone else is too far away to do much good or out of radio range. I opened the armory to distribute weapons." He stared at Jake. "We are going to the rescue, aren't we?"

Jake nodded. "All of us. Send someone to the garage and make sure all the heavy trucks are operational."

"All?"

"All. Everyone that can carry a weapon is going. We'll leave only the security guards."

"You have a plan?"

"Yeah. It involves shooting the hell out of a horde of zombies."

Deacon smiled. "Count me in. I'm tired of paperwork."

"How many automatic weapons do we have in the armory?"

Deacon scratched his head. "Oh, a .50 caliber BMG and an M60 mounted on two of the jeeps, five or six M27 IARs, and twenty or so M16s."

"Strip the jeeps. We don't need them. They can't carry many people and are too vulnerable. Make sure we have plenty of ammo for each weapon. The IARs and M16s use 5.56 mm. Issue everyone ten magazines. We're going to be doing a lot of shooting."

"How about something that goes boom?"

Jake considered Deacon's suggestion. Grenades could be useful, but dangerous in close quarters. "Make sure only trained personnel get M67 frag grenades. Break out that case of M116/A1 stun grenades you've been slavering over. We'll find out if zombies can be stunned."

"What about taking Big Bertha?"

Jake hesitated. Big Bertha was the name most of the Rangers used for the 6x6 Desert Chameleon Armored Personnel Carrier the military had loaned them. With its 30mm cannon and 7.62mm machinegun, it was a formidable weapon, and Deacon had been itching to try it out since the day it had rolled onto the Ranger premises.

"No good. It's out of commission. Rust in the fuel tank or something. The engine keeps dying."

Deacon was crestfallen. "That's a shame. I was looking forward to rolling over a few zombies with it."

Jake was as disappointed as Deacon. The APV would have made things much easier. "Maybe next time."

It was nearly an hour before the volunteers and the vehicles were ready to roll. Jake was disappointed in the response time, but the one thing they had not included in their regular drills was relieving a siege. They had only one chance at it and had to do it properly, or he would simply be sending in more people to join the siege.

Alton drove up in a golf cart, flushed from both the heat and the effort of getting things organized. Jake hoped he did not take his remark about taking every able-bodied person in Marana personally. Alton was self-conscious about his debilitating injury, but he had never used it as an excuse. Jake had never questioned Alton's determination not to allow it to handicap him beyond the obvious limitations, but this was one of those exceptions. If all hell broke loose, they would have to move fast and Alton couldn't.

"The army's not coming," Alton reported.

"What?" Jake had counted on the ten-man Marana garrison accompanying them as added firepower. "Why not?"

"They've been ordered to remain here and guard Marana in case we are overrun as well."

"Son of a bitch!" Jake shouted. Heads turned in his direction at his outburst, but he ignored them. "We need them."

"The captain in charge is as confused as I am, but he has his orders. Can't you take the security personnel and let the military handle security here?" Alton suggested.

Jake shook his head. "We can't trust the military. What if Langston orders them out? That would leave no one here. No, we'll just have to manage without them. Damn military assholes! What good are they?" Jake looked at Alton and saw the concern in his face. He regretted unloading his frustration on him. None of this was his fault. "Keep things under control here. We'll be back by morning."

"Is that a promise?"

Jake hesitated. Alton knew he never made a promise he did not think he could keep. "If the creeks don't rise, and Macy's doesn't have a Fourth of July White Sale." He smiled at Alton. "You know how I love a good sheet sale."

Alton smiled back. "I'll consider that a yes. Take care, Jake."

As the first trucks of the convoy left the staging area, Jake felt a sense of relief that they were getting under way, but he could not shake a sense of dread that they would be too late. It would take them over three hours to reach Yuma. They had heard nothing from either Yuma or Luke Air Force Base in two hours, so they would be going in blind. He hoped the train made it on time or all their plans would be for naught.

He stared at the darkening sky with growing concern. It was early for the summer monsoons to start, but they weren't on a fixed schedule. A *haboob* dust storm or a heavy rain would make the trip more difficult and force them to drive slower, eating away at their chances of success.

Just as his truck pulled out onto Tangerine Drive, he was shocked to see Preacher Man walking up to the vehicle. "What now?" he groaned.

Preacher Man looked as pale and gaunt as when Jake first saw him, but he moved with a renewed vigor or sense of purpose as he strode up to Jake's truck. Jake rolled down the window.

"I must go with you," Preacher Man said.

"No. You should be in the infirmary."

"God has given me strength so that I may fulfill his purpose."

"Really? 'Cause you look ready to keel over. We're in for a fight, Preacher Man. I can't spare anyone to watch out for you."

"I have managed quite well these past two years on my own. God watches over me." He stared at Jake as if daring him to contradict him. He continued, "When I met you, I knew the end of my journey was near. I am weary from my heavy burden, and I am eager to lay it aside. God intends me to accompany you. For what purpose, I am not certain. I know only that if I do not go with you, many will die."

Preacher Man's resolve made Jake half believe him. The truck behind them honked its horn. He was holding up the convoy. Jake made up his mind. "No. Stay here. I don't have room for you."

"I must go to Yuma. I see that now. God has made my destination clear to me."

Preacher Man's insistence did not sway him. "Yuma will have to wait." He yelled at the driver, "Go!"

He glanced back through the side mirror at Preacher Man standing beside the road and wondered if he had just made a terrible mistake.

* * * *

July 1, 2017, 9:45 p.m.   Mirada Del Sol Safe Haven, Yuma, AZ—

It was almost ten p.m. before the convoy reached Yuma. Forced to abandon one truck to a flat tire and a second one when the engine overheated, Jake rued the loss of transport space for passengers. The loss of two trucks reduced the number of people that they could carry with each trip. *If any of them are still alive.* He banished that dark thought from his mind. As dark as the skies, he noted. The rain held off, but heavy lightning pierced the heavy gray clouds to the southwest. The storm was coming and it would be a big one.

In spite of the overcast sky, just before setting, the sun dropped below the low-lying clouds in blinding brilliance. Then, as it dipped below the horizon, it washed the entire western sky with streaks of orange and gold. It was a spectacular vista; one he would have welcomed for its beauty if not for the fact that it heralded nightfall, and darkness was an added hindrance to their mission.

As they reached the outskirts of Yuma, he heard gunfire in the distance, but most of it came from farther south near the airport and the Marine base. Two A-10 Thunderbolts, commonly known as Warthogs, visible only by their blinking wing lights, circled the area, making strafing runs with their 30mm GAU-8 rotary cannons. If he had a means of communicating with them, the Warthogs' cannons, firing 65 rounds per second, could clear a forty-foot wide swath through a crowd of zombies and make the job of transporting people to the train much easier. However, all aircraft communications originated from Luke Air Force Base. They would make their firing runs around the Marine base until they ran low on fuel, and then return to Luke.

He was still fuming from the refusal of the Marana garrison to come with them. The Warthogs were just another example of the military watching out for their own first. The approaching storm would ground any further flights that night. Once again, they were on their own.

As they neared South Avenue, they encountered the fringes of the zombie invasion; not yet enough to present a major obstacle, but he knew there would be more nearer the hotels. Where the humans were gathered, he realized grimly. He looked south toward the location on the Union Pacific line paralleling the interstate that they had chosen to meet the train, and then swore to himself. The train was not there. He halted the convoy and spoke over the walkie-talkie each driver carried.

He tried to keep his voice more positive than he felt, as he said, "The train should be here soon. I need one truck to drive peel from the convoy and wait for it. As soon as it arrives, join us at the hotels to help transfer people." One of the trucks pulled out of line and headed south. "Well go in from the interstate and load up as quickly as we can. When we leave, we'll drive north up Pacific Avenue and double back to the train using South Avenue. That way, we can put some distance between us and the zombies and buy some time. No one leaves the convoy. We all stay together. If someone breaks down, call out, and wait for someone to pick you up."

Fires had broken out in several buildings south of the interstate from the A-10 gunfire, casting an eerie orange glow over the dark, moonless landscape. There were no lights on in the hotels housing the Yuma residents, but that did not mean everyone was dead. A single building housing four diesel generators served both buildings. Meant as a temporary solution to provide power to the hotels until the main power grid was operating, its main vulnerability was the inability to refuel them in an emergency such as this one. The lack of lights would only make things more difficult.

He checked to make sure his Uberti .44/40 was ready to fire and placed his Browning A5 12-gauge shotgun on the seat beside him. Jake nodded to the driver. "Let's go."

They drove straight into hell. Within minutes, zombies converged on the line of vehicles from the both sides of the road. Hundreds more lurked among the buildings along the interstate.

"Don't slow down," Jake warned. "Drive through them."

Heeding his advice, the lead truck plowed straight through the crush of zombies, sending them beneath the five-ton trucks' tandem rear wheels. The trucks following mashed the zombies into a bloody pulp staining the pavement like road kill. As the sheer number of the creatures massed around them forced them to reduce speed, Jake ordered the men to open fire. Automatic weapons fire broke out from the cabs and the rear beds of the trucks. The .50 caliber Browning mounted in the bed of the second truck fired through slits between wooden railings, cutting a path through the creatures on the right side. The M60 machinegun, mounted in the middle of the convoy, delivered an equal amount of devastation to the left side of the convoy.

The M16s, .30/30s, and M27 IARs joined in the fray. Most of the shooters had received extensive training under his guidance. Though less dramatic than the heavy weapons' fire, their sheer numbers took their toll on the zombies. Jake added his rifle to the mix, leaning out the window and picking out zombies only on the roadway directly in their path. Slowly, they eased through the creatures and reached the fences around the two hotels.

In the dark, it looked as if the ground in front of the hotels was heaving. Then, outlined by the lights of the trucks, the image resolved into a sea of the dead. However, this Dead Sea was no benign body of salt water; it was a deadly pool of inhuman quicksand that could suck them down into the abyss. The ten-foot, chain-link fences protecting the two hotels were sturdy, but mere metal mesh was no match for the weight of zombie flesh pressed against it. It would not withstand the pressure of a horde of zombies for much longer. Sections already leaned precariously inward at the Holiday Inn. Jake was amazed it had held as long as it had.

Before attempting to reach the people in the two buildings, they had to relieve the pressure along the fence. He chose the Holiday Inn first because of the weakened condition of its fence and ordered the drivers to circle the perimeter of the fence like Indians circling a wagon train, firing into the massed creatures as they drove. After three passes around the hotels, they had barely made a dent in the zombie assault. Jake knew it was useless. Even with an unlimited amount of ammunition, they stood no chance of eliminating the danger. There were simply too many zombies and the steel fences were not foolproof. Instead, Jake changed tactics.

"Concentrate your fire on the area immediately around the gate."

Within minutes, they had cleared a path wide enough to reach the gate, which he saw to his dismay was chained and padlocked.

"Ram the gate," he told the driver.

Just as the lead truck sped up to bust through the gate, a man raced from the hotel waving a ring of keys he held in his hand.

"Slow down," Jake warned the driver. "We'll keep the gate intact if we can."

The man fumbled with the keys for a moment, but managed to unlock the gate. He swung it wide open for them.

The driver needed no encouragement. As soon as the gap was wide enough for the truck, he gunned the engine and shot through. Before the truck had stopped moving, Jake jumped down. He yelled to the young man with the keys, "Get the people moving! Now! We don't have much time."

The man glanced at the twelve trucks and made a rapid mental calculation. "You can't carry everyone."

"We'll make as many trips as it takes. We aren't leaving anyone behind."

The man looked unconvinced but did not argue. He waved back toward the hotel and people poured from the building. Jake counted heads as they rushed for the trucks. At one-hundred-sixty people, the trucks were crammed as full as he dared load them. The tires were dangerously flattened under the load.

"That's all for this trip," he told them. His announcement created instant panic.

"How do we know you're coming back?" one man shouted from the crowd.

"Because I'm staying here with you." He turned to Deacon. "Deacon, you're in charge. Get these people out of here. Keep them safe. Don't wait until all the trucks are empty before sending them back. Keep them in groups of five. A single truck will never make it though."

He slapped the side of Deacon's truck and waved his arm at the others to get them moving. The men in the trucks began firing as the gate swung open, clearing a space around the entrance. Jake pulled the pin from one of the M116/A1 stun grenades and lobbed it over the fence ahead of the trucks. He could not risk using one of the fragmentary grenades for fear of damaging a truck or injuring a passenger. One of the creatures caught the grenade in its hand and stared at it as if deciding if it was food. The grenade exploded in a bright flash of light, blowing off the creature's hand. The concussion knocked several to the ground. The noise and smoke drew attention away from the trucks long enough for them to slip through.

After the last truck left, Jake slammed the gate shut. He trotted to the hotel entrance, pushing through the crowd of people. The sight of so many people was driving the zombies crazy. He wanted to tell everyone to go back inside and stay out of sight, but he understood their concern. At least keeping them in one place would save time loading the trucks when they returned. He would be lucky to keep them from injuring one another in the stampede to escape. A number of people in the crowd were armed. He pointed to several of them and called to them.

"Go to the fence and shoot anything not human. Try to keep the entrance clear."

A few looked skeptical but most did as he asked. Those few reluctant to join in the fray or afraid they would lose their place in line, he asked to guard the crowd. They seemed satisfied with the simple task. He would prefer that they used their weapons on the growing number of zombies crowding the fence, but holding them in reserve kept them happy and served a useful purpose.

He checked his watch. He estimated that the round trip to the train, unloading the passengers, and returning would take a little over thirty minutes, if they ran into no obstacles and if the train was there. If it was not, his plan would crumble like a rotten log, and he would have succeeded only in trapping himself with the five hundred or so people left to rescue.

He thought briefly of searching for Jessica in the crowd, but he didn't know which hotel she lived in. He was of mixed emotions concerning his ex-lover. He had a lot he wanted to say to her but didn't know if he could find the right words, or if she wanted to hear them, or if now was the time to do it. He would settle for knowing that she was safe. For the briefest moment, he wondered if Alton had come to him with the news on the attack on Yuma because he knew that the thought of Jessica in danger would urge him to action. *No. Even Alton wasn't that devious.*

The Staggers-infected zombies had resumed massing at the gate again in spite of the concentrated gunfire. The faster Lopers were forcing the starving, weaker Shamblers away from the gate, trampling many to death in their eagerness to feed. Disregarding their mandatory weapons training in their panic, most of the Yuma defenders were simply firing blindly into the crowd of zombies, not following *Jake's Law #1 — Aim high; shoot straight.* In spite of their poor aim, the sheer number of bullets fired was taking a toll on the creatures. *Not enough,* Jake worried.

He joined them with his Browning 12-gauge shotgun. His aim was more accurate. At close range, the double-ought buckshot pellets left little of the creatures' heads on their shoulders. The zombies at the edge of the wide pellet pattern suffered serious wounds that would have killed or incapacitated a normal human, but eyeless, earless, or bleeding thick black blood from gaping chest wounds, the injured creatures still zeroed in on the living, breathing human flesh for which they so hungrily craved.

Jake's basic Staggers philosophy entailed killing them all and letting the hot desert sun shrivel the worms into dead husks. However, it was night and the leading edge of the storm was upon them. He felt the first tentative drops of rain on his skin. It would soon become a raging torrent. He stopped firing long enough to check his watch. It was well past the estimated thirty minutes, and the trucks still had not returned.

"Where the hell are they?" he growled to the uncaring mass of zombies. He then shoved the barrel of his shotgun into the face of one zombie pressing against the fence and pulled the trigger, taking satisfaction in the spray of blood and gore that drenched the surrounding zombies.

* * * *

Deacon was as worried as he was sure Jake was. It had taken longer to make the trip up Pacific Avenue to Highway 95, across, and back down East Avenue than they had planned. Zombies surged north across the border and through Yuma in numbers far greater than they had anticipated. The sound of gunfire drew them from their mindless trek north and back toward the hotels. Threading through the massed creatures without wasting precious ammunition had been like skiing the slalom course in the Winter Olympics. When the convoy finally reached the open fields northeast of the hotels, he pushed the trucks to the max, urging every extra revolution and every extra mile per hour that the drivers could squeeze from them.

Passing the ruins of the Love's Travel Stop with the charred remains of dozens of semis in the gravel parking lot, he searched the tracks vainly for the train but saw no sign of it or of the truck Jake had sent ahead. He stopped on the bridge spanning the railroad. Its height offered an extended few of the tracks in both directions. To his dismay, he saw no train. The steeply sloping sides and concrete rails of the bridge forced the convoy to drive south to E. 24th Street and back up Industrial Avenue to reach GH Processing, their destination. The dairy processing center's railroad trunk line provided the best location to load people onto the cars. The area surrounding the tracks was clear with good line-of-sight for shooting zombies.

A soon as he stopped the truck, Deacon slammed his palm on the steering wheel. "Where the hell are they?" he asked his passenger, who acted as his shooter.

The young man, barely out of his twenties, stared back at him with panic edging into the corner of his dark brown eyes. "The train or the truck?"

"Both, damn it!"

"I don't know, but if that train doesn't get here soon, we're screwed."

He could not simply unload the passengers and go back for Jake and the others. He didn't have enough armed men to protect the passengers and to protect the trucks on the return trip through the horde of zombies around the hotels. He considered driving east along the tracks until he met the train, but that would waste fuel. He checked the gas gauge. It was past the halfway mark. They had brought extra gas cans for the return trip, but refueling in the middle of a zombie horde did not appeal to him.

"I can't just keep driving around. We'll run out of gas."

"We can do what Jake suggested. You know, drive out into the desert."

Deacon shot the young man a scornful look. "I ain't leaving Jake," he snarled. "I'll give it five more minutes. Then we'll head back to the hotel and fight from there."

He saw headlights flash and spotted the other truck emerging from behind two grain silos.

"There the fools are," he said, sighing with relief.

The truck pulled up alongside his, and the driver rolled down his window. He saw that the driver was fellow Ranger Mitch Andrews. His face was expressionless as he stared at Deacon. The first thing Deacon noticed was that he looked much older than his twenty-six years.

Hell, we all do, Deacon thought. "Where's the train?" he asked.

"Fuck if I know," Andrews answered. "We drove along the tracks for a couple of miles but didn't see shit. What's the plan?"

His relationship with Andrews, never close because of Andrews' aloofness, had cooled after the recon mission to Hatch,

New Mexico. At the time, he had attributed his animosity to Andrew's cold and callous shooting of Gerald Cray when bitten by a zombie. Cray had been the closest thing to a friend he had. Later, he realized his anger and resentment was not born of the mercy killing itself, but from Andrews' accusation that he lacked the courage to do the job himself. Andrews had been right. Despite the certainty of his friend's inevitable death from the bite, he had desperately tried to cling to any shed of hope. He had seen in Cray's senseless demise the randomness and the casualness with which death crept unbidden from the dark shadows. Death was a mirror into which men were hesitant to peer for fear of seeing their own reflection.

Damn, he thought, shuddering as if someone had stepped on his grave, *Jake should have placed Andrews in charge instead of me.*

"We give the train a few more minutes," he decided. "After that, we head back to help Jake."

Andrews said nothing, but from his grim expression, Deacon guessed he did not think much of the plan. "We could secure the building here," Andrews suggested, "leave the passengers with a few guards, and go back for another load."

"And it the train doesn't come?"

"In that case, we're all fucked anyway."

Andrews' cold statement delivered without rancor but with the conviction of inevitability, alarmed Deacon. The young Ranger's constant dark mood set him apart from the other Rangers, making it difficult to befriend him, and this seemed to suit Andrews. No one knew much about his past beyond a few veiled references to his family. He did not drink, play cards, or join in the bullshit sessions with his fellow Rangers. He did his job when called upon, but otherwise kept to himself. No one questioned his courage or abilities, but Deacon feared Andrews' casual acceptance of death might lead him to plunge others into dire circumstances with him.

Andrews' plan had merits. If the train came in the meantime, they could board it. If zombies showed up first, it would be no more difficult to escort the civilians from the building to the train than from the trucks. It was tempting, but splitting the armed men was a dangerous move.

"No," he replied. "We wait. If the shit hits the fan, we'll have two groups of civilians under siege."

"You're in charge," Andrews replied.

"Yeah, fuck it all. I'd rather be taking orders, but there it is. We wait," he repeated. He hoped he was right.

12

July 1, 2017, 11:30 p.m.   Mirada Del Sol Safe Haven, Yuma, AZ —

The first tentative drops or rain heralded the savage downpour that followed. Sweeping in from the southwest like an avenging angel, the storm descended on Yuma with a cannonade of thunder that shook the ground and illuminated the black sky with the false dawn of unremitting streaks of lightning. Each strobe-like flash revealed the ghastly, once-human faces of the creatures that snarled and growled like savage beasts from the darkness. It seemed to Jake as if their numbers increased between flashes, created by the very storm that concealed them.

Two years after the start of the zombie apocalypse, some of the creatures looked truly terrifying. Jake didn't know if anyone had ever done a study of the physiognomy of zombies, but certainly, they looked as fierce as did any ancient warrior tribe of Central Africa or the 3rd Century Celts whom the Roman army so rightly feared. The physiological differences went beyond the creatures' original race, sex, or physical build.

The Lopers, people who had turned zombie in the last few months, were fast and agile, possessed with an animal cunning and strength that made them the most dangerous. Except for their bedraggled attire and fierce animal expressions, they were closest in appearance to normal humans. Even the hard rain drenching their bodies could not wash away the accumulated filth and layer-upon-layer of crusted blood painting their savage faces as effectively as war paint.

During the last, deep coma stage of the Staggers disease, as the cerebrum died, the parasitic worms burrowed into the hindbrain, hijacking its functions to keep the host alive, releasing the human host's animal instincts for survival, and creating an insatiable lust for flesh. The autonomic nervous system originating in the three separate parts of the hindbrain controlled breathing, heart rate, biting, chewing, digestion, vision, and hearing. It also negated normal human sleep patterns. Zombies never slept. They were 24-hour, seven-day-a-week predators.

Older zombies or zombies that did not feed often deteriorated quickly in appearance, as outer layers of skin rotted away and internal organs atrophied. The cerebellum, which controls sensory input/motor control coordination, deteriorated, making them slower and less coordinated, but nonetheless dangerous. These slower moving Shamblers, in sufficient numbers, were as deadly as Lopers. No one was certain how long a zombie lived, but Jake had seen creatures trapped in houses last for several months without feeding, slowly wasting away. During the last stages of the disease, the creatures become less mobile, standing as rigid and motionless as statues while the mature Staggers worms worked their way through the rotting flesh to escape in search of fresh hosts. Even these creatures retained sufficient strength to lunge or grab at any perceived source of food or threat.

Around him, the people he had promised rescue were becoming disillusioned. The trucks still had not returned. Each minute that passed with no sign of the overdue vehicles increased their concern. The storm had ionized the air, making communication by walkie-talkie almost impossible. The shrill squeal of static each time he tried the walkie-talkie seemed to drive the zombies into a mad frenzy. His deepest fear, that the train would not come, he held in abeyance, concentrating instead on the act of firing his weapon, reloading, and firing again. Around him, the sound of gunfire diminished, as people tired of the seemingly futile task of killing all the zombies. He had heard no gunfire from the Springhill Suites in some time. Conversely, he had heard no screams and hoped that meant they were still safe.

He did not doubt Deacon's ability to lead the convoy. If anything, he was overly cautious, underestimating his abilities. In situations where lives depended on circumspection and not boldness, he was the man for the job.

But where the hell is he?

The man with the keys who had opened the gate, a young man named Lawrence McNamara, one of the members of the local council came to him, warily keeping his distance from the leaning, overstrained fence. "People are concerned. They are wondering what is taking so long."

He stared sheepishly at Jake, as if fearing Jake would lift the hot barrel of the Remington shotgun and shoot him instead of the zombies. Jake realized that his mien, which others, most notably Alton, had described as ferocious when riled, or during the heat of battle, might make him appear more menacing than the zombies. He tried to relax his clenched jaw and narrowed eyes. He decided to be honest.

"So am I."

Clearly, this was not what Lawrence wanted or expected to hear. His chest tightened on a sharp intake of breath and his face paled.

"Something has delayed the train and the trucks are waiting." He glanced up at the storm roiling overhead. "Maybe the track washed out. I don't know. If it doesn't arrive, we'll dig in here and hold out until help arrives."

"Can we?"

Jake had witnessed the aftermath of a zombie attack. The creatures were mindless but relentless. They would not stop assailing the fence until it eventually gave way. The hotels had too many glass doors and windows on the ground floor to offer much protection. Each building contained an armory and an adequate supply of ammunition under normal circumstances, but no one had anticipated an all-out zombie assault. Ammunition was running low. He had only what shells remained in the shotgun for it. He still had his M2010 ESR rifle and Colt revolver, but he had left the Uberti .44/40 in the truck, an action he was certain he would regret.

"We have no choice."

"The military will come soon."

Whether meant as a question or a statement, Jake could not answer.

"I mean, they're here for our protection, aren't they?"

Jake sighed. "Sometimes I think we're just here to feed them."

Lawrence stared incredulously at Jake, as if saying anything derogatory about the military was blasphemy. Jake decided he had pushed the young man too far. He just wanted some assurance so he could calm his charges.

"Yeah, they'll come. They'll break the siege at the airport soon and send help."

This seemed to satisfy Lawrence. He walked slowly back to the hotel. However, as if sensing his doubts, the people defending the fence began retreating toward the hotel, at first by ones and twos, but then groups peeled away and raced to safety. The creatures, emboldened by the site of their intended prey running, pressed harder against the fence. It began to sway and buckle. Jake knew it would not hold them out much longer. If help did not come soon, the zombies would overrun dwindling defenses, break into the hotel, and massacre everyone inside. He walked back to where he had laid the case containing his M2010 rifle atop a concrete planter, removed it from its case, and took a position halfway between the gate and the entrance to the hotel. He would retreat no farther. He would not allow people under his charge to die, nor would he go home if everyone didn't. He invoked *Jake's Law #11* — *Be willing to lose it all.*

"Where the hell are you, Deacon?" he shouted into the darkness.

13

July 2, 2017, 12:15 a.m.   G.H. Processing Plant, Yuma, AZ —
Deacon knew he could wait no longer. It was after midnight,
well past his self-imposed five-minute deadline. The train was not
coming. Because of the fury of the storm, he couldn't reach Jake
on the walkie-talkie and didn't know if he or anyone at the safe
haven was still alive. He could make the easy call and save the
people in the trucks, drive them back to Marana. It might have
even been the wisest move, but he couldn't abandon the others,
even it meant risking everyone's lives. He picked up his walkie-
talkie and keyed the mic.

"The train's not coming," he told the other drivers. "We can't
sit here hoping any longer. We're going back to the hotel."

He heard the uproar from the back of the trucks as the drivers
informed the passengers. He didn't blame them. They had escaped
possible death. Now, he was delivering them back to a dubious
future.

"Wait," Andrews replied over the radio.

"We can't wait. We have to go. Now." He braced himself for
Andrew's objections.

"No, I see lights. I think it's the train."

Shouts of joy erupted from the passengers, and Deacon felt a
heavy weight lifting from his shoulders. "God, let us save at least
these few," he prayed.

He opened the door to climb out of the truck for a better view.
A strong gust of wind propelled a sheet of rain inside the cab,
soaking both him and the driver. He stepped into an ankle deep
stream of water flowing across the parking lot. Through the

deluge, he spotted a triangle of bright lights coming toward them. Flashes of lightning revealed two bright blue locomotives pulling a string of boxcars as they had requested, but spaced among the cars were four flatcars. Two of them were empty, but upon one sat a large yellow bulldozer. Behind it was the twenty-two-foot-wide blade. The flatcar behind it bore the strangest machine Deacon had ever seen, a cross between an excavator and a giant lawnmower.

"What the fu…?" he groaned.

The train moved maddeningly slowly, almost creeping, as the engineer brought the massive metal behemoth to a screeching halt directly in front of the waiting line of trucks. Two armed, uniformed soldiers stepped out of the driverless drone locomotive coupled behind the lead locomotive, and took up positions on the small deck at the rear of the cab, but made no move to aid in the transfer of passengers. They were there to protect the engineer.

The engineer leaned out the window. "Name's Dan Delany, Loco Dan, some call me," he yelled, smiling at his own joke. When Deacon did not respond to his attempt at levity, he continued, "Sorry I'm late. I had to take it slow and easy through a flooded section of track. I thought the water was gonna wash old Number 2121 off the tracks. She was rolling like a rowboat."

Deacon wondered what kind of flood it would take to derail a 6,000 horsepower, 200-ton locomotive. He pointed to the flatcars. "What's with the heavy equipment?"

"Oh, that. They need the D11 Caterpillar dozer for the Freemont copper mine in Morenci. The territorial government is trying to reopen the mine. The DAH boom mulcher is for a forestry project in Payson up on the Mogollon Rim." He shrugged his shoulders. "God only knows what they need it for. I didn't have time to disconnect the cars."

"Get rid of them. We don't need them to slow us down."

"I can't. No spur here to drop them off."

Deacon swore. "Well, keep the engine running," he replied. "We're pulling out soon." He turned to the trucks and waved his arm. "Everybody out of the trucks!" he shouted.

Grateful people spilled from the back of the trucks as if someone had opened a floodgate. Some tumbled from the trucks in their eagerness to leave and fell to the ground. Others stumbled over their prostrate bodies, creating bottlenecks of writhing bodies splashing around in the water. The crowd ignored the fallen, parting around the pile of bodies in their fervor to reach the ramp to the loading platform. The wooden loading platform was the length of three boxcars, but it could not hold all the people fighting for a place in the boxcars. Jostling and shoving quickly escalated into shouting matches and fistfights. Trying to make room for the brawlers, the crowd succeeded only in pushing more people off the edge of the platform. A few ignored the platform and the melee altogether and raced for the remaining boxcars, scrambling aboard as best they could.

Many of the passengers were armed. Deacon knew he had to step in before scuffles, cuts, and bruises led to serious injury or murder. Using the walkie-talkie, he directed the trucks that had yet to unload to back directly to the open boxcar doors to transfer their passengers. To quell the growing panic, he fired his pistol into the air. A dead hush fell over the crowd.

"That's better," he shouted. "Now, stop fighting and get in the boxcars. You're all residents of the Mirada Del Sol Safe Haven. Act like it. Help each other. No one's leaving 'til we all do. The next person who throws a punch, I'll shoot dead on the spot."

Between Deacon's threat and his reminder that they were friends, the group of refugees became more orderly. The panic did not vanish altogether, but submerged beneath the thin veneer of civilization that held it in check. The boxcars began filling.

Deacon watched, smiling. *Now, I can go back for Jake and the others.*

Almost as if he had called down disaster by voicing his optimism, someone shouted, "Zombies!" What small measure of calm he had coaxed from the crowd vanished in an instant. Frenzied cries for help mingled with muttered prayers and curses. Many of the armed passengers, in their renewed panic, began firing blindly into the darkness. A bullet whizzed past Deacon's head.

"Stop shooting!" he yelled, but few heeded him. They were too frightened to think clearly. He was afraid the situation would escalate out of control. He needed to restore some sense of order. "Rangers! Guard the perimeter."

The half-dozen Arizona Rangers and the rest of the armed men from Marana fanned out, and using the trucks for cover, formed a defensive perimeter around the loading passengers. Deacon was glad for Jake's organizational skills. He had placed each Ranger in charge of a squad of four civilians. The small groups anchored by a trained professional were more effective than a large group of individuals shooting every which way. Flashes of lightning revealed the shadowy shapes of zombies lumbering down both sides of the tracks. He did a quick count, stopping at seventy, but more were arriving from the darkness, drawn by the noise of the passing train. Unlike the riotously vocal citizens of Mirada Del Sol Safe Haven, the zombies were eerily silent. A few premature shots rang out.

"Wait until they get into range," he advised the trigger-happy shooters.

Suddenly, one of the soldiers on the drone engine screamed in agony. The second soldier began firing his weapon at a zombie that had climbed up the steps from the far side of the track and attacked them from behind. The zombie ignored the second soldier's wild shots as it sank its teeth into the first soldier's throat and yanked its mouth away with a mouthful of bloody flesh. The soldier's screams faded to a soft, pathetic gurgle as his throat and mouth filled with his blood. Another zombie climbed up to join in on the killing, attacking the second soldier before he could reload his rifle. Witnessing this, Loco Dan the engineer retreated to his engine compartment and locked the door.

The men and women from Marana, led by the Rangers, began firing into the group of zombies. Better trained than the Mirada Del Sol Safe Haveners, their well-aimed concentrated shots took down the front members of the zombie line. The M60 machinegun and the .50 caliber BMG opened up from the trucks, spreading death and destruction in a wide arc, but zombies had reached the far side of the rear of the train where the machineguns' intense fire was ineffective. Deacon realized they faced the distinct possibility that the creatures might overrun the train. People inside the boxcars frantically tried to close the doors on others pushing to get inside.

WWJD. What would Jake do?

He sighed. There was only one thing he could do. When the last of the people were aboard and the boxcar doors closed, he waved for the engineer to start the train moving. He ran up to the engine as it began to pull away. "Go to the Union Pacific Depot up the line and wait for us as long as you can."

Loco Dan's wide-eyed stare showed his concern. He glanced at the zombies swirling around the train, and then back at Deacon. "What if you don't show up?"

Deacon frowned. He didn't want to think about that possibility. "Then you're on your own, Loco Dan."

"What about my guards? They're dead. I can't do much with my little .25 caliber pistol."

Deacon swore under his breath. So many decisions. "I'll send men with you."

The depot was less than two miles away. At the speed the zombies were moving, they would reach the depot in an hour or less. That left barely enough time for the convoy to rush back to the hotel and pick up more people. No matter how quickly they loaded the trucks, the zombies would reach the station before they could they return with a third group. Still, it was the only choice. Stopping the train farther north added more distance for each trip. Any closer placed it in the middle of the invading zombie horde.

Andrews trotted up to him. Despite the shooting and frenzy of fighting off zombies, he was as calm and his face as expressionless as always. He nodded at the train just beginning to pull away from the platform. "That's not going to buy us much time."

"It'll buy us enough," Deacon replied, praying he was right. "Choose four men and go with the train to protect the engineer. Make sure he doesn't get cold feet and decide to run."

Andrews nodded. He picked out the four men closest to him and joined them as they raced to catch up with the moving locomotive. Deacon watched until all five men clambered aboard. With the train rapidly receding, the zombies began to focus their hungry attention on the men around the trucks. They had killed almost half the creatures in the first group, but many more ambled along the tracks from the east and from the south.

"Get the trucks rolling!" he shouted.

The firing slowed; then ceased altogether as men hurried to their vehicles. Twelve of the thirteen trucks followed him from the parking lot. One did not. They lost a truck when zombies surrounded it and overwhelmed the driver. Even so, they had been lucky. They had delivered all the passengers safely to the train. He regretted the driver's death, but the loss of the truck reduced the number of people they could carry by a dozen. *And I just sent five men away. I hope that decision doesn't come back to bite me in the ass.*

* * * *

July 2, 2017, 12:40 a.m.   Holiday Inn, Mirada Del Sol Safe Haven, Yuma, AZ—

The fence was doomed to failure, its inevitable demise written in the slow press of the zombie horde. One section slowly gave way as the metal posts supporting it pulled from the rain-soaked soil. Prepared for just such an eventuality, Jake hustled forward two small groups of men and women slightly less frightened than their fellow residents. They carried lengths of 2x4s and sheets of plywood to construct a temporary brace. Hands held the plywood in place against the top of the fence, keeping away from the eager arms and hands thrust through the openings in the fence, while others wedged 2x4s against it and drove the other end into the ground at an angle. The braces held, but the wooden boards could not find solid purchase in the muddy soil, digging a furrow as the zombies pushed against the fence.

"It won't hold," Lawrence groaned. He had helped Jake organize the fence repair squads.

Jake could only agree. The emergency quick fix had been their only hope. He silently cursed the engineers in charge of the project. Due to an oversight or simple laziness, the builders had constructed the temporary fence outside the asphalt parking lot in the open ground surrounding the hotel. The drenching rain was loosening the soil around the metal fence posts. They were now unable to support its weight. If they had dug holes in the asphalt and secured the posts by adding cement to the holes, the fence could have withstood a hurricane. The oversight would be in his next report. *If I write one.* He wished he had one of the trucks they had brought or even a jeep to help brace the fence. However, he decided it probably would not have made much difference, as he watched two more sections of the fence bow precariously inward under the weight of massed zombies.

Most of the residents, sensing that help would not come in time, had retreated to the imagined safety of the hotel. Only the dozen or so standing by with more wood remained outside. The lack of victims within their visual range did not diminish the zombies' craving to reach them. With their enhanced sense of smell, they knew more human flesh was hiding within the building.

"Get everyone inside," he told Lawrence. "We'll have to evacuate the first floor and barricade the stairs."

Jake sighed. He was angry with himself. The weight of his failure threatened to drive his feet into the mud. Was his overconfidence in his abilities going to kill not only the residents of Mirada Del Sol, but thirty of his own people as well? For all he knew, the people in the trucks were already dead. Was he beginning to believe his own hype, his aura of infallibility? Maybe it would be best if he made his last stand with feet firmly planted in the dirt, shooting zombies until he ran out of bullets, or they overwhelmed and ate him. Such an end would be preferable to facing a future with a failure of this magnitude on his conscience. If he could only convince himself it was a heroic effort and not the coward's way out, death by zombie.

No! He dismissed the idea before it found purchase in his mind. It might ease his conscience, but he could not give up trying to save lives as long as he could draw a breath of air.

He followed everyone inside the building, noting the profusion of ground floor windows and the massive glass doors of the entrance. They could seal off the ground floor rooms, but barricading the entrance was impossible. He was glad to see Lawrence herding the last of the residents up the stairs, noting as he crossed the lobby floor the best way to build a barricade by stripping furniture from the rooms. He would have preferred something heavy and solid, but they would have to make do with mattresses, sofas, and desks.

Just as he mounted the first step, the blaring of a truck's horn cut through the din of zombies. Then, the heavy machineguns began chattering. To him, it sounded like a Fourth of July celebration. Headlights bathed the lobby in bright light. He shielded his eyes against the glare. The trucks were pushing through the zombies, but they were moving slowly. Some of the creatures were pulling themselves onto the back of the trucks.

"The key!" he yelled to Lawrence.

He caught the tossed key with one hand and raced for the gate. He ignored the creatures pushing against the gate, as he unlocked the padlock and swung the gate open. The first truck crushed two of the creatures beneath the wheels. He shot two more with his revolver. He counted only twelve trucks but did not have time to speculate about the fate of the thirteenth. He slammed shut the gate after the last truck rolled through.

Deacon leaped down from the lead truck. "Jake! Thank God, you're still alive."

"We won't be if we don't hurry."

He did not have to wait for the residents. Seeing the arriving trucks, they poured out the doors of the hotel before the last truck stopped moving. There were too many. He read their panic in their frightened faces and knew they could not endure much more.

"We'll have to double up," he told Deacon. "Cram as many in as you can. They can sit on one another's laps. We won't have time for another round trip."

"We had to move the train. Zombies overran the original loading site. I sent the train and five men to the Union Pacific Station. It's closer. If we hurry, we can make two trips."

Jake appreciated Deacon's optimism, but he knew it was a race against time to get the trucks rolling before the fence collapsed entirely. No amount of shoring could keep it up forever. He watched the trucks fill, knowing deep down that there wasn't enough room for all of them. The Holiday Inn housed almost three-quarters of Mirada Del Sol Safe Haven's six-hundred-fifty residents. Even with four people in the cab and twenty stuffed into the rear of each truck like size-42 breasts in a B-cup training bra, over fifty would have to remain behind. He could not choose who would go and who would stay. How could he estimate one person's worth to the community over another's? Was a baker worth two field workers or an electrician more valuable than a plumber? Was one child worth two elderly people?

The machineguns kept the area around the gate clear for their exit, but the increasingly loud groaning and rattling of the weakened fence, interspersed with the sharp cracking of the wood support beams spelled the fence's certain demise. Some, hearing the fence giving way under the crush of zombies, scuffled for a spot in the already overcrowded trucks. Others stood by meekly, as if they had already accepted their fates. He noticed a disproportionate number of elderly people among those waiting. The residents had sorted out the potential worth of individual problem among themselves, condemning the elderly to die. Jake intended to prove them wrong.

"Get them out of here," he told Deacon. "Don't come back. If you can't reach the train, get these people out of the city. If you make it to the train, take the trucks back to Marana. They may need them."

Deacon sensed Jake's desperation. "Jake, what are you going to do?"

"Take these people to the roof and hope we can get some choppers in here before they die."

"We can put people on top of the trucks. We can throw out the extra gas cans. We can take them all, including you."

Jake shook his head. "The trucks are overloaded as it is. More weight and they might crack an axle. You'll need the additional gas to get home." A crude plan formed in his mind. "On second thought, leave me two cans of gas. Now, go on. I'll be fine. Just don't forget to send help." Deacon didn't budge. "I said go!" Jake shouted. Deacon shifted into gear and started toward the gate, still staring at Jake. Jake stopped the truck he had ridden in and told the driver, "Toss me down my .44/40." The driver handed him the Uberti through the open window. As the truck pulled away, someone tossed two five-gallon cans of gas out of the back of the truck. They plopped into the deep mud near the gate.

Jake leaned the Uberti against a planter and ran to the gate with his shotgun under his left arm. He lobbed one of his M67 fragmentary grenades as far as he could. He did not have time for niceties. He hoped his arm was strong enough to lead the trucks. Unlike the stun grenade, the army had designed the M67 to kill and maim. The apple-sized sphere held 6.5 ounces of high explosives and had only a five-second delay fuse once he released the handle, so he hit the ground as soon as he tossed it. It exploded, sending a storm of white-hot shrapnel shooting though the zombies crowded around it. Severed heads and limbs flew through the air and showered down on the mob of creatures. He leaped up and opened the gate, and then stood aside as the convoy rolled out over the bodies of zombies in the way. He slammed the gate shut after the last truck exited but had no time to secure it properly.

Zombies rushed the gate, pushing up against it and widening the gap between the gate and the fence post. The chain and padlock would not reach. He lunged at the gate with his entire weight, back braced against it, digging his feet into the muddy soil. He fired the shotgun over his shoulder without taking aim until he emptied it into the zombies trying to push through the gap. He created just enough space to close the gap between gate and post and threaded his empty shotgun through the links of both gate and fence as a crossbar. He stepped back as the gate buckled inward under the push of zombies behind it. It held, but he feared it would not hold for long.

Jake turned to the people remaining outside. "Into the hotel! The original plan still stands. We barricade the stairs and wait for help." He pulled two men carrying M16s from the crowd. "You two patrol the fence perimeter and look for weak sections. I'll check this front section."

As long as the fence held, they stood a chance. If it still provided a barrier against the zombies when morning came, the jets and helicopters the military would eventually send would be able to distinguish zombies from the living and target them. If, as he suspected, the Mexican Army was deliberately herding its plague of zombies north across the border as a prelude to seizing the Colorado River Basin for its water and productive farm lands and the copper mines near Tucson, the military would have fires to put out all over southern Arizona. If the creatures swarmed the hotel, or both hotels, the pilots might decide to take no chance and carpet bomb the entire area, killing everyone.

His inspection of the fence revealed that it was giving way at an alarming angle under the mass of zombies. The super-saturated soil was just too muddy to support the fence posts. It was time to move inside. As he waited for the two men to return with their report, he heard one of the M16s barking in a long burst that emptied the magazine. The second M16 fired two short, controlled burst before it too fell silent. Then, he heard the men's sickening screams. Zombies had already breached the fence, and he had sent both men to their deaths.

He slung his rifle over his shoulder, grabbed the two gas cans, and ran for the hotel. Before he reached the door, the screech of shearing metal announced the end of the fence. A twenty-foot section on both sides of the gate collapsed inward, spilling zombies into the compound. The surge of zombies shoved forward over the fallen bodies, pushing them deep into the muddy ground until they became part of the landscape and entangling others in the wire mesh of the fallen fence. He had focused his attention on the gate and almost missed the pair of zombies rushing at him from the darkness around the side of the building. Only the low, throaty growl gave them away. They quickly moved between him and the door. He dropped the gas cans at his feet. He did not have time to unslung his rifle and take aim. Instead, he drew his knife and waited.

He sidestepped the first zombie, jammed the blade into the side of its neck, and twisted. Still holding the handle of the knife, he used the creature's momentum to turn it and send it crashing into the second creature. When he pulled the blade free, it stumbled and fell, as the driving force keeping it moving died. The second creature recovered quickly, leaped over the first zombie's body and rushed at him, snarling with its arms outstretched. He stooped, grabbed one of the gas cans, and used it as a bowling ball, sending it flying into the creature's legs. When it landed face first on the asphalt, he leaped upon its back and slid the knife into the back of its neck, severing its spine.

The other zombies were halfway across the parking lot, their hungry attention focused on the only living creature in sight—him. This time, his knife would not help him. He sheathed it and removed his Uberti. He cocked and fired from his hip without taking aim. The heavy .44 caliber slugs fired from close range did not have to hit the creatures' heads to be effective. The dead and the dying entangled in a frenzy of flailing limbs. When he emptied the Uberti, he rammed the barrel into the forehead of the nearest zombie. The creature swung around, hitting several other zombies in the head with the rifle butt until it collapsed dead. Jake grabbed the two gas cans, and ran for the door. On the way, he picked up his M2010 and tucked it under his arm.

At the entrance, he jammed the knife into one of the cans to split it open and poured gasoline in a line across the cobblestone entranceway. It ran down the slope toward the driveway. As the first creatures waded into the stream of fuel, he pulled out his lighter and touched it to the edge of the pool. The gasoline erupted into flame, singing the hair on his arm before he could leap back. At first, the zombies ignored the flames, but as the heat dried out their pants legs, the material caught fire. Flames crawled up their legs and enveloped them. He smiled at the sight of blazing zombies careening into one another.

He did not bother shutting the front door. He raced up the stairs and found people already building a barricade in the stairwell. He tossed his rifle and the remaining gas can over the top, scrambled over the loose pile of chairs and tables, and landed in a heap on the other side.

"They're coming," he warned. "Build it higher. Use anything not bolted to the floor."

He poked the barrel of his M2010 through a gap in the barricade and began shooting the first zombies attempting to climb the stairs. Some were aflame from the gasoline. At close range, he could not miss, but there were far too many to stop completely. The dead flaming zombies rolling back down the stairs tripped those following and slowed their advance, spreading the flames. He hoped they did not set the hotel on fire. He helped two men wedge a sofa against the pile of furniture and surveyed their work. Two or three strong men could have demolished the barricade in minutes. Even an unorganized mob of mindless zombies would pull it down eventually from the sheer number of hands clawing at it.

"Start building another one on the top landing of each stairwell. We'll retreat to the roof."

"It's storming outside," one woman protested.

"Would you rather be wet or dead?" he asked.

She shut up.

He shot one last zombie and herded the people of Mirada Del Sol up the stairs to the roof. Along the way, he had them gather wooden tables, laundry carts, cold drink machines, ice machines, and doors removed from rooms—anything solid—and carry it to the top landing of the stairwell. With it, they would construct their last barricade. If the zombies broke through it, they would have nowhere left to go. The fire escape ladder from the roof led down only to more zombies.

The rain had slackened, but the wind had not. It drove the rain horizontally across the roof into Jake's face. He wiped the water from his eyes and looked around. Few people had time to remember umbrellas. A lucky few held plastic garbage bags over their heads. Most suffered the full onslaught of the storm. They huddled on the leeward side of the air conditioner units, air ducts—anything that could break the flow of the wind. By flashes of lightning, Jake noted their drawn, worried faces. Each clap of thunder, each new flash of lightning caused them to shudder in fright.

Jake braved the fury of the storm, standing on the edge of the roof peering west toward the Union Pacific Station and, hopefully, a glimpse of the train of the trucks. He saw neither. He looked down over the edge of the room at the sea of zombies throwing themselves at the collapsing fence or pushing for a spot in the line entering the hotel. He could see very little of the Springhill Suites in the darkness, but now he could hear gunfire, sporadic at first, but increasing in intensity as that building's fence also fell inward. He hoped they found a secure place to wait for rescue, whenever that might come.

Jake had come to Yuma as a rescuer, boldly and full of confidence. Now, he waited with the other frightened residents for a second, more successful attempt led by someone else. His sense of failure tried to drag him into places as dark as the storm-filled night. It reminded him of the similar stormy night he had lost his ranch, destroying it rather than allow Levi Combs and his cutthroats have it. He had saved Alton, but lost Jessica. Saving her had been another battle, the final battle that he had won and Combs had lost. His friends did not suspect how much the loss of his refuge, his grandfather's ranch, had affected him. He had allowed the ranch to become what he was, how he valued his life. Its loss had been a brutal lesson in life's ironies.

He could not do much to stop the zombies from getting inside the hotel, but he could slow them down a bit. He ripped away a piece of his undershirt, still relatively dry, soaked it in gasoline, and shoved it into the opening of the remaining gas can. Using his lighter, he lit it. At first, he thought his homemade wick was too wet, but to his relief, it caught fire. He punched holes in the side of the can with his knife and dropped it over the side of the building above the covered walkway of the entrance. It hit the ground, bounced a few times, rolled through the water, and went out.

"Damn!"

Drawn by the noise and sudden movement, half a dozen zombies chased after it. Jake used his last stun grenade, pulling the pin and dropping it over the side. It detonated in the pool of gasoline spilling from the can and ignited it. A few seconds later, the can exploded into flame. The concussions sent the zombies, and pieces of zombies, flying across the parking lot. A sheet of flames rode the surface of the water, spreading across the parking lot. The heat flash-dried the tattered clothing the zombies wore and set it on fire. Zombies burst into flame like walking Tiki torches. Within minutes, the entire parking lot around the front entrance of the hotel was ablaze.

All too soon, the flames died away in the rain, but the gasoline bomb had sown confusion among the zombies. Their animal instinct minds, once drawn to the flickering flames, still sought the vanished enticing spots of light. Instead of pushing their way into the hotel, they wandered aimlessly around the parking lot.

There was nothing to do now except wait.

14

July 1, 2017, 6.00 p.m.   Marana Safe Haven, Marana, AZ —

Hollis Boudreaux, aka Preacher Man, had not let Jake's refusal to take him to Yuma as the final word on the matter. God had whispered in his ear, and God had final word on all matters. He was determined to reach Yuma, even if it meant appropriating a vehicle from the motor pool and following the convoy. He had not driven in two years but thought he could manage long enough to reach Yuma. He stumbled and almost fell in the parking lot as a wave of dizziness fell over him. His weak body was betraying him at the time he needed it most. *If only my poor body was a strong as my will*. He knew he could not undertake such an endeavor alone. He needed help, but whom? As if in answer to his prayer, he saw the young Indian boy, Aden, who had tended to his grandfather in the infirmary, walking toward the infirmary and called out to him.

"Aden! May I have a word with you?"

Aden stopped and stared at Preacher Man, finally recognizing him.

"Do you know how to drive?" Preacher Man asked.

Aden wrinkled his brow at the curious question. "Yes. Why?"

"I must go to Yuma. However, it would be best if I placed myself in other more capable hands. Would you take me there?"

"Yuma?" He shook his head and began to walk away. "I'm sorry. I cannot leave my grandfather."

"God has decreed that I must reach Yuma. Lives are at stake."

Aden paused. "Whose lives?"

Preacher Man hesitated. *Whose indeed?* "I do not know," he admitted. "That much of my vision is unclear."

Aden stared at him with renewed interest. "Vision?"

"God allows me to see snippets of His Great Plan. My poor feeble human mind cannot comprehend most of it, but this much is clear: He has decreed that I go to Yuma as He sent Moses back into Egypt. Like Moses, I do not know what I am to do or how I am to accomplish it, but I must go."

Rather than dismiss him outright as crazy, as many had, Aden considered his plea. He felt a glimmer of hope. Native Americans consider the insane touched by the Great Spirit. Perhaps he was. "I must speak with my grandfather. He will tell me what I must do."

Preacher Man nodded. "Please do. We have little time."

Doctor Von Ross was not pleased to see him when they entered the infirmary. "There you are!" he snapped. "You're in no condition to be up and about. You need rest."

Preacher Man dismissed his concern and pushed by him. "I will find my rest in the bosom of my God."

"You'll find it today, if you don't allow me to help you."

The doctor's words had the ring of prophecy. They sounded in his ears like the Trumpets of Jericho and troubled his soul. He shook off the dark fingers of doubt. "Your concern is commendable, and I am touched by your efforts to heal a sick old man, but my health is of little importance."

"You're not an old man. You're what, fifty-two, fifty-three?"

"Age is not counted in years, doctor, but in experience."

"Do you think the weight of the world is on your shoulders? Do you think you must sacrifice yourself for whatever vision you have? That's a lot of guilt for one man to assume."

"I assure you, it is not hubris on my part that dictates my actions. I have no wish to die. I have died once already. God brought me back, not as one of the afflicted, but as a vessel for his Holy Spirit. I must do as He bids."

He pushed on past Von Ross and entered the room in which the boy's grandfather lay. The boy stood by the old man's side. His grandfather, now awake, lay on his side, propped up by one skinny elbow, staring at Preacher Man with dark eyes that burned with the same fire he had seen in his own eyes in reflections in mirrors and storefront windows. Unlike the burning bush of Moses, this holy fire did consume. Like his compelling flame, it ate at the old man's body and soul, aging him before his time. A shadowy haze clouded his face, a result of the dark visions he had witnessed.

Despite his apparent frailty, the grandfather's voice was strong and commanding. "My grandson tells me you speak with your God."

Preacher Man nodded, feeling as if he were being judged. "You have seen dark things as well. I can see it in your face."

A slight smile creased the wrinkles around the old man's lips. "It is not so difficult to see a dark future for the *Toha*. The Whites create darkness by separating themselves from nature and the spirits. We Tohono O'odham are as dried leaves swept before the winds of a winter storm by the fate of the *Toha*. We no longer have roots to hold us in the soil."

"I, too, am rootless. My God has allowed me to see a small part of his plan. I have crossed this country with a purpose; what it is, I do not know. Yet, I know I must go to Yuma. There, I must do something for which God has been preparing me. Lives are in the balance. I need your grandson to take me. I fear I am too feeble to make the journey alone."

The old man nodded. "I, too, have seen this." His eyes bored into Preacher Man like black obsidian daggers, digging into him as if probing for the truth buried within his flesh. "I see, too, that you have tasted death's bitter tea." Finally, spent by his talking, he lay back on the bed, closed his eyes, and sighed deeply. "I see no good end for you in this."

Preacher Man felt a cold hand grip his heart. "I will accept God's will."

"It is good that a man can rise above his human ego and accept that which the gods decree."

Preacher Man thought the old Indian had fallen asleep, but after a few moments, he opened his eyes and stared at him. "My grandson may go if he wishes, but you must keep him safe."

"I cannot promise that."

"Then, you must go alone."

Defeated, Preacher Man almost wailed in anguish. "I cannot do this alone. It is a burden too heavy for one man. I will give my life to protect him, but that is all I can offer. I cannot promise more."

The old man smiled. "That is enough."

He spoke to the boy in Tohono O'odham. Aden looked at Preacher Man, nodded, and said, "I will go with you."

Preacher Man sagged against the wall as his legs trembled with relief. He said a silent prayer to God. To Aden, he was afraid to speak lest his voice betray his emotions. Instead, he nodded.

After gathering his few possessions, he and Aden went to the motor pool for a jeep. When he saw the Desert Chameleon Armored Personnel Carrier, a spark flowed through his body as if the hand of God had reached down and shaken his soul. He wondered why Jake had not taken it to Yuma. The armored vehicle would have made a formidable addition to the firepower Jake mistakenly thought would win the war against the zombies.

He turned to Aden. "This shall be our chariot."

Aden got down on his knees and looked under the APC. "It looks as if someone has been working on it. I don't think it runs." He rose and looked at Preacher Man. "I'm pretty handy with tools, but I don't know anything about these things. Maybe we should stick with the jeep."

Preacher Man smiled. His hands trembled as if eager to plunge into the bowels of a large engine once again. "I think I can repair it, with your help."

Aden shrugged. "I'm game, but I thought you were in a hurry."

"Sometimes God stays a hurried man's footsteps for a purpose. I believe this is the purpose."

Aden placed his hand on the APC and slid it along the side. "I don't know. It looks like a tank. Are you sure you can fix something this large?"

"In a previous life, I was a Navy mechanic. With God's hand guiding mine, and your young hands assisting, yes, we can repair it."

"If you say so." Aden smiled, staring at the APC. "It certainly would make a badass anti-zombie weapon."

"I have no desire to kill zombies if it can be avoided."

Aden fixed him with a questioning stare. "Are you going to Yuma save the people or to save zombies?"

Preacher Man frowned at the absurdity of the question. "People, of course."

Aden shook his head slowly. "Then you have to choose—zombies or people. You cannot rescue people from zombies without killing zombies."

The boy is right. His reluctance to kill the creatures was a personal issue. He could not expect others to abide by his personal code of behavior. The creatures ignored him because they sensed a kindred spirit in him, something remaining from his brush with the Staggers, but they would not ignore others. Others were simply food.

"You are right, of course. We will kill them if we must to save those trapped. If it was wrong to do so, God would not have sent me on this mission."

"I'll find some tools."

A sense of serenity descended over Preacher Man. It was something he had not felt in many years. He knew deep in his soul that his long journey was almost over.

15

July 1, 2017, 1:30 p.m.   Springhill Suites, Mirada Del Sol Safe Haven, Yuma, AZ —

When word had first come of the zombie incursion that morning, Jessica Hubley had been teaching a yoga class, seven students of various ages and varying degrees of agility searching for a method of calming the fears that haunted them. The fears were different for each, but the effect on the body was the same— anxiety, loss of appetite, irritability, depression, and self-doubt. The centuries-old exercises encouraged proper breathing discipline, physical strength, mental calmness, and channeling energy from the spine to all parts of the body. From Rabbit, Tiger, and Table poses, she led them through Triangle, Five-Pointed Star, and Standing Forward Fold. The latter required more limberness than most could manage, but they tried.

By the end of the thirty-minute session, she was not sure if her students had achieved any of their goals, but she had. She no longer practiced yoga to reach nirvana and disassociation from the physical world, as she had pre-apocalypse; she used it to make her more aware of her surroundings and to achieve a degree of body/mind coordination that could help save her life in an emergency.

As she read the message aloud to her class, she could tell by the tone of the order to remain inside that the threat was worse than the casually worded missive sent around implied. If she had learned anything from Jake's arbitrary set of laws, it was that his rules worked. *Jake's Law #3 — A fool and his life are soon parted,* applied here. Many of the residents chided her for carrying her .45

semi-automatic with her at all times, even keeping it beside her during yoga lessons, a sublime juxtaposition of inner peace and physical preparedness. She ignored their taunts and silent contempt. They, unlike her, had complete faith in the military and the nascent Citizens Council to keep them safe, while she had more faith in her pistol and her ability to hit what she aimed at.

From the yoga class, she went directly to the Springhill Suites council representative and suggested he open the arsenal and issue weapons. He smiled and spoke to her in a condescending manner, as if being a woman entitled him to ridicule her concern.

"This is a minor sighting," he assured her. "The military will deal with it quickly. No need to get all panicky."

From Jake, she had learned not to tolerate fools, especially fools who could cause serious harm through their foolishness. She took a deep breath to suppress her first reaction of causing him serious physical harm, returned his smile, and replied calmly but firmly, "You will issue me a weapon, or I will plant my foot on the side of your head repeatedly until you think the bell for recess has just rung." She pointed to her bare right foot, lifting it slightly from the floor for emphasis.

Her threat startled him. "But I—"

"If there is no problem, I'll return the rifle promptly. If there is one, then you will issue weapons to anyone qualified to use one, or I will come back to persuade you."

"Y-y-yes, ma'am," he stuttered, and fumbled for the keys to the storage room arsenal.

She smiled at his back as he opened the door. Two years ago, she would never have considered asserting herself. Today, she had threatened a man if he did not accommodate her. Jake would have been proud of her. She frowned at the thought of Jake. Whatever their personal issues, he was a good man to have around if there were zombies present.

The makeshift arsenal was small but stacked with cases of ammunition and wall racks that held M16s, M27IARS, a handful of shotguns, and several makes and models of semi-automatic and single-shot rifles. A rookie might feel safer with an automatic rifle, but she understood the value of accuracy over firepower. Instead of an M16 or IAR, she chose a Ruger SR-762 because of its accuracy and because it fired .308 Winchester rounds, which were the equivalent of the 7.62mm NATO rounds of which they had a large supply. The Ruger had a rail for adding a flashlight and a scope, and the butt and handgrip adjusted to fit her smaller stature. The Ruger had the firepower to stop a zombie at 800 yards, but if the threat was as bad as she suspected, she doubted she would need that kind of accuracy. She picked up two additional magazines and a box of ammunition. The representative stared dumfounded at her as she checked out the rifle's sights for bends or scratches that could affect accuracy, and then unloaded and reloaded the magazines to assure they were loaded properly.

"Are you going outside?" he asked.

She shook her head. "No, I just want to be ready when the shit gets deep."

"But the military is dealing with the problem. You can hear them shooting."

Just as he spoke, a loud explosion in the distance brought a look of surprise to his face. "Does that sound like a minor incursion to you?" she asked. "If you want my advice, be ready to issue these weapons," she waved her hand around the arsenal, "and hope they are enough." She turned and left before he could argue or agree.

Her room was on the third floor facing south and offered a good view of Yuma. She pulled up a chair and sat facing the window, watching an alarmingly increasing number of fires spring up in the city and listening to the pockets of gunfire getting closer to the safe haven. Through her binoculars, she could see movement, zombies, moving north through the streets and alleys. This was no small incursion. Her heart pounded in her chest at the thought of going through it all again, the running and hiding, barely surviving. She wasn't sure she could take it again, but she was prepared.

Living with power, running water, and hot meals was nothing new to her. With Jake, she had enjoyed the niceties of post-apocalyptic life in a world otherwise reduced to campfires and canned goods. She had gotten used to it, but Jake had never let her forget how easily it could all go away. Almost as if proving a point, he had destroyed it all, his life's work, to try to save her from Levi Combs. She wasn't sure he had entirely forgiven her for the necessity of it. Perhaps that was at the root of their problems. During their brief relationship, some of Jake's prepper mind-set had rubbed off on her. In her room, she kept two flashlights, spare batteries, an assortment of Bic lighters and matches, an army K-Bar knife, bottles of water, and freeze-dried food for an emergency. Some thought her a hoarder, but she considered it a bug-out kit, knowing someday it might save her life. She hoped today was not that day.

As the morning went on, the chatter of small arms fire changed to the thunder of large caliber weapons fire and the dull thud of explosives—mortars and RPGs. The fact that no helicopters were in the air concerned her. She had not even seen one making its usual daily rounds patrolling the city. She sat, her SR-762 across her lap, watching all morning.

By mid-afternoon, she knew they were in trouble. More zombies than she could count had reached the railroad tracks running parallel to I-10, and the military was nowhere in sight. She returned downstairs to grab some sandwiches before they were all gone and found an angry mob clogging the dining room and lobby. She stood on the fringes and listened as they discussed the situation among themselves. Most whined about the inconvenience, little understanding the danger they faced.

"My tomatoes are ripe," one agitated woman complained. "If I don't pick them today, they'll get mushy."

One man, wearing shorts, a white Polo shirt, and a red sweatband around his head, said, "We were playing tennis when they chased us off the court. I scheduled that court time three days ago."

"Where is the army?" another man demanded. "That's what I want to know. This is their job, isn't it?"

"Why can't we just leave until the military gets everything under control?" a woman carrying a small child in her arms asked. The child, oblivious to the noise outside and the adult tensions in the room, slept peacefully.

"We will be fine," one man tried to assure them. "We have a fence around the hotel. The military must be busy, or they would be here by now, though they could have sent someone to apprise us of the situation. We just have to be patient. They will come. I'm certain."

Hearing the tone of the crowd, Jessica stepped forward and spoke up. "I wouldn't be so certain of that."

The man glared at her, becoming a little nervous when he saw the SR-762 casually cradled in her arms, and demanded, "Who the hell are you?"

"A woman with a rifle," she replied, glaring at him. "If you bother looking out a window, you'll see hundreds of zombies just across the interstate coming this way. I haven't seen a helicopter, a jeep, or a uniform all morning. The military's got bigger concerns than us."

"Don't try to start a panic," the man warned. "We're safe here."

She shook her head at his incredulity. "When a zombie nibbles on your ear, don't believe he wants to whisper sweet nothings. They're coming here. Now. No one is going to stop them." She turned to the crowd. "If any of you can fire a weapon, I suggest you get one and be prepared."

"I don't know who you think you are, young lady, but you're frightening my son," the woman carrying the child snapped at her.

Jessica just stared at her until she backed away.

"We should contact the Arizona Rangers," one man suggested. "What are they doing? Why aren't they here?"

Jessica smiled. "I'm sure Jake would be the first to tell you to be prepared."

A woman stepped from the crowd. Jessica noted that the woman was a few years older than she was, and that her curly red hair was a shade or two lighter than her own hair. Something about the way the woman looked at her sent shivers running up and down her spine. The feeling was disconcerting, but what bothered her more was that she didn't know why.

"Do you know Jake?" the woman asked.

The question startled her. She stared at the woman for a moment. Unlike most of the others in the room, she didn't look frightened, merely curious. "Yes. Do you?"

The corner of her mouth turned up slightly in a wry smile. "He saved me from a bad situation."

"That sounds like Jake Blakely. He's good at that." She paused, curious. Had this woman and Jake had a fling? She was pretty, but she didn't look like Jake's type. She shook her head. *Hell, what do I know about Jake's type. I wasn't.* The woman smiled, as if reading Jessica's unspoken question. "What's your name?"

"Hilda. What's yours?"

"Jessica."

"Well, if you know Jake," Hilda said, "I'm throwing my lot in with you. What's your plan?"

Jessica relaxed, deciding she liked Hilda. She seemed a no-nonsense woman. "We prepare and we wait."

Hilda nodded at Jessica's rifle. "I'm not much good with one of those." She pulled a small .25 caliber from her pocket. "Jake gave me this. I can shoot it ..." She paused, glanced away, and shook her head, "but I think I might be more comfortable with a shotgun if we're going to fight off zombies."

Jessica laughed at Jake's present to Hilda. A gun. It was so Jake. "In that case, we'll find you a shotgun." She looked at the others. "I suggest you all find something to shoot with."

"Nonsense," one older man with thinning gray hair replied. He looked as if he might have been someone important in the old world, but standing there in dirty, green, one-piece coveralls, a two-day stubble of beard, and calloused hands, he looked out of place, a relic of the past. "You're pandering to everyone's fear." He straightened his posture and glared at her. "You're not in charge here."

Jessica shrugged. "Suit yourself. You have got the right to die any way you choose." She looked over the crowd watching the exchange between them. "If any of you change your mind, I'll be in room 314." She narrowed her gaze and stared the older man in the eye. "But knock first," she warned, "or I'll shoot you through the door. Come on, Hilda, let's get you situated."

Hilda smiled, as the crowd moved aside to allow them to pass. "You sure know how to liven up a party, Jessica."

The armory was still open. She scanned the room for just the right weapon for Hilda, just as she would in considering a new pair of shoes. It had to be comfortable, and yet functional. Style was not as important as function. They were getting ready for a fight, not a ball. She chose a Remington 12-gauge shotgun. It had a five-round magazine and was easy to fire. She handed the shotgun to Hilda, who handled it somewhat awkwardly, as if intimidated by it. Then, she ran her fingers over the polished wooden stock and along the length of the barrel. She stared at the gun for a moment and grinned at Jessica.

"Now I know why men like big guns. I just had a penis envy moment."

Hilda roused Jessica's curiosity. She seemed out of place in the safe haven among the widows, housewives, and Millennial teenyboppers. She didn't look like a woman who would hide from a challenge. *Like I'm doing.*

As they climbed the stairs to Jessica's room, she asked, "If you're from Hatch, how did you wind up here?"

"Oh, I'm not from Hatch. I was just passing through when … I was on my way to Albuquerque. Jake convinced me it was too dangerous. The people in Hatch who were setting up the new safe haven asked me if I wanted to come to Yuma to study nursing." She shrugged. "I said, 'Why not?' It beats the hell out of picking cotton or working in a factory."

Jake again. Am I jealous? If so, am I jealous of her or of Jake? She suppressed the thought. In her youth, she had experimented with the idea of bisexuality and found it enticing, but had decided she was definitely hetero. *Am I?*

"How do you know Jake?"

Hilda's reaction surprised her. Her face paled, and a scowl formed on her lips, but Jessica did not think Jake was the cause of whatever caustic memory her question had raised. She felt an immediate sense of empathy for Hilda.

"I was being held captive in Hatch by three men." She took a deep breath and released it slowly as a sigh. "Jake killed them." She smiled. "First time I've ever been glad to see a cop. I wasn't real nice to him, but I was still mad." She stared at Jessica for a moment. "From the way you said his name, I take it you and him were a little more, ah, intimate."

Jessica's cheeks reddened at Hilda's perceptiveness. "We were lovers for a time. He saved me much the same way he saved you.

He broke one of his beloved Jake's Laws to teach me how to survive. He's a hard man to figure out."

Hilda nodded, as if Jessica's the last sentence summed up her assessment of Jake as well. "He's a hard man period. He's cocksure and unsociable as hell, but he's totally no-nonsense." She stared at Jessica and smiled. "If he taught you, I made a wise move to hook up with you."

Hilda's compliment embarrassed her. "We'll see," Jessica replied. They reached her room. His hands trembled slightly as she slid her keycard through the card reader. As she pushed open the door, she said, "Here we are," and stepped aside to usher Hilda inside.

What am I getting myself into? Then she remembered *Jake's Law #21 — Trust your instincts.*

* * * *

July 1, 2017 10:00 p.m. Springhill Suites, Yuma, AZ—

They now had no power. The hotel was dark, and without air conditioning was getting hot. Because of the storm, it was humid as well. Zombies encircled both hotels. Jessica knew that without the military, they were in a dangerous situation. The hotel and the chain-link fences surrounding it were adequate against an occasional zombie incursion or a handful of armed attackers, but not a zombie army. *Where is our damn army*? she wondered angrily.

When she heard firing, she thought her unspoken question had been answered; but then, she realized the trucks approaching the hotels were not military. The dozen or so trucks circled the Holiday Inn, killing zombies by the score, before entering the compound. She watched the people load into the back of the trucks and leave. She thought she recognized Jake at the gate, but the rain was coming down too hard to be certain. *It would be typical of him to be out front where the worst danger was.* She could not fault him for his courage. Or his taste in women.

She glanced at Hilda sitting in the chair behind her sipping from a glass of tequila with the last of the ice and a lime twist. Her face betrayed none of her thoughts, but Jessica felt as if she were in them. They had not spoken much since meeting except of general, innocuous things, as if both were afraid to let down their guard and broach the subject that filled the room as much as the zombies outside. Hilda had made no overt move, and for that, Jessica was glad. As much as she was attracted to Hilda, and believed the attraction was mutual, she was not sure she wanted to invest herself in another relationship, especially at a time when her mind needed to be unencumbered by emotional baggage. Because of the humidity and sweat, Hilda's blouse clung to her body, outlining the shape of her large breasts. She noted with some jealousy that in spite of her age, Hilda's breasts sagged less than her younger ones.

Stay focused.

Hilda sipped slowly, not trying to drink away her problems. Jessica thought the tequila was more a focal point than a need, something to take the edge off any emotional turmoil she might be going through.

Hell, she might just be thirsty.

Her fellow residents downstairs were growing more nervous with each passing hour. She had watched twenty or more leave the building a few hours earlier before the power had gone out. Where they were going, she could only guess. The warehouse at the trucking depot north of the hotel was a secure cinder-block building. Perhaps they believed it safer there than in the hotel. She hoped they made it, but if the number of zombies now milling about outside the fence were any indication, their chances were dismal.

As she watched the rescue operation of her neighbors in the Holiday Inn unfold, her frustration with her fellow Springhill Suites residents grew. A crowd had gathered outside in the pouring rain, but the presence of so many people drove the zombies mad. She watched two men she recognized from the Citizens Council herding them back inside the hotel and threw them a silent curse.

She had earlier suggested fighting their way across the twenty yards separating the two compounds and joining the people in the Holiday Inn to those same two men. It would make any rescue attempt easier, and by combining their strength in arms, provide a more effective defense. The council members had refused her suggestion as 'foolish' and 'premature.' Now, it was too late. The residents at the Holiday Inn, who under Jake's leadership showed some backbone by defending themselves, were likely to mistake them for zombies in the storm and shoot them.

Hilda, whom she had since learned was not very tolerant of stupidity or of men bullying women, suggested shooting both of them. It had been a tempting thought, but Jessica feared crossing the hair-thin line between killing in self-defense and killing for a supposedly good cause. Jake would not have hesitated. She hoped that she was better than Jake was.

As the hours passed, she watched the trucks come and go one more time, fighting their way through the zombie horde. She sensed the finality with which Jake sent them away. *At least most of the people in the Holiday Inn got away safely. We're not going anywhere.*

A dozen or so men, women, and children had locked themselves in the small galley kitchen downstairs, refusing to unlock the door to allow anyone else to get water or food. Jessica had considered shooting out the lock, but Hilda had surprised her by restraining her.

"Let them be. They're frightened. I don't think anyone will starve before this is all over. Besides, you've got water, protein bars, and tequila in your room. What more do we need for a party?"

Others sought shelter behind the locked doors of their individual rooms. Against one or two of the creatures, such shelters might suffice, but against an army of hungry zombies, the doors were useless. The sheer weight of the massed creatures would force a door from its hinges or break the lock. *At least we have weapons when that time comes.* Most did not.

She wished Jake were there, but he had his hands full doing what he did best. She was not Jake, but neither could she sit idly by and allow over a hundred people to die senselessly. She turned to Hilda.

"I have to do something," she said,

The lantern on the nightstand threw a shadow across her face, but Jessica detected a slight smirk on her lips. "I figured you would. You're a lot like Jake."

Jessica started to deny the comparison, but realized with a start that she was. She had tried to change Jake and had failed miserably. Instead, he had changed her, not by force of his personality, which was admittedly considerable, but from sheer necessity. Jake had the qualities necessary to survive in a post-apocalyptic world. The realization that she could not continue as she had been doing had forced her reluctantly to team with him. She had learned from him. He had made her harder. He had stripped away her innocent notions of right and wrong and replaced them with a dose of hard reality. In a few years, people would call him a barbarian, but right now to the people next door, he was a savior.

Beginning with their floor, she and Hilda patrolled the halls of each floor trying to coax people from their rooms or hiding places and to a more secure area they could collectively defend. Most refused. In the end, she rounded up less than thirty people willing to listen. She led them to the hotel's Sunridge Conference Room, the larger of the two meeting rooms. They stockpiled water, weapons, ammunition, and any food requiring no refrigeration or cooking, and then constructed barricades against the doors and windows using overturned conference tables. Behind the tables, they piled the heaviest furniture from the hotel lobby. With no air conditioner or ventilation from open windows, the room was stifling, but the clamminess was the least of their worries.

Of the twenty-six men, women, and children in the room, only six professed any proficiency with firearms. Every resident was required to take one thirty-minute weapons class each month, but most did nothing beyond that. She was not sure of Hilda's ability to hit anything with the shotgun, but at least she was willing to try. To those who wished only a safe place to hide, she said, "Everyone except the children take a weapon and keep it handy."

One young woman, perhaps nineteen, who Jessica had seen working in the cafeteria, said in a loud voice filled with anger, "Why should we have to fight? You have a gun. Protect us."

Inwardly, she smiled. Jake had warned her that in a crisis, people always looked to someone else to protect them. She had vehemently disagreed at the time, believing it just his excuse to avoid helping others. Now, she understood what he meant.

"Yes, I do, but if zombies break in, you'll be the last person I chose to protect." She pointed to three children and two men in their seventies. "These people have no one else to protect them. You're capable of firing a weapon. Do it or die."

She did not waste any more time on the girl. She hoped the others took heed. If push came to shove, she would do what she could for the helpless, but she was not going to sacrifice herself for people she did not know or particularly like. She saw Hilda suppress a chuckle when the girl and several others took M16s from the stack of weapons against the wall.

When the sound of breaking glass came from the lobby, some of her charges began crying. A hard knot like a poorly digested meal settled in her stomach. Zombies were inside the building.

"Suck it up!" she snapped. Her gaze covered each of the people in the room. "The children aren't crying. Try to be at least as brave as a ten year old."

Dozens of dead hands hammered at the door of the conference room. The door shook and bounced on its hinges, but it held. Jessica aimed her rifle at the door, glad to see Hilda and several others doing the same. After a few minutes of intense apprehension, the hammering lessened as many of the creatures moved on. Others in the hotel were not as lucky. A loud crash echoed from down the hall, followed by several gunshots, and then a series of horrifying screams from several throats. The galley kitchen refuge had fallen. Those hiding inside had no means of escape and died horribly. The screaming of the young children inside and the sounds of their death agonies steeled her to fight until the end, with teeth and fingernails if necessary. She vowed her last breath would not be wasted in screaming, but in fighting.

It sounded as if every zombie gathered outside the compound had finally found its way inside the hotel. Clumsy footsteps tromping the corridor of the floor above raised everyone's gaze toward the ceiling, as if fearing their weight would send them crashing through the floor above and land them in their midst. More screams erupted from above them, as doors meant to keep out casual intruders failed to stop determined, hungry zombies.

"If the zombies are inside the hotel," one young man suggested, "shouldn't we use the opportunity to escape?"

Jessica looked at him. He looked very young, perhaps nineteen or twenty, with short black hair and beard, but his hazel eyes blazed with excitement. Unlike the others gathered in the room, he had shown no fear at the zombies at the door. Instead, he had scribbled furiously on a piece of paper. She had thought he had been writing his last words or a will, but the paper he held in his hand contained roughly sketched diagrams and a series of calculations.

"Escape to where? They're all around us."

He pointed to a diagram of the hotel, and then to a dot in the parking lot. "This is where we are. Here is a converted UPS van. I'm the driver. I use the van every day to haul workers to the fields. It has seats for fifteen people plus room for tools." He looked around at the people in the room. "I'm sure we can all fit inside."

"But it's in the parking lot, outside," one man protested.

The young man smiled and pointed to one of the windows in the room. "It's only thirty feet beyond that window. I have the keys and I gassed it up this morning. Surely, we can manage thirty feet," he said, as if challenging anyone to contradict him. "Once in the van, I'll drive straight through the fence to the interstate. From there, we just drive until there are no more zombies."

His plan had merit, but Jessica was still unsure. To convince the others to leave a secured room, she would have to be certain. "Can the van break through the fence?"

"That's what I was working on. The van is one of the older diesel models—a 7.3L Cummins with 215 horsepower engine—not one of the later hybrids. It has an all-metal body. I estimated the amount of rain we've received so far and determined that the loose, sandy soil is fully saturated. Around Yuma, the layer of dense calcium carbonate, white caliche it's called, is just a few centimeters below the surface. When they scraped away the soil for the hotel, they removed this layer, leaving only loose sand and gravel. So, basically, the fence posts are jammed into a child's sandbox. No wonder the zombies could break the fence down so easily. The van should have no problem with it."

She stared at the young man in wonder. "What were you?"

He glanced away in embarrassment. "I was an engineering student at U of A majoring in hydrology."

"And you're driving a van?"

He shrugged. "They need van drivers more than they need an engineer at this point."

Jessica felt a spark of hope growing in her chest. They could not depend on the military to save them, and Jake had problems of his own with the group from the Holiday Inn. Remaining where they were was a short-term solution to what could become a long-term problem. Without power, food, or water, the zombies could outlast them.

She addressed the group, some of whom had been listening. "We need to remove the barricade from the window. If it is at all possible, we need to heed this young man's advice."

As she expected, some were vehemently opposed to the idea. One was the young girl who had protested earlier.

"We're safe," she whined. "That's why you brought us here, right?" She turned to the others seeking support. "I mean, we followed you here because we believed you."

"We're safe," Jessica agreed, "but we might get hungry or thirsty before any help arrives. *If* any arrives," she added.

"They were taking people away from the Holiday Inn."

"That was hours ago. Now, they're hiding on the roof in the rain. We can stay here and hope for the best, or we can try to save ourselves. If there are too many zombies outside, we stay where we are, but if it looks doable, I say we go for it."

"No," the girl said. Her hands trembled with fear.

"Yes," Hilda answered, glaring at the girl.

Hilda's show of support heartened Jessica. The intimidating stare with which she swept the crowd withered their arguments. Reluctantly, all but three agreed to try the young man's plan. "You can seal the window after we leave," Jessica told the doubters, "but if you come with us, you're carrying a weapon, and you're going to use it. We need to protect one another. If you don't like the rules, I suggest you remain behind. If I see someone throw down his or her weapon and run, placing everyone else in danger, I'll shoot them. Clear?"

"That's … that's murder!" the girl replied.

"Call it what you will, but if anyone gives up, I'll shoot them dead. There are no free rides here."

Jessica knew she was bullying some of them into agreeing with her, but people sometimes needed a shove when they planted their feet too firmly in the past or the present. The future was what counted. If tomorrow was not better than today or yesterday, why go on, why struggle so hard to survive? She felt a strange thrill coursing through her body as she issued her warning. She felt empowered. *Is this how Jake feels?*

She turned to the young man. "What's your name?"

"Dag."

"All right, Dag. Let's take a look."

After pulling the barricade from a window, Jessica was relieved to see only a handful of zombies on the south end of the hotel. Most were around the entrance or inside one of the two hotels. If they did not try to break out now, the creatures would eventually wander back outside.

"We can make it," she told the others.

Very carefully, making as little noise as possible, she broke the glass in the window and cleared it out of the frame.

"I'll go first. Don't make any noise," she warned.

Outside the window, she kept watch while the young man upon whose idea she was staking all their lives crawled toward the truck. She sighed with relief when Dag slid open the door, only then realizing she had been holding her breath. One by one, the others climbed through the window until they all crouched beside the wall concealed by a row of saw palmetto plants. She signaled Dag and he cranked the truck. The noise immediately drew the attention of the zombies in the side parking lot.

"Okay," she said. "Go for the truck."

Jessica stood and shot the closest zombie in the head, and then began firing at the others. Hilda leaped up and stood beside her, holding her shotgun at her side and pulling the trigger. She almost lost it from the recoil, but quickly learned to press it against her hip to steady it. Her first shots were wild, but she managed to hit one zombie in the upper torso. Several others used their weapons as well, but most simply clutched them tightly in their hands and ran for the truck. One of the men, who had shown more hatred toward the zombies than fear, marched straight at the zombies as he fired. Before she could warn him, two zombies attacked him from the side, taking him to the ground. She dismissed him from her mind and immediately focused on saving the others.

Dag backed the van toward her, Hilda, and the man helping to hold off the zombies. "Go!" she shouted, pushing Hilda toward the waiting van. When Hilda and the man were in the van, she fired one last shot at one of the few remaining zombies and joined them. To her astonishment, as the van began to pull away, the girl who had complained the loudest and had chosen to remain in the conference room, leaped from the window.

"Wait!" she shouted. "I want to go too!"

Jessica cursed under her breath, leaned out the open door, and yelled, "Hurry!"

The girl raced toward them, but Jessica saw that she would never make it. A zombie emerged from behind a car to cut her off. The girl saw what was happening and tried to retreat to the room. With no clear shot at the zombie, Jessica watched on in mute horror as the girl began screaming, "Help me!"

Dag moved his foot toward the brake. She stopped him. "Don't. We can't do anything for her."

He grimaced, but nodded and pressed the accelerator. Jessica watched the zombie knock the girl to the ground and begin tearing at her flesh before looking away. She braced herself in the open door, as the van raced down the embankment toward the fence. As Dag had predicted, the metal post pulled easily from the ground, taking the fence with it, and the van shot through. They bounced along the open ground between the hotel and the interstate, cleared a concrete drainage ditch, and hit the pavement. Dag headed the van east, switched on the headlights, and gunned the engine.

"Oh crap," he said, while slamming on the brakes.

Jessica looked out and saw a wall of zombies across the highway, too many to force their way through. "Turn around. Go west."

Dag pressed the accelerator, swung the van in a tight turn, and drove west.

Jessica hung her head. Instead of the relief at escaping she should be experiencing, she felt spent, exhausted, as if she had left part of herself back in the hotel with the others. She had saved herself and twenty-three others, but many more were trapped and probably dying in the hotel. Their lives were not her responsibility, but she could not help feeling as if she had failed them.

She felt a hand slip into hers to grasp it. She looked up at Hilda. "You did good, dear," Hilda said in a soft voice. "If they had listened to you, maybe more would have made it."

As Jessica nodded, her eyes burned from the tears she fought to hold back. "It's just that every life is precious now. There are so few of us left. To lose so many ..." She could not continue. The pain was too great for her to bear. The tears broke past her barricades and flowed down her cheeks, each one representing a life lost. Hilda held her in her arms and let her sob.

How can Jake stand it? Is this why he came up with Jake's Law #14 — The heavier the burden, the less likely someone will want to share it. Now, she understood his loneliness, his reluctance to become involved in the world around him, to suffer the pain and the heartache of others. She had unwittingly taken that from him, believing she was making him a better person. *Oh, God! How could I have been so wrong?*

16

July 2, 2017, 2:15 a.m. Union Pacific Station, Yuma, AZ —

Mitch Andrews saw the sudden flash of flame to the southeast toward Mirada Del Sol, but he did not have time to ponder its meaning. He was too busy uncoupling cars. Under Loco Dan's cryptic directions, Andrews and the four men with him fumbled with the unfamiliar Janney couplers between the cars, trying to get out of the way, as the engineer used the locomotive to push the flatcars onto the siding. To Andrews, it was taking much too long and making far too much noise.

"Why are we doing this?" he yelled at the engineer, as he waved Andrews to throw the switch to close off the siding from the main track.

"The dozer weighs 16 tons. Between it, the mulcher, and the four flatbeds, we're towing over 160 tons of useless weight. Weight means speed, and your boss man wants a lean, mean fast train."

"He's not my … Oh, the hell with it." He spotted zombies appearing from the darkness moving toward the train. "Back the train onto the bridge. We'll have better protection there."

He hopped onto the lower step of the locomotive and hung on, as the engineer backed the train onto the elevated railroad bridge over Harold Giss Parkway near the station. With men stationed at each end of the train, they shot zombies as they neared the bridge. His plan worked for almost twenty minutes, but as the creatures' number grew, they poured onto the tracks at both ends of the bridge faster than he and his men could shoot them down. If Deacon did not get back soon, it would be too late. The passengers inside the boxcars were screaming and crying for the train to move. The commotion drew the zombies to them, but Andrews was too busy to try to quiet the passengers. He could have used help from the armed passengers inside the cars, but they were content to remain behind the locked doors of the boxcars. From the number of zombies appearing from the south toward the city, it did not matter. A few extra rifles would not greatly affect the odds.

Loco Dan, the engineer, leaned out of the locomotive window and yelled up to him as he stood atop the drone engine coupled to the rear of the locomotive. "If we don't leave now, we're not going anywhere. The tracks are slick enough already from the rain. If I have to push my way through zombies, the wheels won't get any traction on the blood and guts."

The engineer was rightfully concerned, but Andrews was determined to wait until the very last moment before abandoning the others to their fate. He hadn't come all this way to give up so easily. He would not fail, not again. He had been unable to save his wife and child, but he would save the passengers.

"Not yet," he answered.

The engineer shook his head slowly, probably cursing him for a fool. He heard a loud, sharp scream, as zombies attacked one of his men at the far end of the train as he was reloading his weapon. They dragged him to the ground and ripped him to pieces. The scent of blood drove the zombies mad. Their hunger heightened by the smell, the mob of zombies pounded on the boxcar doors, eliciting more screams from the frightened passengers inside. He did not think the zombies could break into the car, but he did not want to put the theory to the test.

He jumped down from his perch for a better shot at the creatures attacking the boxcars, and then hesitated as he saw how numerous they were. The handful had become a mob. Now, the mob was quickly growing into a horde. More creatures than he could count advanced on the train up the sloped sides of the bridge from the city to the south. The zombies they had left behind at the processing plant would soon reach the station. They were more than five men—four, he corrected himself—could handle. He went to the locomotive.

"Start the train moving, but slowly," he told the engineer. "We're not leaving yet, but we need to keep these things off balance."

"Which direction?" the engineer asked, eager to move the train.

"East. We'll get the zombies to follow us for a ways, and then reverse directions and come back here to meet the trucks."

"And if the trucks aren't here?" the engineer asked, glaring at him.

He stared hard at the engineer. "They will be," he said.

The engineer looked unconvinced. He returned Andrews' stare for a moment, but then nodded. "You're the boss," he said.

The boss. Being in command was a situation he had actively avoided. When asked why he would not fly a helicopter as he had in the National Guard, his answer had been bad nerves. That had been a lie. He did not want the responsibility. He had lost his desire to be in charge of anything. Now, he had no choice. He enjoyed being an Arizona Ranger, but just a simple officer following someone else's orders.

In the early days of the plague, he had been in charge of the small group of survivors, trying to find food and shelter. The group had included his wife and six-year-old son. It had been his decision for them to take refuge in a service station while he scouted around for some place more secure. It had been his decision to leave an untested fourteen-year-old boy on guard with a rifle. He had not been present at the beginning, but by piecing together the details afterwards, he understood what had happened. Zombies had shown up at the gas station. His family and the others were secure inside the cinder block garage, but the young boy panicked and began shooting through the windows. One of his shots pierced the tank of a propane-fueled city bus in for repairs, abandoned when the city fell to the zombies. A spark from a stray round ignited the escaping highly combustible propane. Within moments, the entire service station was in flames.

He arrived and heard the screams of his family and the others trapped inside. He began killing zombies at a frenzied pace, fighting his way through the dense smoke to his family. As he crossed the parking lot, one of the underground fuel tanks exploded. The ground beneath his feet heaved upward, as the asphalt buckled, sending him flying over the hood of a truck. The truck saved his life by protecting him from the massive concussion and fireball that sent chunks of asphalt, concrete, and metal shrapnel flying in all directions. When he recovered sufficiently to look, the garage was gone, blown away as if it had never existed, leaving only a fire-blackened expanse of concrete and an oil change pit where it had once stood.

Though he searched the smoldering rubble for hours in a mind-numbing daze, he found no remains of his family or of the others with them. He had not given up until more zombies arrived, drawn by the noise of the blast. It was the single lowest point in his entire life, and the memories of that dark day it still haunted his sleep and most of his waking hours.

Now, he was in charge again.

The train shuddered and steel wheels squealed in protest, as the train began inching along the tracks. The couplings rattled as they reached their limits and jerked the cars forward.

"On top of the cars!" he yelled to his remaining me, and then climbed up the steel ladder on the side of one of the cars.

The train backed slowly down the rails, crushing zombies that did not get out of the way. He and his men fired down on the creatures with M16s and Winchester .30/30s, but the zombies ignored the men with rifles, intent instead on the moving train smelling of human flesh. As the train passed the Home Depot, he spotted headlights on the interstate—the trucks. The walkie-talkie in his back pocket startled him as it crackled to life.

"Andrews, where are you going with my train?"

He smiled pulled out his walkie-talkie. The ionization from the lightning during the height of the storm had rendered it almost useless for keeping abreast of the situation. Now, he could relinquish command to Deacon.

"Deacon, keep driving to the station. We'll reverse direction and meet you there. Careful of the zombies." After a pause, "Is Jake with you?"

Deacon sighed into the mic. "No. He stayed behind with about fifty people. I just saw a flash that direction. I think he doused the zombies with the gasoline we left him."

Andrews shook his head in dismay. Jake had a bigger death wish than he did. He applauded Jake's courage and sense of responsibility in remaining with the last few people, but Jake did not realize that without him, the Arizona Rangers would fall apart. Only his drive and sense of purpose kept them going. He should not be the one taking all the risks.

"Give me a couple of trucks, and I'll go back for them."

"No, Jake said to get these people to safety, and then take the trucks back to Marana."

Deacon's reply stunned him. Was he abandoning Jake? Was Deacon giving up? That didn't seem like him. "We can't just leave him."

"We can't do him any good now. He's taking the others onto the roof and waiting for the military. Our part in this rescue is done."

Andrews wasn't giving up so easily. He understood Jake and that made them kindred spirits. He knew Jake would not give up on him if the roles were reversed. "What if the military doesn't come?"

"We have no choice. We'll be lucky to get these people aboard the train without losing some of them. Jake reminded me that we have to think of Marana as well. They might need the trucks."

Damn it! Deacon was right, and Jake was right, but he didn't like it. If the zombies hit Marana, they would need the trucks to evacuate the people there. Jake was risking his life to save as many people as he could, but he did not forget where his priorities lay. As he liked to say, it was all in the numbers. Risking three hundred to save fifty was poor math.

Andrews was not ready to give up yet. He tried one more tactic. "What about the people in Springhill Suites? Are we leaving them too?"

He heard a catch in Deacon's voice, although he did not know if it was for Jake or for the people they were leaving behind. "We don't know if anyone there is still alive. It doesn't matter. We can't help them."

Andrews sighed in defeat. Deacon was right. The risk was too great. "Okay. We're coming back. Get ready. We'll have to make this quick."

He walked down the top of the cars to the engine, carefully leaping the distance between cars, and climbed down, first shooting a zombie that had made it aboard the locomotive and was pounding on the glass of the compartment door. He kicked its corpse off the platform.

"Take it back to the station. Go beyond the bridge. We'll need as much space as possible to transfer people from the trucks."

The engineer nodded and hit the brake. The train shuddered to a halt amid a squeal of wheels. Then, the diesel electric motor roared as the train pulled forward. The wheels spun, steel on steel, until they found traction. The cars strained against the couplings and screamed their resistance to the sudden change of direction. Heedless of the passengers inside, ignoring their yells and bruised complaints as they were tossed about inside the boxcars like bones cast on a goatskin to read the future, he pushed the lever forward to increase speed, leaving the zombies behind.

Andrews' face tightened. *I hope they have a future.*

The trucks, much faster than the train, raced ahead up the interstate until their taillights disappeared in the rain. The train rolled over any zombies standing on the tracks or unlucky enough to trip over the rails. Andrews watched the top half of one zombie's torso shoot from beneath the locomotive like a clown from a circus cannon and roll across the ground. The zombies that had attacked the train on the bridge minutes earlier had tried to follow and were gathered on the south end of the bridge. Now, the train returned as an object of revenge, plunging through them like a snowplow through a mountain pass avalanche. Andrews and his men fired among them, taking their toll on the creatures as they passed.

Ahead, he spotted the headlights of the trucks just north of the station leaving the road and driving onto the sloping embankment, cutting cross-country; crashing through fences and jumping ditches on the most direct path to the tracks. Deacon's decisiveness would have brought a smile to Andrew's face, if he were predisposed to smiling. He hoped Jake's placing Deacon in charge would spur Deacon to step up and assume more authority. Jake was a good man, but the weight of his authority would eventually break him if he did not learn to delegate responsibility. Deacon was a good man to have around.

He didn't mind that Deacon and the others thought him cold and distant; that was how he preferred it. However, he regretted earning Deacon's resentment toward him for shooting Cray. He had liked Cray, but he knew that Deacon or even Jake would have had a difficult time sparing Cray from his inevitable fate as another Staggers victim. He had taken that guilt upon himself. The guilt of one more death weighed no more heavily on him than that which he already bore.

The engineer had also spotted the trucks arriving. Loco Dan sped across the bridge without slowing and on past the station. Just as Andrews thought he was not going to stop, he hit the brakes hard. If the train had been an automobile, it would have fishtailed off the road, but the rails kept it straight. Andrews suffered a little of what the hapless passengers were enduring in the boxcars, as the abrupt reduction in speed slammed him against the side of the drone locomotive and tumbled him off the car onto the gravel ballast below. He skidded hard, knocking the breath from his lungs, but he held onto his rifle. He had enough presence of mind to roll away from the tracks and the deadly singing steel wheels passing by just inches from his face.

Do people call him Loco Dan because he drives a locomotive or because he's bat-shit crazy? he wondered.

Andrews ached all over. He wanted to lay there long enough for the pain to go away, but zombies were approaching from the direction of the station. He sucked in a breath of air and fought his way to his knees as a preliminary to standing up. When a wave of nausea swept over him, he decided that kneeling would suffice for the time being, and began shooting. His right arm groaned in protest each time he cocked the .30/30, but his aim did not falter.

Behind him, on the other side of the train, he heard the 7.62mm roar of the M60 and the .50 caliber BMG machineguns on the trucks and forced a grin to his scraped and bleeding lips. His feint of moving the train away from the station, and then reversing directions, had given them some lead-time. If they hurried, they could load the new group of passengers and be away before the zombies massed again.

The last boxcar was passing him. He looked up and saw Simon Wiggins, one of the Rangers he had chosen to accompany him, standing atop the boxcar, waving furiously at him. At first, his befuddled mind could not grasp why Wiggins was waving; then, he saw two zombies rushing at him from the darkness as the end of the boxcar swept by. He leveled his rifle and shot one in the chest and head. It stumbled over the tracks and fell dead at his feet. The second one was a Loper, fast and eager to feed its insatiable appetite. It leaped over its dead companion's body and lunged at him before he could fire again. Still on his knees, he pushed it away with the butt of his rifle, but the creature did not fall. From the corner of his eye, he saw Wiggins taking aim, but he and the zombie were too entangled for a clear shot. Then the darkness swallowed both boxcar and Wiggins. He was alone.

The zombie was strong and Andrews had not completely recovered from his fall. He fought to keep its gaping mouth away from his neck and arms. Its teeth snapped like ivory castanets played by a Mexican flamenco dancer, but this was no lovely senorita, and he had no desire to be a zombie's dance partner. The creature's breath on his face was like a vent from the bowels of hell, stinking of rotten flesh, fresh blood, and the diseased corruption within the creature's own body. It was enough to spur him to greater effort. If he could not clear enough space to raise the Winchester, he decided, he would try something more radical. Andrews released his hold on the rifle. Taken off guard by the sudden release of pressure, the creature stumbled over him and fell, allowing him just enough time to pull his Colt revolver from his holster. He pulled back the hammer with his thumb as the gun cleared the holster, his finger already on the trigger. The zombie got to its feet quicker than he could and raced at him again. He jammed the barrel into the zombie's stomach, pointing upward, and emptied it.

One .44 caliber bullet exited the creature's shoulder, breaking its arm and spraying Andrews with foul smelling blood. A second blew a hole in its upper chest just above the sternum and passed through its lower jaw, shattering teeth and bone, before exiting above its left ear. Still, the creature did not die. One of his last four bullets found the creature's spine, severing it. The Loper groaned one last time and fell over backwards as its legs went numb. Andrews grabbed the rifle from it with one hand before it fell and holstered his pistol with the other. He stood, fired one shot from the rifle into its head, and then wiped his wet sleeve across his face to remove the zombie's blood.

Just as he turned to race after the train, he felt a searing pain in his right ankle. He looked down to see a third zombie, its lower legs amputated by the train wheels, sinking its teeth into his ankle. It had crawled up unnoticed during the fight. A blinding rage enveloped him. He slammed the butt of the rifle into the top of its head until the creature's brains were nothing but gray, bloody pulp on the ground and coating the butt of his Winchester.

"Son of a bitch!" he groaned, wiping the stinking slime from the rifle's butt in the dirt.

The bite was not deep, only painful, but even a mere scratch from a zombie was fatal. With Yuma under siege, the chances of reaching an infirmary in time to begin anti-parasite treatments was dismal, if not nil. Even then, the odds were stacked against him. Instead of the rage or the fear he expected at such a realization, he felt strangely at peace.

I'm a dead man, just like Cray. I'll bet Deacon won't hesitate at putting me out of my misery. He chuckled. *No, I'll take care of that matter myself, but first, I have a job to do.*

He limped toward the station. He reached the train just as the first trucks pulled up. The passengers spilled out, splashing through the mud and knee-deep puddles as they dashed for the boxcars. Some of the trucks on slightly higher ground backed up to the boxcars doors and unloaded directly into the cars. In spite of the danger all around them, they did not scream or panic. It was a controlled exodus.

The men in the trucks and on the train poured a steady stream of bullets into the gathering zombies. The creatures fell one on top of one another, forming low mounds of dead zombies, but more surged forward, crawling over the bodies when they could not walk, a relentless horde of hungry predators with one goal—sating their appetites. A few made it through the line of weapons and fell among the embarking passengers. Two passengers went down with zombies on top of them. Armed passengers began firing wildly, killing a third passenger with their crossfire. If he did not do something fast, more passengers would die by misaimed gunfire than from zombie attacks.

He glanced back at the leading edge of the zombies they had left at the GH Processing plant ambling up the tracks toward the train, and then, looked at the train. Four trucks had not yet unloaded. They were rapidly running out of time.

"If I'm going to die, I'll die for a purpose," he said to himself. He had been looking for a way to die since the deaths of his wife and son, but suicide was against the tenets of the Catholic Church. *If there still is a Catholic Church and a Pope*. He was not a good Catholic, but his wife had been. "I wonder if the Pope would consider this suicide."

He stopped, turned, and faced the zombies, barely noticing that the rain had stopped. "Hey! You slack-eyed Mother Fuckers! How you would like some nice, tasty black meat? I grew up on chitlins, chili peppers, and cornbread with hot pepper sauce, so I might be a little spicy for your taste."

Taking his knife, he sliced it along his side, wincing at the sharp, intense pain, as the blade bit deeply into his flesh. He ran the blade from his stomach to his back, and let the flow of blood join that of the wound in his ankle. Rather than fight the pain, he accepted it, let it flow through him in a welcomed rush of relief and completion. He had felt as if living on borrowed time since the deaths of his wife and son, precious time borrowed from them. He cupped his hand beneath the wound, filling it with his blood. Then, he flung the blood in the zombies' direction. Now that the rain had stopped, their keen sense of smell was sharper than ever. A chorus of low growls rose from their collective throats, as the scent of blood reached their nostrils.

"Follow me to Paradise," he shouted and began walking toward the zombies and away from the tracks at an angle. His goal was to draw as many away as he could. *The closer the meat, the sweeter the treat*. He smiled when he saw a large number of them veering away to follow him. He heard shouts and someone calling his name from the direction of the train, but he ignored them. He was already growing faint from loss of blood. He could never reach the train before he collapsed. He had decided on the perfect ending to his life of misery, one of which his wife would approve.

He had almost reached the Union Pacific Station before he ran into zombies coming in his direction. The zombies following were almost upon him. He was surrounded. He stopped and glanced up at the sky, noticing for the first time that the rain had stopped, and the storm had passed. The night sky was still full of clouds, but he thought he saw a faint glimmer of a star shining through a small rift before it disappeared. *Angie looking down on me.* He pulled two M67 fragmentary grenades from his pocket and pulled the pins. Clutching them in his hands, he held them in outstretched arms as a welcoming gesture for the zombies.

"Come and get it, boys and girls," he said to the zombies, "a hot, black snack chock full of vitamins and minerals. Don't be bashful, now. Gather round."

Just as the first zombies grabbed at him, their teeth sinking into his flesh, he dropped both grenades. He watched the released handles flying through the air.

"Here I come, Angie."

Andrews did not hear the explosion or feel the searing heat of the blast. His mind did not register the hot pieces of metal shrapnel piercing his body. He was beyond the pain of life. He did not see the dozen or so zombies propelled into the air like wheat chaff from a thrasher or burst apart like a piñata at a child's birthday party. Mitch Andrews had finally gone home.

17

July 2, 2017, 4:30 a.m.   Holiday Inn, Mirada Del Sol Safe Haven, Yuma, AZ —

The rain had stopped, but the screams from the Springhill Suites next door had not. The short but intense rounds of sporadic gunfire from various places in the hotel throughout the night came less frequently as dawn approached. One daring group had escaped the hotel during the night through a window and had driven a UPS van through the fence and away from the milling zombies. Jake doubted many of the other one-hundred-plus people living there still survived. Designers of hotels had not had zombie hordes in mind while constructing them.

He tried to keep his mind from wandering to thoughts of Jessica. He had been disappointed that she had not been among the residents of the Holiday Inn. If so, he would have insisted that she be one of the first evacuated. He owed her that much. He clung to the thought that she was still alive. He had taught her well. She was now tough, resourceful, and capable of recognizing the danger she faced. Her major shortcoming in his eyes had been her insistence on helping others. *Like I'm doing*.

The thought almost brought a chuckle to his lips. He had come with a grandiose plan to save everyone, a less-than-perfect plan that had fallen apart upon execution. He had failed to save anyone in the Springhill Suites. Anyone that survived there had done so with no help from him. He didn't even know if the train had gotten away safely, or if survivors on the roof with him were the only ones left alive in Yuma. That was the dark thought that ate at him most. Was it just him and the miserable, wet, and exhausted group of people scattered across the roof? He glanced around. No one had slept. They sat in small huddled groups or, like him, sat alone in their misery along the edge of the roof. They were safe, but Jake wondered for how long.

With the storm over and dawn approaching, General Langston would send jets and helicopters from Luke Air Force Base to break the siege at the Marine base and the airport southeast of Yuma; then, they would concentrate on the zombies that had taken over the city. The pilots would be in a killing rage, eager for revenge, taking little time to differentiate between human and zombie targets. Jake suspected their orders would be to drop their explosive payloads on any concentration of the creatures, such as the zombies packed around the two hotels. There were plenty of empty buildings in Yuma to use for rebuilding the safe haven once they had neutralized the zombie threat. The loss of two hotels would matter little in the grand scheme of things. He and the others were sitting on ground zero.

They needed off the roof, but as Jake looked over the edge down at the zombies milling below, he wondered how. He had no more tricks up his sleeve. *Is that true, or am I just afraid to try again? Once bitten; twice shy?* A sense of fatal resolve came over him. He would not sit and wait for death. He would take any of the others of like mind and fight his way through the zombies waiting below. They would either make it to safety or die trying. Burning to death in a napalm bath or disintegrated by an AGM-130 bunker buster missile loaded with a ton of high explosives seemed like a poor option.

At first, he thought it was just the sound of distant thunder; the storm trying to renew itself, but as he listened more intently at the second echoing explosion, he recognized it as the report of a 30mm cannon. Had the military arrived early? If so, he need to get moving now before it was too late. Others had heard the cannon fire as well. They lined the edge of the roof facing the direction of the sound.

"I see it!" one man shouted excitedly, pointing east.

Jake peered in the direction he was pointing, smiling when he recognized the dark green Desert Chameleon APC. As it got closer, he recognized the man standing in the open top hatch—Dax

Kauwe, the big Hawaiian captain of the garrison at Marana. His girth filled the hatch like a two-sizes-too-small shirt. Behind the APC, two five-ton trucks followed; the two trucks they had left broken down on the side of the road. He did not know if Captain Kauwe was disregarding his orders to remain in Marana, or if his orders had changed, but he was glad to see the burly Big Islander.

The heavy APC plowed through the massed zombies like a tractor tilling a field, sending bodies flying in opposite directions away from the truck. The 7.62mm machinegun mounted in the APC spewed a steady stream of lead into the zombies in front of the vehicle, while men in the trucks took down their fair share of the creatures on each side of the small convoy. The 30mm cannon fired once more, blasting a crater in the parking lot and hurling a cloud of asphalt chunks and metal shrapnel outwards in a twenty-yard-wide swath of destruction.

The armored vehicle raced for the hotel entrance, turning in a tight arc at the last moment and skidding to a halt parallel to the building. The two trucks stopped on each side of the APC forming an open box protecting the entrance. Men spilled out of the vehicles.

Jake turned to the people on the roof. "We have to go meet them. I'll take the point. Stay close together as we go down the stairs. Watch the landings."

He knelt in front of the roof door and signaled two men to open it. As soon as the door swung open, three zombies rushed onto the roof, their savage eyes searching for a victim. He took careful aim, firing a round into each zombie's head. One by one, they dropped to the roof.

"Okay, we go now," he said.

He hoped they took his advice seriously to stay together. They would not have time to return for stragglers. Their rescuers were outnumbered and would not be able to keep the zombies away for very long. He encountered two of the creatures on the second landing. To save ammunition, he slid his knife from his scabbard and stabbed the first zombie in the side of the head. He yanked out the blade and in one fluid motion, reversed it and backhanded it into the forehead of the second creature. He shoved the dead zombie over the railing with his foot to extract the knife.

Gunfire erupted behind him. He turned to see one creature sinking its mouth into the soft flesh of a man's upper arm. The man screamed and slung his arm to dislodge the creature, but succeeded only in losing a large chunk of flesh as the zombie yanked away its head. He dropped his rifle and clamped his hand over the bleeding wound. A woman fired her pistol into the creature's head; then, to the bleeding man's horror, she shot him in the head as well. Both fell in a heap across the stairs.

One of the soldiers, a boy barely eighteen, whose too-large helmet bounced around on top of his head with each step, met them on the next landing. "Hurry, sir," he said in a voice high-pitched and shaky with fear. "We don't have much time."

"Gotcha, son," Jake replied, raising his rifle and pointing it past the boy's head. The boy's eyes went wide, but Jake brushed past him and shot the zombie that had followed him up the stairs. He saw the dead zombie and grinned at Jake.

"Thanks, sir."

"Don't call me sir. The Queen hasn't knighted me, and I'm not in your army."

As he rushed down the corridor toward the entrance, Jake was astonished to see Preacher Man standing there with Aden Ortega behind him.

"What the hell are you doing here?" Jake demanded of Preacher Man.

"He fixed the armored car," Aden answered.

Chagrined for his outburst, Jake looked back and forth between Preacher Man and Aden for a moment. "Well, I'll be damned to hell and back."

"Hopefully not," Preacher Man answered. "Captain Kauwe kindly decided to join us with his men. I thought the APC might come in handy."

"You're forgiven," Jake answered. "You pulled our chestnuts out of the fire."

Preacher Man frowned. "I regret the loss of so many of God's children, but I suppose it cannot be helped."

At first, Jake thought he was referring to the people Jake had been unable to save, but then realized he was speaking of the zombies. "Don't worry about them. A lot more are going to join them soon enough."

Captain Kauwe walked up. His gaze appraised Jake in a professional manner, taking in the blood on his clothing and the badge on his chest. "Perhaps we should leave. Shit's getting deep out there."

"One stop before we go," Jake said.

"We don't have time …"

"There are survivors at the Springhill Suites next door. We have to take them with us."

Kauwe checked his watch and frowned. "Okay, but we don't have much time. Luke launched a squadron of F-16s about three minutes ago. We shouldn't be in the vicinity when they arrive."

Jake sensed something more in Kauwe's words than he was saying. "What?"

"They've called *Broken Arrow*."

"Son of a bitch!" It was Jake's worst nightmare. Someone had deemed the situation so severe that the pilots would drop their payloads as close as possible to the buildings they were trying to secure. To Jake, it meant the military was willing to write off any friendly-fire casualties as unavoidable, even their own. He had expected something similar, but hearing it from Kauwe set his teeth on edge. It was going to be close. It would take the jets less than 20 minutes to reach Yuma, line up on target, and drop their ordinance.

"Let's haul ass!" he yelled at the people behind him.

The soldiers were as eager to leave the area as the civilians were. They began loading people into the trucks, sometimes not as nicely as Jake would have liked with the older people, but they got the job done in record time.

He joined the captain in the APC. "Did the train get through?" he asked.

"Yes, with about 450 passengers."

Jake shook his head. "Not nearly enough. What about the trucks?"

"We saw twelve of them along the way headed back to Marana, but we didn't stop to say hello."

Relief flooded over Jake. Deacon and the people from Marana had made it, and so had most of the people from Yuma, but over a hundred had died. More, if Deacon had encountered any problems at the train.

"There they are," Kauwe called out a few minutes later.

Jake peered out the window and saw six F-16s pass overhead. He did not follow their path with his gaze, but he heard the bombs dropping behind them a few seconds later. The explosions shook the ground, and the post-dawn sky lit up as if the sun had gone from morning to noon in one brief burst of speed. Hellfire was raining down on the zombies from above.

To save time, the captain ordered the APC straight through the fence between the two hotels, while blasting the horn to alert the people inside they were coming. Zombies turned to stare at the sudden sound, only to be crushed beneath the vehicle's six massive tires. The trucks pulled beneath the covered entranceway, while the APC took up a covering position.

Jake, Captain Kauwe, and six men entered the building, shooting anything that moved that wasn't human. Alerted by the firing, people left their refuges and met them in the corridors eager to escape. Jake saw bodies and parts of bodies lying in blood-smeared rooms whose doors had not proved a match for the determined zombies. Some of the creatures were so satiated from devouring their prey they could barely move and proved easy targets for the soldiers. Yelling as they raced down each of the hotel's three main corridors, they rounded up and escorted the survivors back to the lobby. Altogether, they found only thirty three people. By the time everyone was aboard the two trucks and the APC, it was standing room only, but no one complained.

With the heavy APC leading the way, the convoy plowed a bloody furrow straight through the zombies. Jake felt like applauding every time the vehicle bounced over a body. Each creature they killed was one less danger to humans. At the expressway, Kauwe turned the APC onto the westbound ramp. To Jake's questioning stare, he replied, "The orders are to prevent any zombies from escaping Yuma. They'll concentrate on the interstate and railroad line first, starting east to west." He added, "They should be able to see three moving vehicles."

Jake did not bother answering. His nagging fear was that the pilots could see them but would not hesitate at collateral damage to get the job done. He silently urged the APC to move faster. In his imagination, he could already feel the heat from napalm and incendiaries roasting his ass.

Exhaustion, combined with end-of-mission fatigue sought to force him to close his eyes, but each time he did images of butchered corpses in Springhill Suites assaulted him. Later, he would rehash his mission to see if he could have done anything differently to have saved more lives. To the survivors, it had all been worth the effort. To the dead, he could offer only his apology.

The driver's white-knuckled grip on the steering wheel matched the grim expression on his face, as he dodged knots of zombies and avoided lines of wrecked automobiles. Jake cursed the fixed military mentality that had concentrated securing the miles of asphalt lifelines between safe havens, but had neglected the short length of road from Yuma into California. Now, they had to run an obstacle course of rusting hulks. On the jets' second bombing pass, the roadbed convulsed as if dozens of seismic tremors triggered simultaneously beneath them. Jake expected the asphalt to crack open and swallow them. The fire behind them billowed into an all-consuming inferno.

His blood went cold and his breath caught in his throat as he watched an F-16 approaching them from the rear at a height barely above the streetlamps. The aircraft moved so slowly, for a brief moment he thought the pilot was attempting a wheel's-up landing on the interstate. Then, at the last moment, it released a pair of two AGM-65 *Maverick* missiles and banked sharply to the right. Jake held his breath expecting to die. The missiles skimmed over the top of the vehicle and struck the bridge over the Colorado River less than a hundred yards ahead of them. The roadway collapsed, taking a large number of zombies with it.

The driver of the APC slammed on the brakes, sliding the vehicle off into the eastbound lane. The sudden deceleration threw Jake off balance. He flew forward and hit the floor chest first, sliding toward the front of the vehicle beneath pairs of outstretched legs. Kauwe's beefy hand reached down and grabbed him just before he face kissed the driver's metal seat.

The drivers of the trucks behind the APC, caught off guard by the APC's sudden braking, split to pass on each side of the stopped vehicle. One split left, clipping the rear of the APC and throwing the truck into an uncontrolled spin. It slid sideways off the road and down the steep embankment. The tires hit a water-filled concrete drainage ditch and flipped onto its side straddling the ditch, the engine still revving and the rear wheels spinning.

The second truck fared little better, careening down the embankment on the right side of the road toward the Yuma Territorial Prison Historic Park. The brakes were useless in the muddy, sloping soil. The truck slammed nose first into a palo verde tree. The tree splintered under the impact, but the broken stump impaled the fuel tank. Diesel fuel spewed from the ruptured tank, soaking the ground around it. The driver died on impact, thrown head first through the windshield. As shaken and injured passengers spilled from the rear of the truck, one of the rattled soldiers began firing his M16 at zombies drawn by the noise. When he emptied the magazine, he fumbled and dropped the fresh magazine as he pulled it from his ammo belt. He knelt to pick up the magazine and slapped it into the M16, but in his nervous haste, he pulled the trigger as he rose, firing a burst into the side of the truck. The spark of metal on metal ignited the spilled diesel fuel.

Flames engulfed the truck and anyone still trapped inside. People scattered in all directions to escape the conflagration. The screams of the dying cut off abruptly as the fire ignited the hand grenades on the soldiers still in the back of the truck. The burning canvas billowed outward from the explosion. The soldier who had caused the blaze died from flying shrapnel. The popping of sound of 5.56mm ammunition continued for several minutes.

Jake extracted himself from the tangle of feet and bodies and limped out the APC's open rear hatch. His battered right knee throbbed from the pain of impact with the floor. He did not know which hurt worse, his banged up knee or his bruised ribs.

Captain Kauwe had already exited the armored car. He stood staring at the burning truck. He turned to Jake as he walked up to stand beside him. "They're sealing off the exits. We waited too long."

Jake noted the accusatory tone of Kauwe's voice and could not argue. It was his fault they were late. He wanted to save as many as possible, but once again, he had only made things worse. How many had escaped death by zombies only to die just as horribly in the burning truck? *Failure seems to be a pattern lately.*

He tore his gaze from the carnage at the truck and looked to the east. Flames swelled from the hotels they had just vacated and several other buildings on both sides of the interstate. A second inferno burned southwest of the city near the Marine base and the airport. The firestorms only added to the rising heat of the summer day. "We're boxed in."

"Well, it's a cinch we're not going that way." Kauwe pointed to a mass of zombies moving north toward the river, quelling any thoughts of escaping in that direction. The explosions and the sudden appearance of the three vehicles now drew them toward the interstate.

Jake counted seven people running toward the APC from the burning truck, mostly elderly and pre-teens. He closed his eyes to erase their frightened faces. He had done this to them. Maybe not directly, but his arrogance had led him to believe he could do what others would have rightfully balked at. He clung to the thought that had he not come, they might have all died in the bombing, but it offered little comfort as he listened to their terrified screams. He opened his eyes and watched people climbing from the overturned truck on the other side of the interstate, dazed, bewildered, and staggering from injuries as they splashed through the water in the ditch and climbed up the sloping sides on hands and knees.

One of the injured was Preacher Man. Blood ran down his gaunt face from a head wound as Aden helped him from the ditch. Preacher Man had saved his life. Perhaps that had been his mission from God all along, the reason he had insisted on coming, though why the Almighty would take an interest in him, Jake could not fathom. Whatever the reason, he would return the favor. These two, at least, he would save. He walked back into the APC and retrieved his M2010. He climbed on top of the vehicle and sighted the closest zombie in the crosshairs of his scope. He felt the numbness of remorse fade away from him like the discarded skin of a molting rattler, as he gently squeezed the trigger. The cold steel felt almost a part of him, as it came alive in his hands.

The first zombie dropped in a spray of blood. His pulse quickened with each shot, with each dead zombie. *Take that*, he yelled silently; then, he gave voice to his frustration, his anger. "Eat this, bastards!" he screamed. "Come on! Take it like a man!" His heart thundered against his bruised ribs, but he ignored the pain. In fact, he welcomed it. The pain proved he was alive. His ears roared from the sound of blood rushing through his body and from the sharp snap of his shots. "No more!" he yelled. "No more." His mind and training took command of his body. He did not think about his shots. Aim. Shoot. Aim. Shoot.

He barely heard Captain Kauwe's voice cutting through the noise ordering the APC's gunner to open fire with the 7.62mm on the zombies. Seconds later, the 30mm cannon exploded into action, firing high-explosive shells beyond the truck and into the midst of the zombies. The recoil bounced the vehicle's roof, jarring his knee and ribs. He emptied his weapon, but the people from the truck had reached the APC safely, all except Preacher Man and Aden. Burdened by helping the injured Preacher Man, zombies had overtaken them, but just as on the night he had first seen Preacher Man, the creatures paid no attention to him. They parted and passed around the pair as if they were mere obstacles and not prey.

The soldiers continued firing until the last zombie in the first wave fell. Many more were moving their direction. Jake looked down from his perch at Preacher Man held upright by Aden's strong arms. The side of his face was battered and bruised. One eye was swollen shut. A deep laceration in his temple spilled blood onto his emaciated face. In pain, half-dead, he looked up at Jake and smiled.

"He's hurt bad," Aden said. His pained face revealed concern for Preacher Man.

Jake slid down from the APC, birthing a fresh wave of agony as his damaged knee buckled when he hit the ground. He groaned at the pain, but let it spur on a surge of adrenaline from his endocrine system. He felt as charged as a 500-megawatt reactor.

"Get him inside," he said. "Get everyone inside." Even as he said it, he knew it was impossible. The APC had already been carrying more people than the specs called for, but at least its machinegun and cannon offered protection. *As long as the ammunition lasts,* his mind supplied, reminding him of the dire situation.

The remaining six soldiers from both trucks took up positions around the vehicle. They could not hold off the zombies for very long, even if the jets did not decide to bomb everyone into oblivion. Jake searched for a way out, cursing his *Jake's Law #9 — Always have an exit strategy.* He had ignored it so many times in the past twelve hours that one more time would not make a difference. He had created the situation. It was his duty to extract them from his folly.

This is my last leap into the fray. After this, no more responsibility. The world can live or die without my help.

His gaze fell upon two pieces of heavy equipment sitting on flatbeds at a siding in front of the Union Pacific Station a hundred yards away. He dismissed the giant Caterpillar dozer as too slow to be of much use. The blade could be deadly, but he could never keep zombies from climbing up onto the tractor. However, the boom mulcher was another matter. He had once seen one in operation, the twenty-inch barrel knives reducing a tree to sawdust in seconds. For a forest of rampaging zombies, what could be more apt than a de-foresting tool?

"I'm going for the cavalry," he told Kauwe, who looked at him as if he had just lost his mind. He pointed to the mulcher and saw the captain's grim face break into a wide grin.

"I'll come with you," he said.

"They need you here."

"In about fifteen minutes, they won't need anyone, unless, of course, the Air Force decides to unload on us first."

He didn't have time to discourage the captain. Besides, Kauwe wasn't his responsibility. He had come to Yuma when he could have remained in Marana. If he wanted to risk his life, Jake would not hinder him. "Okay."

They started racing to the siding. Jake had forgotten about his knee, but the agony of running quickly reminded him. He bit down on his lip and broke into a stiff-legged Walter Brenan hobble to keep up with the much younger and fitter Kauwe. Normally, he could have covered the hundred yards in twenty seconds. Now, it seemed to take an eternity. He pulled his Colt revolver and shot two zombies closing in on him. Kauwe proved himself equally competent with his military-issue 9mm, shooting any zombie in his path. He glanced back, saw Jake lagging behind, and slowed to help him. Jake waved him on. He would make it. He had to make it. This was his last act of attrition.

They reached the siding. Kauwe held off more zombies as Jake scrambled atop the flatcar. He smiled when he saw that the DAH mulcher was secured strictly according to Army regulations with chains, sliphooks, pin anchors, and turnbuckles. *Right out of TEA Pamphlet 55-19,* he mused. He released the turnbuckle, slid the sliphooks from the pin anchors, and tossed aside the chains. He climbed inside the cab and stared for a moment at the unfamiliar controls. *Can't be that difficult. I hope like hell there's fuel in it.*

To his immense relief, the mulcher cranked. He ground gears trying to engage the treads but managed to ease the machine to the edge of the flatcar. With no ramp, he would have to roll off the edge and hope to remain upright. If he flipped the heavy machine, even if it did not crush him immediately, he would be easy pickings for the zombies.

Here goes.

He held his breath as he watched the front end of the treads roll out over empty space. The machine pitched forward at a dangerous angle until the extended boom touched ground. The jarring thud of impact sent shooting pains up his leg. He used the boom to ease the mulcher's wheels off the flatcar. He heard a sickening crunch as the treads ripped away part of the flatbed. Nothing could prevent the bone-jarring shaking as the treads left the flatcar.

"Climb aboard," he yelled at Kauwe.

As they rolled toward the APC, he swung the boom to knock aside two zombies. The force of the blow knocked one's head cleanly from its body. In spite of the suppressing fire from the soldiers, the ring of zombies pressed more tightly around the APC. Jake extended the boom and engaged the 57-inch-wide cutting platform. The blades of the twin barrel knives spun at 3000 rpms.

He met the first zombies with the cutters held vertically like a fan. He felt hardly any impact, as the rotating blades shredded the zombies into bloody confetti. Blood, flesh, and powdered bone sprayed from the cutting assembly.

He extended the boom over the outer ring of creatures to reach a knot of zombies closing in on the open rear door of the APC. He lowered the cutters horizontally from above. When he lifted it, the creatures had disappeared as if he had performed a magic trick. Using the mulcher like a bulldozer with the blades extended vertically in front of the machine, he made several passes around the APC, mowing down zombies like pruning overgrown hedges. Captain Kauwe shot the occasional stray zombie from the open cabin door.

Jake's primitive hunter blood lust rose until his vision narrowed to the creatures directly in his path. He was no longer fully human. He was an ape-man freshly down from his African savannah tree. The sharp, tangy odor of blood quivered his nostrils, speaking to his ape-man brain. He wanted to rend flesh, devour it just as the mindless zombies were doing. The primitive beat of a drum not yet invented pounded in his ears; the music forming in the proto-human brain long before the ability to express it through opposable-thumb hands developed. He did not stop until Captain Kauwe tapped him repeatedly on the shoulder, the rhythmic taps slowly replacing the beating drum.

"It's finished," Kauwe said. "Back off."

Jake sat back in the control seat, his arms throbbing from gripping the control stick and his right knee blazing with pain from operating the foot pedals. When he released the controls, his hands shook so badly he had to place them under his armpits to stop the tremors.

"You did it," Kauwe said.

Jake nodded numbly. He could barely comprehend Kauwe's words. The controls looked like mystical apparitions to his animal mind. He feared them, feared their unfamiliar smell. With a shudder of revulsion, he escaped the cabin and stood on the ground, letting the familiar world reassert itself. The African savannah faded around him, replaced by a swatch of bloody ground specked with bits of flesh, hair, and bone. The gunfire had ended, but the shocked looks of revulsion and loathing directed at him struck him like a volley from a firing squad. Their unspoken accusations were the leather flails of a Spanish Inquisitor's whip scoring his recalcitrant flesh.

Only Preacher Man's eyes held any hint of sympathy. The old man sat at the edge of the APC's ramp as Aden treated the wound to his head. From the drawn, far off expression on the itinerant preacher's face, Jake knew he was not long for the earth. He stumbled toward him, eager to kneel at Preacher Man's feet and beg forgiveness.

"You did as you must," Preacher Man said. His voice was weak, but there was no accusation in his voice, only blessed understanding.

Jake fumbled for words to express himself. Somewhere along his evolutionary journey from primitive ape to human being, he had lost the ability to speak coherently. His mind raced with thoughts that had rattled around in his mind for years. Voices of his dead comrades in Afghanistan spoke to him. Other voices to which he could assign no faces assailed him with snippets of past conversations he wished he could go back and change. The past was gone. The future was beyond his grasp. He had only here and now, the bloody present. He stared down at Preacher Man and shook his head. Preacher Man raised his hand and made the sign of the cross in the air, just as he had that night at the rail yard.

"I bless this man in the eyes of God and absolve him of all blame." His hand fell limply to his side.

Jake's legs betrayed him at the last act of absolution of a dying man. He fell to his knees and wept. When he raised his head, Preacher Man's head lay cradled in Aden's lap. Tears rolled down the youth's cheeks. "He's dead. It was too much for him."

With Preacher Man's death, Jake found his voice. "He came for this moment. He's at peace now."

The idea of peace called to Jake, but he knew it was something he could never have. He lived too much in the world to be a bearded ascetic and too far removed from humankind to fit in. He was a remnant of the past, almost as much as the primitive he had just become, but he was a relic that the world badly needed in a time of great strife and turmoil.

"What do I do?" Aden asked.

The sounds of explosions continued around them, but it seemed they were safe for the moment. He noticed armored vehicles moving along the streets. The siege at the Marine base had been broken. Now the clean-up would begin. He wasn't sure how the general would react to the Mexicans destroying the fence and herding their zombies over the border, but he suspected it would end in war. He didn't know what kind of army Mexico had left, but men would die on both sides, too many men and for too little reason. He knew he would not participate in the coming battle. He no longer had the stomach for wholesale slaughter of men or zombies. He had washed that craving from his soul with the forest mulcher, and his heart no longer ached for things as they had been. He would settle for better than they now were. He knew he could no longer function as part of the safe haven project or as a leader of men. He had lost that right.

He looked down at his great-great grandfather's Arizona Rangers badge. His fingers traced the outline of the five-pointed star as if summoning his great-great grandfather's spirit to guide him. He knew that would not happen. He was alone, as he always had been and always would be henceforth. He had enjoyed brief interludes of companionship. Perhaps they had helped save him from becoming the monster he now knew lurked within him, that lived inside all men.

The badge was his link to the past and his guide toward the future. He could not abandon his need to serve a greater entity— the Law. He simply understood the futility of trying to establish law and order in a lawless land. The safe havens could not bring law with them. The law had to be there first and the safe havens built upon its foundation. His original concept of Ranger judge, jury, and executioners needed modifying, but not tossing entirely. He could not enjoy the comforts of a safe haven and dabble at dispensing law and justice. Preacher Man had given him the proper idea.

He would travel the far reaches of the countryside, the places well beyond the scope of any law or organized system of true justice. He would confront evil in its domain—petty criminals, gangs of looters, thugs, robber barons, hired guns—anyone who felt themselves above the Law and entitled to the fruits of another's labors. He had no qualms about killing in the name of the law. That much had not changed, but he would leave the judging and the punishment to the victims. He would facilitate their right to justice, not assume it. The law could not be given to someone. It had to be assumed, as a right and as a responsibility.

Alton would not approve. He could never approve anything outside of his rigid concept of right and wrong. That could work where the seed of the law had taken root, but not on barren soil. That would be his domain—the desert wastes, the vast open plains, the concrete jungles of the deserted cities.

He answered Aden's question. "Find a place beside the river and bury him. Mark his grave with a cross."

"Will you help me?"

Jake shook his head. "I can't. I don't deserve the honor of burying him. You do. You brought him to this place. You helped him achieve his goal. I refused him."

Aden stared at him as he would an apparition, an ancestral spirit summoned by a Tohono O'odham ritual. "Are you a spirit warrior?"

At any other time, the question would have sent Jake into raucous laughter. Now, he did not know how to answer. His knee ached and his breathing set his ribs on fire. He was human enough. "I'm flesh and blood."

Aden took his answer at face value. "You look ... you look different."

Jake nodded. "After the apocalypse, we're all different. Some people changed only slightly. Others ... others became someone else."

"Who are you? What have you become?"

What indeed? His fingers touched the star on his chest and the answer came to him as if his great-great grandfather's ghost had finally reached out to him. He wondered why he had never asked himself that question. *Who am I?* Hilda's name for him came to his mind.

"I'm Jake Law," he answered, now certain who he was.

"My grandfather will pray for a spirit guide to show you the way."

Jake nodded. He knew he had one already. He now believed such things were possible.

"Are you going back to Marana?"

To see Alton one last time? To try to explain what he intended to do to Deacon? He could not face Alton's disappointment. "No." He turned to face the Colorado River. "My path lies out there."

He ignored the people around him, and they ignored him, all except Captain Kauwe. He watched Jake retrieve his M2010 rifle, pack a small bag with water, rations, and ammunition for both his rifle and the Colt pistol, but said nothing. The sun was well above the horizon, sucking the previous night's moisture from the soil. The day would be hot and humid, but Jake knew he could endure the heat as he had everything else the world had thrown at him over the past two years. He had learned to live off the land. Those skills would serve him well in the days and months ahead.

"Here, you might need this." Aden handed him his ash bow and quiver of arrows. It was a gift fit for a spirit warrior. *Or a man,* he thought wryly.

"Thank you," he said.

Biting back on the pain from his knee, he settled the bow and the quiver over the same shoulder as the rifle and the pack on the other; then, he took his first step north and into his future.

18

September 20, 2017, 9:00 p.m.   Marana Safe Haven, Tucson, AZ —

Alton massaged his stiff leg as he sat on the front porch of his home. The night still held onto the day's heat, but with the sun gone, it would cool quickly enough. The day had been hectic. Until Yuma could be resettled, Marana and Hatch safe havens would absorb the surplus population. He had made time in his busy schedule for lunch with Jessica and Hilda, noting the looks of intimacy passing between them as they spoke of the past. She seemed happy and that was all he had ever wanted for her.

There was talk of war with Mexico. He was against it. He wondered how two nations, so ravaged by the plague, could even contemplate such a horrendous thing. He was hoping for some kind of diplomatic solution, but, like zombies, the sight and smell of blood sometimes drove men insane. He would work to stop it, but men had always done foolish things and seemed determine to do so again.

Jake was alive. He had already grown to the status of legend, the Man with the Gun—Jake Law. His methods were not ones the military or the Territorial Government would approve, but they were effective. He convened people's courts and presented lawbreakers to them. Often, they dealt with the criminals themselves, under Jake's supervision and guidance, all according to the Law. Everywhere Jake went, he appointed deputies; people entrusted to uphold the Law. Little by little, the Law was spreading, and with it stability.

"He always wanted to be a Ranger," Alton said to the night, wondering if Jake could hear him. Probably not, he decided. "Now he's a Ranger in the truest sense of the word, a traveling lawman."

Aden now worked with Deacon at the Ranger station. Through him, Jake's legend grew. He swore Jake had simply changed shape as he walked away from Yuma, became a hawk, a shape shifter. Alton knew it was silly, but it fitted Jake's image as bigger than life. When the country once again became even a small portion of what it once was, it would be because of men like Jake. He recalled *Jake's Law #11 — Be willing to lose it all.* Jake had reached 21 in his list of Jake's Laws. Alton wondered when he saw him again, how many more he would have added.

One day, he hoped, Jake would walk out of the desert, sit down, and share a bottle of *Dos Equis* with him. Alton kept two bottles in the refrigerator for that day.

If, he reminded himself, legends drank beer.

 SEVERED**PRESS**

CHECK OUT OTHER GREAT ZOMBIE NOVELS

DEAD ASCENT
by Jason McPhearson

The dead have risen and they are hungry...

Grizzled war veteran turned game warden, Brayden James and a small group of survivors, fight their way through the rugged wilderness of southern Appalachia to an isolated cabin in the hope of finding sanctuary. Every terrifying step they make they are stalked by a growing mass of staggering corpses, and a raging forest fire, set by the government in hopes of containing the virus.

As all logical routes off the mountain are cut off from them, they seek the higher ground, but they soon realize there is little hope of escape when the dead walk and the world burns.

CHAOS THEORY
by Rich Restucci

The world has fallen to a relentless enemy beyond reason or mercy. With no remorse they rend the planet with tooth and nail.

One man stands against the scourge of death that consumes all.

Teamed with a genius survivalist and a teenage girl, he must flee the teeming dead, the evils of humans left unchecked, and those that would seek to use him. His best weapon to stave off the horrors of this new world? His wit.

SEVEREDPRESS

CHECK OUT OTHER GREAT ZOMBIE NOVELS

RUN
by Rich Restucci

The dead have risen, and they are hungry.

Slow and plodding, they are Legion. The undead hunt the living. Stop and they will catch you. Hide and they will find you. If you have a heartbeat you do the only thing you can: You run.

Survivors escape to an island stronghold: A cop and his daughter, a computer nerd, a garbage man with a piece of rebar, and an escapee from a mental hospital with a life-saving secret. After reaching Alcatraz, the ever expanding group of survivors realize that the infected are not the only threat.

Caught between the viciousness of the undead, and the heartlessness of the living, what choice is there? Run.

THE DEAD WALK THE EARTH
by Luke Duffy

As the flames of war threaten to engulf the globe, a new threat emerges.

A 'deadly flu', the like of which no one has ever seen or imagined, relentlessly spreads, gripping the world by the throat and slowly squeezing the life from humanity.

Eight soldiers, accustomed to operating below the radar, carrying out the dirty work of a modern democracy, become trapped within the carnage of a new and terrifying world.

Deniable and completely expendable. That is how their government considers them, and as the dead begin to walk, Stan and his men must fight to survive.

CHECK OUT OTHER GREAT ZOMBIE NOVELS

DEAD PULSE RISING
by K. Michael Gibson

Slavering hordes of the walking dead rule the streets of Baltimore, their decaying forms shambling across the ruined city, voracious and unstoppable. The remaining survivors hide desperately, for all hope seems lost... until an armored fortress on wheels plows through the ghouls, crushing bones and decayed flesh. The vehicle stops and two men emerge from its doors, armed to the teeth and ready to cancel the apocalypse.

TOWER OF THE DEAD
by J.V. Roberts

Markus is a hardworking man that just wants a better life for his family. But when a virus sweeps through the halls of his high-rise apartment complex, those plans are put on hold. Trapped on the sixteenth floor with no hope of rescue, Markus must fight his way down to safety with his wife and young daughter in tow.

Floor by bloody floor they must battle through hordes of the hungry dead on a terrifying mission to survive the TOWER OF THE DEAD.

CHECK OUT OTHER GREAT ZOMBIE NOVELS

Z BURBIA
by Jake Bible

Whispering Pines is a classic, quiet, private American subdivision on the edge of Asheville, NC, set in the pristine Blue Ridge Mountains. Which is good since the zombie apocalypse has come to Western North Carolina and really put suburban living to the test!

Surrounded by a sea of the undead, the residents of Whispering Pines have adapted their bucolic life of block parties to scavenging parties, common area groundskeeping to immediate area warfare, neighborhood beautification to neighborhood fortification.

But, even in the best of times, suburban living has its ups and downs what with nosy neighbors, a strict Home Owners' Association, and a property management company that believes the words "strict interpretation" are holy words when applied to the HOA covenants. Now with the zombie apocalypse upon them even those innocuous, daily irritations quickly become dramatic struggles for personal identity, family security, and straight up survival.

ZOMBIE RULES
by David Achord

Zach Gunderson's life sucked and then the zombie apocalypse began.

Rick, an aging Vietnam veteran, alcoholic, and prepper, convinces Zach that the apocalypse is on the horizon. The two of them take refuge at a remote farm. As the zombie plague rages, they face a terrifying fight for survival.

They soon learn however that the walking dead are not the only monsters.

www.ingramcontent.com/pod-product-compliance
Lightning Source LLC
Chambersburg PA
CBHW031332170626
46807CB00002B/657